SUSAN KYLE

AFTER MIDNIGHT

WARNER BOOKS

A Time Warner Company

WARNER BOOKS EDITION

Cover design by Diane Luger
Cover illustration by Franco Accanero
Hand lettering by Carl Dellacroce

Warner Books, Inc.
1271 Avenue of the Americas
New York, NY 10020

A Time Warner Company

Printed in the United States of America

First Printing: November, 1993

10 9 8 7 6 5 4 3 2 1

"No holds barred?"

His chin lifted. "I've heard all about you, over the years. They say you're one of the brightest young hostesses in politics. I might have recognized you in one of those designer gowns you wear. Insiders say you're the brains and drive behind your brother. But you don't look so tough to me."

"Pneumonia will make the toughest of us mellow, just briefly," Nikki said inclining her head. "So it's war, is it?"

"That's how I fight," Kane returned, ramming his hands deep into his pockets.

"Fair enough. But there's one condition. No mudslinging."

He lifted an eyebrow. "You know better."

She felt her face color with bad temper and her own hands clenched. "No mudslinging about what we did together," she said, forcing the words out.

He wanted to hit her where it hurt most. She'd made a fool of him.

"We had a one-night stand," he said. "And I'm not running for public office. If I were, you might actually worry me."

Nikki had once been warned, "Men love in the darkness and are indifferent in the dawn." Now that phrase came back to her with vivid force . . .

"No one, absolutely no one, beats this author
for sensual anticipation."
—*Rave Reviews*

Also by
SUSAN KYLE

ESCAPADE
NIGHT FEVER
TRUE COLORS

Published by
WARNER BOOKS

AFTER MIDNIGHT

CHAPTER ONE

Seabrook Island had long been an island community for many of Charleston's oldest and wealthiest families. The beautiful and exclusive island included a marina, two golf courses, and a private club. More importantly, it offered seclusion from the hectic pace of the nearby city and the local tourist resorts.

Although Nicole Seymour wasn't a millionairess, the Seymour name granted her entrée into this private beach society, and in many ways the peace and quiet it afforded her now was equal to any fortune the Seymour family ever had had. Exhausted from her efforts for the Spoleto Festival and organizing a political fundraising gala for her brother's reelection campaign, Nikki wanted only to enjoy a few lazy afternoons in the sun.

Tall and slender, and perfectly proportioned, her body was as sensual as her pure green eyes and the bow curve of her pretty mouth. An enchanted society columnist had once said she sparkled when she was happy, and despite her height, she had the mischievous disposition of a pixie. With her thick black hair cut in a wedge around her soft oval face, she even had the look of one. Behind her beautiful face was a quick mind and an impeccable reputation. If others thought her a bit too wary and cautious, Nikki knew these qualities helped make her a valuable hostess and companion for her bachelor brother's political obligations. Clayton was as ambitious as their late father had been and Nikki had played a significant role in each man's success.

It was early June and unseasonably cool, but Nikki was enjoying a quiet afternoon in the sun. Her small breasts lifted and fell slowly as she lay breathing in the delicious sea air. She shaded her eyes and watched the silvery glitter of a float plane as it landed near her house, not far from the old Settles place. Nikki had heard that a Houston oilman had purchased the property because it was near the automobile manufacturing company he had recently acquired. No one knew much about Kane Lombard, but Nikki had noticed his yacht in a slip at the marina, and she'd read of his wife and son's violent death in Lebanon not long ago. Unlike the Seymours of Charleston, the Lombards of Houston and New York still had their money—and the bloody tragedy it had inspired.

As the sound of the plane faded, Nikki drifted off to sleep. The sun was lower when she woke, but still bright enough to burn her skin. Stretching drowsily, she stood up and was slipping a soft white robe over her green and gold bathing suit when, suddenly, something on the beach caught her eye. She went to the railing to look out over the ocean. Something black bobbed in the surf. She leaned over the balcony's railing, straining for a better look. A head. It was a head!

Without even thinking, she darted down the steps and ran across the beach. As a teenager she'd had Red Cross lifesaving courses, and CPR. She knew there wasn't a lot of time to spare. Her heart raced madly as she neared the water.

As she darted into the foaming surf and felt the water swirl around her calves and the hem of her robe, she saw that the body washing up on the beach was a man's. He was huge, muscular and very tall, with darkly tanned skin and dark hair. She'd never be able to carry him to safety, but thankfully she could see that he wasn't unconscious or dead. As she bent over him, his powerful arm muscles rippled as he tried to pull himself through the surf onto the beach. He coughed violently and his whole body shuddered.

She helped him just past the surf and then stopped to breathe while she watched him for signs of respiratory distress. He was panting hard, but steadily. Something shone on the sand just beneath him. She reached down to retrieve his watch, and, without looking at it, slipped it into the pocket of her robe.

"Easy does it," she said gently, helping him to sit up. "What happened?"

"Hit . . . my head . . . I think," he choked. "Oh, God!"

He was violently ill. He retched, and what looked like a gallon of sea water came out of him. She spoke to him quietly, reassuringly, while she felt for his pulse. It was strong, and he was now breathing rhythmically. After another minute, he relaxed onto his back and Nikki bent over him to examine him. There was a deep gash on his forehead that needed immediate attention. She examined it with deft hands, tracing it back up into his thick black hair.

"Open your eyes, please."

He did, and she met them with a shock of pleasure. They were so dark a brown that they were very nearly black. The size of his pupils was hard to discern, so she put her hands on his cheeks and turned his head toward the light. There was no difference that she, a lay person, could find. She'd need a doctor to make an exact diagnosis, though she was fairly certain the nausea had resulted from a mild concussion.

The feel of his face in her hands, and the piercing quality of those dark eyes, disturbed her. She dropped her hands quickly and moved back.

"Will you be all right while I call for an ambulance?" she asked.

"No . . . ambulance," he said firmly. He coughed and managed to sit up again, wincing. He put a hand to his head and groaned. "God, what a headache! I hit my head. I remember that." His thick brows drew together. "Funny. I can't remember anything except that I was going to drown if I didn't reach the shore. I can't even remember my name!"

Nikki sat very still. It was a miracle that he hadn't drowned in this condition. The current could easily have carried him out to sea if there'd been a bad undertow.

"Can you walk?" she asked with sudden decision. If he refused an ambulance, she could at least call a doctor for him. Chad Holman was a long-standing friend of the family and he was an internist. He'd come if she asked him; he lived just down the beach.

"I . . . think so."

He was badly disoriented. That disturbed her. "Come on, then," she said. "I'll get you up to the house."

He looked straight into her eyes and she felt a shock all the way through her. He looked very familiar. She couldn't place him, but he looked like someone she knew. Perhaps she'd seen him at the Spoleto Festival.

"I couldn't have come far," he said slowly.

"Yes, that makes sense. When you've rested, you'll probably remember who you are. I believe temporary amnesia isn't unusual after blows to the head."

"Are you a nurse?"

She lifted her eyebrows as she studied him. "Why not a doctor?"

"Why not a nurse?" he shot right back, his dark eyes and his tone challenging.

She glowered at him. "I can see that you're going to be a problem patient either way. Come on, I'll help you. Oh, for a wheelbarrow," she groaned as she got under one huge arm.

"If you're trying out for standup comedy, don't give up your day job," he said heavily.

His deep voice was amused, even through the pain. He stumbled a little and there was a muffled curse. He was obviously a man who wasn't used to being vulnerable, and he didn't whine. She liked him already, and she was dying to know who he was.

He wasn't a neighbor, not one she'd ever seen. He was wearing designer trunks and he was too old to be a college student. The streaks of silver in his dark hair told her he must be almost forty, older than Clayton for sure.

She slid her hand around his back and felt her fingers tingle. His skin was olive tan and silky, rippling with muscle. Her eyes dropped involuntarily to the broad chest with an incredibly thick mass of curling black hair that ran in a wedge from his collarbone all the way down into the low-slung white trunks around his lean hips. Nikki hadn't been attracted to a man for ages, but she couldn't keep her eyes off this stranger's almost nude body. In an odd way, he seemed familiar. With his arm drawn over her shoulder, she held his hand for balance. Although his hand was large and rough, his oval nails were immaculately kept. He wore no jewelry except for the watch she'd stuck in her pocket.

"Easy does it," she said gently.

"I'm sure that on normal days, I can walk by myself," he assured her with droll humor.

"I'd never doubt it," she said. "One step at a time, now. You're injured, that's all. It's bound to affect your balance."

"Are you sure your first name isn't Florence? Maybe it's Pollyanna."

"You're not being very pleasant for a man the ocean spit out," she remarked. "Obviously you left a bad taste in its mouth."

He didn't smile, but Nikki was certain he repressed a laugh. "Maybe so."

"Do you feel sleepy or nauseated?" she persisted.

"Just dizzy."

She nodded, her mind running quickly through possibilities.

"*Are* you a nurse?" he asked suddenly.

"Not really. I've had some Red Cross first-aid courses, though, and," she added with a mischievous glance upward, "a little training with beached whales. Speaking of which . . ."

"Stop right there while you're ahead," he advised. "God, what a headache!" His free hand went to his head and he groaned.

Nikki was getting more nervous by the minute. Head injuries could be serious and she didn't have the expertise to diagnose this one.

He looked down and saw her troubled look. He glowered even more. "I'm not going to drop dead on the beach," he muttered. "Are you always so transparent?"

"In fact, I've been told I have a poker face," she said without thinking. She looked up into his dark eyes and found herself staring into them.

"You have green eyes, Florence Nightingale," he chided. "Green, like a cat."

"I scratch like one, too, so look out," she said with far more bravado than courage.

"Point taken." He eased the pressure of his arm around her neck and went the last few steps up to the deck under his own power. He stopped, holding his head and breathing deliberately for a few seconds. After he rested, she helped him into the house.

"I know enough first aid to bandage that head," she informed him briskly. She helped him into a chair at her kitchen table. "But first I'm calling Chad. He's a friend of ours," she said without mentioning Clayton.

"Are you planning to exhibit me?" he mused darkly.

"There's a thought. I could advertise you as a merman and sell tickets." She was smiling, but her mind was in high gear. Head wounds were dangerous, and he'd been badly confused. She needed expert advice, quick. "Chad's a doctor," she added. "A very good one."

She picked up the receiver. Taking charge was what Nikki did best.

He watched her through narrowed eyes. Her self-confidence impressed him, and he couldn't help stealing a second look.

Nikki felt his gaze and met it head-on. She didn't flinch or blush. Since her divorce from Miles, she'd had little interest in men, and while she sometimes felt sad about what had happened, she didn't let the past infringe on her life.

"Hello?" a pleasant but abrupt voice spoke in her ear.

"Chad! Thank goodness you're home. Could you step over here for a minute? I've got a near-drowning victim on my hands with a head wound and possible concussion." She described the condition she'd found the stranger in, and what she'd done so far.

"Give me five minutes and I'll be right there. How is he now; any headache, vomiting, unequal pupils, confusion . . . ?"

Nikki put the questions to the dark man.

He leaned forward, frowning. "My head hurts. I'm a bit nauseated, but not much."

She looked into his eyes and still couldn't tell if the pupils were unequal. All she saw was that they were very dark—almost black. And whenever she looked into them, a curling sensation spread through her stomach.

"I can't tell if they're unequal because they're so dark," she told Chad. "Headache and a little nausea. He's full of sarcastic commentary," she added with a laughing glance at her guest, "so I suppose you could call him lucid. There's no indication of shock."

"Good sign. Put a cold compress on the wound and keep him quiet. See you soon." He hung up.

She got the first aid kit and did a quick bandaging job on his forehead. He had darkly tanned skin, and when she had him hold the bandage in place while she secured it, she felt the fingers of one of his big hands briefly against hers. They had calluses, she noted. He must not be a man who sat at a desk. But he didn't seem the sort of man who did manual labor, either.

"You'll be all right," she assured him when she finished.

"Of course I will. I'm sure that I'm tough as nails normally." He rested his elbows on the clean surface of her kitchen table and held his head in his hands. "Do you really spend your life rescuing strange men on your beach?"

"You're my first, actually," she replied. "But considering the size of you, I'm hoping for an ocean liner tomorrow."

"Ha, ha," he enunciated.

"How about a zesty, refreshing cup of coffee?" she asked, and got up to make some.

"Coffee causes cancer," he assured her. "I think I read that somewhere, just before I bought a new can of it."

She grinned at him as she busied herself filling the drip coffeemaker. "I have it on the best authority that most things will kill you these days."

"Have you lived here long?" he asked conversationally.

"We've had the place a few years."

There was a stillness about him. "We?"

"The man who lives here with me," she replied noncommittally. It wouldn't do to tell a total stranger that she was single and on her own. "He drives down on Friday evenings," she lied.

Friday was tonight, but he didn't seem to register the information. Perhaps he didn't know the day.

"Today is Friday," she added, just in case. "My friend is very nice, you'll like him." She glanced over her shoulder. "Any nausea yet? Drowsiness?"

"I haven't got a concussion," he said firmly. "I'm not sure how I know that I'd recognize the symptoms. Perhaps I've had it before."

She noticed his eyes on the repairs that had been made to the windows. "Hurricane Hugo paid us a visit, although we were hardly touched, compared to the damage it caused Charleston," she assured him. "We're still trying to get the place back in order." She didn't tell him how difficult it was to find the money. Even with Clayton's salary, they barely made ends meet.

She perched on a stool at the counter, exposing her long, bare legs. When she noticed his blatant stare, she glared at him.

He saw the look and smiled. "Don't worry. I'm absolutely sure that I don't like green-eyed women," he assured her. He sat back in his chair with a rough sigh. One hand idly rubbed the thick hair on his chest. He looked aggressively masculine and that disturbed her. She fidgeted.

"I can find you something to put on, if you'd like," she said after a minute.

"That would be nice. Your male friend leaves some things here when he isn't, I suppose?"

She slipped easily off the stool. "The shirt may be a

bit tight, but there are some pants with an elastic waist that will probably fit you. I won't be a minute.''

She darted into Clayton's bedroom and borrowed the biggest shirt he owned. There was a pair of twill putter pants that had belonged to her late father; she'd never had the heart to throw them out. She took those, too.

She carried the clothing back to her guest. "The bathroom is through there," she nodded down the hall. "Third door on the right. You'll find a razor and soap and towels if you'd like to clean up. Are you hungry?"

"I think I could eat."

"I'll get everything together and you can have something once Chad's examined you."

He got to his feet very slowly and hesitated as he turned to leave the room, looking very big and threatening to Nikki. "I don't remember anything. But I'm not a cruel man, if it helps. I do know that."

"It helps." She smiled.

"I'm certain that I'm not used to accepting help from strangers," he added.

"Good thing. I'm not used to offering it to strangers. Of course, there's a first time . . .''

". . . for everything," he finished for her. "Thanks."

He showered and shaved before he changed into the dry clothes and joined her in the kitchen. He was still barefoot, but the pants fit. The shirt showed off muscles that had obviously not been obtained by any lengthy inactivity. He was fit and athletic. Nikki had to remind herself not to stare at him.

He'd just come back from the bathroom and sat down in the kitchen when they heard the sound of a car.

Chad was in his late forties, a tall and fit bachelor who was just about to settle down. He and Nikki had been friends for a long time.

"Who's the patient, you or the guy in the kitchen?" he asked, glancing over her shoulder at the distant figure sipping coffee. "You look worse than he does."

"I'm just over pneumonia," she said.

"I know that, and you're overdoing it, again. At least try not to get chilled," he returned firmly. "Let's see about your patient."

He introduced himself to the stranger and shook hands, his manner changing to professional courtesy and expertise. He found what Nikki hadn't: a faint difference in the dilation of pupils. "Mild concussion," Chad said after a minute, replacing his stethoscope in his black bag. "I think the amnesia will pass in a few hours. Don't worry about it. As for that head injury, I'd like to have you X-rayed. We'll see about putting you in for the night . . ."

"I'm not going to the hospital, to be X-rayed or anything else," the man said easily, but there was sudden authority in his voice. He sounded like a man who was accustomed to giving orders.

Chad hesitated. He made a soft whistling sound and looked concerned. "Do you know how dangerous concussion can be?"

"I could drop dead. But I don't think I will."

"I have to agree," Chad told Nikki. "If he won't go

13

to the hospital, he'll have to be awakened every two hours tonight. Can he stay here so you can keep checking his condition?''

The man's dark eyes narrowed. "Talk to me. I'm the one with concussion.''

"Yes, but she's going to be the one with all the responsibility," Chad murmured dryly. "Sure you want to take it on, Nikki?''

She pursed her lips and studied the angry man at the table. "I'm sure," she said.

The dark man lifted an eyebrow. She grinned at him.

"All right," Chad said. "I'll leave you with him.'' He dug out some sample packets from the black bag and handed them to Nikki. "If he makes it through the night without any problems, he can have one of these for the headache in the morning. Feed him liquids tonight, too. Watch for nausea or unconsciousness. At the first sign of either, call an ambulance, then call me.''

"Thanks," the man said curtly.

Chad smiled at him. "No problem. I taught Nikki all about first aid. You're in good hands. If that amnesia doesn't pass by tomorrow or the next day, you may need to see a doctor; if not me, the hospital has several good ones on staff.''

"I'll do that. Your fee . . . ?''

"Get your brain back on line, then worry about money," Chad said, chuckling. "This one's my good deed for the day. I used to be a Boy Scout.''

"Sure you were," Nikki teased cheerfully. "But I'll recommend you for a new badge, anyway.''

14

"Thanks. I'll see myself out. Hope you do well," he added.

After closing the front door, Nikki returned to her brooding houseguest.

"Worried about your memory, aren't you?" she asked bluntly. "It will come back."

He frowned at her as she moved pots and pans around in the kitchen. "I hope so. I realize the spot I'm putting you in. I must have relatives, friends . . ."

"Today, you have me. Fortunately for you, I'm at loose ends and bored to death. I'll cook you an omelet and then you can eat it and drink your coffee and go to bed. You look terrible."

"So do you," he returned, noticing the dark shadows under her eyes. "Why?"

"I had a bad bout of bacterial pneumonia," she said. "I'm over it, but it takes a long time to recover from the weakness. I guess I've been overdoing things again. Funny," she mused, "I haven't had pneumonia since I was first married . . ." She broke off, remembering the occasion, and what had caused it. She had to watch her step. It was senseless to pour a potential scandal into the hands of a stranger.

"You're married?" he asked abruptly. "The man you share this cottage with is your husband?"

"I'm divorced," she said, giving him an unblinking, level stare. "And I don't talk about my ex-husband. Ever."

He didn't reply. She turned away and he watched her prepare an omelet with new curiosity. He didn't ask any

15

more questions. But he wondered about her, just the same.

"What do you like in your coffee?" Nikki asked as she poured it into thick white mugs and set them on the spotless green and white tablecloth.

"I think I like cream."

"I'd have thought you were a man who never added anything to his coffee," she murmured with amusement.

"Why?"

"I don't know, really. You seem oddly familiar to me, as if I knew you. But I know that I've never seen you face to face before," she said quietly.

He shrugged. "Maybe I have that kind of face."

Her eyebrows arched. "You?"

He smiled, just faintly. "Thanks." He sipped his coffee before he added anything to it. It tasted just right. "Very nice," he said. "Just strong enough."

"I make good coffee. It's my only real accomplishment, except for omelets."

"What does your poor friend eat?"

"He lives on fast food and restaurant chow, but he isn't home much."

"What does he do?"

Careful, she told herself. "He's . . . in energy," she said, which was the truth. He sat on the Energy and Commerce Committee.

"Oh. He works for a power plant?"

"Not exactly," she evaded, hiding the amusement in

16

her eyes as she thought about the power which that particular congressional committee wielded nationally.

"And what do you do?"

"Moi?" she laughed. "Oh, I sculpt."

"What do you sculpt?"

"People."

He looked around at the living room, but the only artwork visible was a print or two on the wall.

"I sell my work from galleries," she explained.

He decided to reserve judgment on that pat reply. The house was a dump, and she had to know it. She obviously had little money and lived with a man who had even less. He sensed he couldn't afford to trust her, but he didn't know why. "Do you have any of your work here?"

"A bust or two," she said. "I'll show you later, if you like."

He sampled the omelet she'd set before him. It was Spanish, with peppers and onions and salsa. "This is good!"

"Thanks." She watched his face. It was pale, and he seemed to have a hard time keeping his eyes open. "You're drowsy."

"Yes. I don't know how I know it, but I'm pretty sure that I haven't been sleeping well lately."

"Woman trouble?" she asked knowingly.

He frowned. "I don't know. Perhaps." He looked up. "I can't stay here . . ."

"Where would you go?" she asked reasonably.

"You can't wander up and down the beach around here. The security people will pick you up for vagrancy. Do you remember where you live?"

"I don't even know my name," he confessed uneasily. "You can't imagine how intimidating this is."

"Perhaps I can, in a way." She smiled. "Finish that," she nodded toward his food, "and I'll show you to the guest room."

He hadn't realized how tired he was until he finished the excellent omelet and coffee and she led him to the cozy guest bedroom. The clean sheets were turned down, and a magnificent quilt looked invitingly comfortable.

"I put your swimming trunks in the dryer while you were eating the omelet. I'm sorry, I don't have any pajamas that would fit you . . ."

"The trunks will do nicely," he replied. He looked around while she went to get his trunks. There were pretty priscilla curtains at the windows, with antique furnishings and a four-poster bed.

She was back a minute later. She handed him the trunks with a smile. "I'll check on you in a couple of hours," she said. "Need anything else?"

He shook his head. "Thank you," he said sincerely. "I don't remember anything, but I'm reasonably sure that I'm not a rapist or a serial killer."

"I'm delighted to hear it," she returned, tongue-in-cheek. "I'd hate being the subject of a movie-of-the-week."

He burst out laughing. She liked the sound of it, rich

and deep. Her ex-husband had laughed much like that. The smile faded from her face, and just for an instant, her torment showed through.

"Sing out if you feel sick," she said, wrapping her arms over her chest as she moved back toward the door.

"Sure." He watched her go with a narrow gaze, certain that impish mask she wore hid nightmares. He wondered why.

Two hours later, to the second, Nikki opened the door of the guest bedroom and stood watching him. He'd kicked the covers off and his body was sprawled in oblivious abandon. He wasn't distastefully hairy, but he had a nice thick wedge of curling dark hair on his broad chest that ran down to a narrow swath where it disappeared under the low waistband of his trunks. He had broad, thick legs with a deep tan and a feathering of hair, like his well-muscled arms. Stripped, he was the most beautiful man she'd ever seen. She looked at his body and wondered with a shock of pleasure what it would feel like to lie naked in his arms.

She walked briskly to the bed and shook him gently.

His eyes opened, unseeing. "Christy," he said.

So there was a woman in his life. She wasn't surprised. But she was oddly disappointed.

"How do you feel?" she asked.

He blinked and seemed to regain his senses. "My head hurts," he said with a frown.

"Badly?"

"No. It just hurts. And before you ask, I'm not nauseated."

"Okay." She smiled. "Go back to sleep."

He caught her hand as she started to move. "Don't take this the wrong way, but wouldn't it be easier to keep an eye on me from in here? It's a damned big bed, and I don't have designs on you."

Her heart skipped. "That wouldn't be wise."

"Pull that armchair closer to the bed, then, and curl up in it."

He didn't look frightened. But perhaps he was. He couldn't remember who he was, where he came from, and a doctor had told him that he could die in the night.

"I'll get a blanket," she said. "It's warm here, but the nights can be cool."

He managed a faint smile. He wasn't afraid, he told himself. But she looked so fragile. He disliked the thought of her losing sleep over him. He should have gone into the hospital, he supposed, but he was sure that he hated hospitals. If only he could remember why . . .

She was back. She had a robe around her and she pulled the armchair up and curled up next to the bed. She had a small travel clock in her hand, which she set and put on the bedside table. "If I drift off now, it won't matter," she said dryly.

He studied her small oval face with curiosity and a strange pleasure. "You'll roast in all that gear."

She shrugged. "Not really. I get chilled easily, and that could halt my recovery."

"I could sit up in the chair and you could have the bed," he offered.

"Don't be silly." She smiled at him gently. "Go to sleep."

He lay back and closed his eyes. He was sure that no one had fussed over him like this since he was a boy. In a minute, he drifted off to sleep.

It was daylight. Nikki felt exhausted, but her houseguest was sleeping much less restlessly now. She was sure that he was going to be all right. Just the same, she woke him to make sure he was as fit as he looked.

She bent over him and touched his broad chest. During the night she'd only pushed at his shoulder to wake him, but now her fingers lingered.

The effect her touch had on the man in the bed was immediate and startling. He caught his breath as she stroked him, and he arched with a faint moan.

She jerked her hand back and froze in place. He stirred, frowning. But after a minute, he relaxed again and his breathing became steady and regular.

Feeling reprieved, Nikki sneaked out the door and gently closed it behind her. She still had time to manage an hour or two's sleep before it would be time to prepare breakfast.

CHAPTER
TWO

For those two hours, Nicole slept fitfully, haunted by images of her houseguest sprawled in magnificent abandon on the bed in the guest room. She woke up reluctantly when the alarm she'd set again went off.

She brushed her teeth and hair and slipped into a neat blue patterned sundress. A brief check of the guest room told her that her guest was breathing normally. She closed the door and went to the laundry room to start a load of clothes. When she picked up her discarded beach robe from the day before, a watch fell out of the pocket.

She stared at it curiously. It was a Rolex. She turned it over and back again, surprised that she hadn't noticed it before. Her houseguest must be a very successful man to afford such a watch. She put it on the shelf and started the laundry before she went to the kitchen, barefoot as usual, to make breakfast. It was a good thing that she had plenty of provisions, she thought. Judging by his size and build, the man in the guest room had a more than ample appetite.

She'd just dished up scrambled eggs to go with the sweet rolls and sausages when he entered the living room. Wearing the slacks she'd found and the shirt whose edges didn't quite meet in front, he still managed to look elegant.

The man also looked headachy, out of sorts, and vaguely confused.

"Are you all right?" she asked immediately.

He glowered at her. "I feel as flat as an overdrawn account. Otherwise, I suppose I'll do." He spoke without any particular accent, although there was a faint residual drawl there. His was not a Charleston accent, though, she mused; and she ought to know, because her own was fairly thick.

"How about some coffee?" she asked.

His thick eyebrows jerked. "Do you have a caffeine fixation? Every time I see you, I'm offered coffee."

She grinned. "They say that the universal panacea in England is tea. Here, it's coffee. But I do have some aspirin, if you need them," she added.

"I could use a couple, thanks. My head isn't pounding, but I still have a sizeable headache."

She got the aspirin while he sat down at the table and poured coffee into his cup and hers. Cream and sugar were already in place, but she noticed that today he didn't add either to his cup. She grimaced at the chipped sugar dish. It had once been good Haviland china, the pattern a favorite of her late mother's. It was a relic of bygone days that should have been thrown out. But Nikki had a hard time giving up keepsakes.

She noticed her companion eyeing the sugar bowl, no doubt contemplating the relative poverty of the house's occupants. And he wasn't far wrong.

She handed him the aspirin bottle and watched him shake two white tablets into the palm of his large hand. She watched him swallow them down with black coffee. "I'll bet you're a straight-up whiskey man with no larcenous traits and a tendency to obey signs."

"What?"

"I make a hobby of watching how people take their coffee," she continued, grinning at him. "You like yours black, with no flourishes, nothing fancy. I like mine with cream and lots of sugar; company for the coffee, you see," she added, tongue-in-cheek. "Which means that I like people."

"And insinuates what about me?" he asked with a lifted eyebrow.

"You don't like people," she said, and then sat waiting for him to contradict her.

He didn't. He scowled into his coffee. But he didn't remember that; not consciously.

"Do you still not remember anything?" she asked bluntly, concerned.

"I remember how I hit my head," he began slowly, warily. His eyes were very watchful when he looked at her now, because he remembered quite a lot more than the accident. He knew who he was, but he didn't plan to tell her. She was obviously a lady in need of money, and a man in his position couldn't afford to leave himself too vulnerable. In the past he'd found too many people cared more about his money than himself. He did find her attractive; too attractive altogether in that skimpy blue sundress she was wearing. It left her long, tanned legs very bare and emphasized the firm, enticing curve of her breasts without being blatant. He deliberately averted his eyes to the table.

"How did you get hurt?" she prompted gently.

"I was swimming. Too far out," he added a little ruefully. "I guess I was being reckless. A jet ski came too close. I barely avoided it, then the wake knocked me into some rocks. I remember not being able to catch my breath, then darkness. The current must have dragged me here. Hell of a thing that I didn't drown."

"Yes, the undertow can be deadly," she said, recalling other incidents from days past. "You must have an angel on your shoulder."

"Are there angels?" he asked with a cynical laugh. "If there are, I haven't been blessed with their company much in my life."

"You've remembered, haven't you?" she persisted.

"I've remembered a few things," he confessed. "Not a lot." He felt for his watch and frowned. Hadn't he had one when he he'd gone into the water? A diver's watch?

"Oh, I almost forgot!" She jumped up and reached onto the counter by the stove, producing the missing wristwatch. "Here. This fell off your wrist when I found

found you. I stuck it in my robe pocket and didn't notice it until this morning when I started to put the robe in the laundry. Good thing I didn't wash it,'' she laughed. "However do you tell time with something so complicated?''

She didn't recognize a diver's watch. Did that mean she didn't realize how expensive it was?

He took it from her. "Thanks,'' he said slowly.

"It still works, doesn't it?'' she asked idly as she ate her eggs. "I didn't know they made waterproof watches.''

"It's a diver's watch,'' he informed her, and then waited for her reaction.

"I see. Do you skin dive?'' she asked brightly.

He did, occasionally, when he wasn't sailing his yacht. He didn't want to mention that. "Sometimes,'' he said.

"I wanted to learn, but I'm too afraid of being under water for long periods of time,'' she told him. "But I love living near the ocean, especially in a place like this. We have a golf course and tennis courts and there's a marina nearby . . . what is it?''

"Does the man you live with own this house?''

She saw the way he was looking at her and interpreted it correctly. That watch wasn't cheap, and he'd apparently remembered more than he wanted her to know. So he thought she was a golddigger, did he? She was going to enjoy this.

"Why, yes . . .'' she stopped suddenly, not wanting to give too much away. His face was all too familiar, more so this morning. "He lets me stay here when I like."

He glanced around at the room and then back at her. His expression spoke volumes.

He didn't say anything else. He concentrated on the meal Nikki had prepared. His dark eyes slid over her pretty face and narrowed.

"What did the doctor call you? Nikki?" he asked curiously.

"Yes, Nikki," she replied. Even if he knew of her family, he wouldn't know of the nickname, which was used only by family and very close friends. "Do you remember yours?"

He studied her quietly, thoughtfully, while he wavered between the truth and a lie. She was obviously a transient here, in her boyfriend's house. He lived across the bay and he was new to the area. It was highly unlikely that she'd even know who he was if he introduced himself honestly. He kept a low profile. In his income bracket, it paid to do that.

He laughed at his own caution. This woman probably didn't even know what the CEO of a corporation was. "It's McKane," he said offhandedly. "But I'm usually called Kane."

Fortunately, Nikki had her eyes on her coffee cup. The Rolex watch was suddenly explained. She didn't show it, but inside she panicked. The familiar face she hadn't been able to place earlier now leaped vividly into her consciousness. She knew that name all too well, and now she remembered where she'd seen the face:

Forbes magazine. Kane Lombard was reclusive to the point of being a hermit, and the published photograph of him had been a rarity for such a successful businessman.

She also knew that her brother had just butted heads with Kane Lombard over an environmental issue in Charleston. Lombard, she knew, was backing the leading Republican contender for Clayton's House seat.

Her mind worked rapidly. Now she couldn't let him know who she was. They'd spent the night together, albeit innocently. Wouldn't that tidbit do Clayton a lot of good in an election? Issues of morality were still enough to make or break a politician here. And Lombard was helping the opposition.

Her fingers closed around her coffee cup and she lifted her eyes with a schooled expression on her face. Everything would be all right. All she had to do was ease him out of here without letting on that she knew him. Since he didn't travel in the same circles as Clayton and she, chances were good that she'd never see him up close again anyway.

"It's a nice name. I like it." She smiled as if she genuinely didn't recognize him. "You've remembered everything, haven't you?" she added.

"Yes. Especially a speeding jet ski."

She smiled. "I'm glad. It must have been frightening."

"Somewhat." His firm mouth tugged into a smile. "Thanks for taking care of me," he added. "It was a risky thing to do, for a total stranger."

"Oh, I make a habit of dragging half-drowned strange

men up from beaches,'' she said saucily. ''But next time, you might watch more closely for jet skis when you decide to go swimming—just in case I'm not looking.''

''I'll do that.''

He finished his coffee and reluctantly, she thought, got to his feet. ''I'll return your friend's clothes. Thanks for the loan.''

''I can run you home, if you live nearby,'' she offered, knowing full well that he wouldn't risk letting her see where he lived. Everything in his mind was easily read on his face right now. He was afraid she'd be after his money. She could have laughed out loud at the very idea.

''No, thanks,'' he said quickly, smiling to soften the rejection. ''I'll walk, or hitch a ride if I see any of the security people patrolling. You've been very kind.'' His eyes were shrewd. ''I hope I can repay you one day.''

''Oh, that's not necessary,'' she assured him, standing. ''Don't we all have a moral duty to help each other out when we're in need?'' She looked at her slender, well-kept hands. ''I'm sure you'd do the same for me if I needed help of any kind.''

That last bit was meant to rattle him, but it didn't work. She looked up, impishly, and he was just watching her with a lifted eyebrow and a faintly indulgent smile.

''Of course I would,'' he assured her. But he was wary again, looking for traps, even while his eyes were quietly bold on her soft curves.

"It was nice meeting you," she added.

"Same here." He gave her a last wistful appraisal and went with long, determined strides toward the front door. He walked as if he'd go right over anything in his path, and Nikki envied him that self-confidence. She had it, to a degree, but in a standing fight, he was going to be a hard man to best.

The rambling beach house where Kane lived was in the same immaculate shape he'd left it. His daily woman had been in, apparently unconcerned that he was missing. He realized that there wasn't anyone who would readily notice if he lived or died.

He chided himself for that cynical thought. Women did agonize over him from time to time. He had a mistress who cared, in her way, in return for the expensive presents he gave her with careless affection. But no one cared as much as his son had. He closed his eyes and tried not to remember the horror of his last sight of the young boy.

There was a portrait of his son with his late wife on the side table. He looked at that, instead, remembering David as a bright young man of seven years, with his mother's light hair and eyes and her smile. Although he and Evelyn had grown apart over their ten years together, their son David had been loved and cherished by them both. He had taken them on what should have been a routine business trip. He had planned to check on some negotiations one of his attorneys was conduct-

31

ing with an oil minister from another Arab state. There had been no recent trouble in Beirut, so Kane took his family along, expecting to fly them on to Paris afterwards for a holiday. But they had no sooner arrived when all hell had broken loose. He and his family had been caught innocently in a crossfire between two groups of rebels fighting for supremacy in the streets of Beirut, Lebanon.

He'd blamed himself bitterly for all of it, but time was taking away some of the sting. He had to go on, after all.

The new automotive plant in an industrial Charleston suburb had certainly been his salvation. Planned long before the death of his family, it had just begun operation about the time they were buried. Now it was the linchpin of his sanity.

He changed into a knit shirt and shorts, idly placing his borrowed clothing in a hamper so it would be washed before he returned it. Nikki's sparkling green eyes came to mind and made him smile. She was so young, he mused, and probably a madcap when she set her mind to it. For a moment he allowed himself to envy her lover. She had a pretty body, slender and winsome. But he had Christy when he needed a woman desperately, and there was no place for a permanent woman in his life. Chris knew that. She didn't expect too much from him.

He picked up the telephone and dialed the offices of the Charleston plant. What he needed, he told himself, was something to occupy his mind again. His plant manager was away, but he spoke to a subordinate and was promptly faxed a summary of the past two days' production reports.

Just before quitting time in Charleston, he called the plant again. "Get Will Jurkins on the line," he replied to his secretary's polite greeting.

"Yes, sir," she said at once.

A minute later, a slow voice came on the line. "How's the vacation going, Mr. Lombard?" asked his brand-new chief of waste management.

"So far, so good," Kane said carelessly. "I want to know why you've terminated that contract with the Coastal Waste Company."

There was a pause. On the other end of the line, Jurkins wiped his sweaty brow. "Well . . . uh, I had to."

"Why?"

"I believe I mentioned to you, Mr. Lombard, that I noticed discrepancies in their invoices."

"I don't remember any such conversation."

"Listen, Mr. Lombard," he began in a conciliatory tone, "you're a busy man. You can't keep up with all the little details of a plant this size. You sit on the board of directors of three other corporations and the board of trustees of two colleges, you belong to business organizations where you hold office. I mean, how would you have the time to sift through all the day-to-day stuff here?"

Kane took a breath to stem his rush of temper. He didn't like Jurkins' tone. The man was new, however, and he made sense. "That's true. I haven't time to oversee every facet of every operation. Normally, this would be Ed Nelson's problem."

"I know that, yes, I do, sir. But Mr. Nelson's had kidney stones and he had to have surgery for them last week. He's sort of low. Not that he doesn't keep up with things," he added quickly. "He's still on top of the situation here."

Kane relaxed. Jurkins was chief of the waste disposal unit. He had to trust him to do his job. "All right," he said. "Who have you contracted with to replace CWC?"

"I found a very reputable company, Mr. Lombard," he assured his boss. "Very reputable, indeed. In fact, two of the local automotive parts companies use them. It's Burke's."

"Burke's?"

"They're not as well-known as CWC, sir," Jurkins said. "They're a young company, but very energetic. They don't cost an arm and a leg, either."

Kane's head was hurting.

"All right, Jurkins. Go ahead and make the switch. I'll approve it, if there's any flak," he said. "Just make sure they do what they're supposed to. Put Jenny back on the line."

"Yes, sir! Have a good vacation, sir, and don't you worry, everything's going along just fine!"

Kane made a grunting sound and waited for Jenny.

He wanted her to fax him some contract estimates and correspondence.

While Kane was debating his next move, a relieved Will Jurkins pushed back his sweaty hair and breathed a long sigh, glancing worriedly at the man standing beside him.

"That was a close one," he told the man. "Mr. Lombard wanted to know why I made the switch to Burke's."

"You're getting enough out of this deal to make it worth the risk," came the laconic reply. "And you're in too deep to back out. You don't want to go to jail, do you, Will?"

"No," Jurkins said uneasily. "Are you sure I won't, for this? Mr. Lombard doesn't know that Burke is my late wife's brother . . . You won't let that get out, will you? Of course, I could tell them all about you, too," he added slowly.

"And who'd believe you?" The man laughed at his cohort's worried expression. "Will you stop worrying? I know what I'm doing." He slipped Jurkins a wad of large bills, careful not to let himself be seen. "This ought to ease your mind a bit."

Jurkins grimaced as he counted the money and quickly slipped it into his pocket. He needed the extra cash to help his family, though he felt uneasy about the way he was earning it.

* * *

Clayton Seymour had gone down the roster of Democratic representatives over a new bill that affected cable television rates. He and his legislative committee, not to mention part of his personal staff, were helping his friend, the minority whip, gather enough representatives together for a decisive vote on the issue. But he was going blind in the process. He looked out his window at the distant Washington, D.C. skyline and wished he were back home in Charleston, fishing. He maintained two district offices; only two, whereas most of the other House members had anywhere from two to eight.

Each of those offices back home in South Carolina had full-time and part-time staffers who could handle requests from constituents. In addition, he'd appointed a constituent staff at his Washington office, along with his legislative, institutional, and personal staff. It sounded like a lot of people on the payroll, but there were actually only a handful involved and they were eminently qualified.

During his term in office, he'd remained within his budget. It was one of many feathers in his political cap. In addition, he had seats on the Energy and Commerce Committee and the Ways and Means Committee, among others. He worked from twelve to fourteen hours a day and occasionally took offense at remarks that members of Congress were overpaid layabouts. He didn't have time to lie about. In the next Congress, more than eleven thousand new pieces of legislation were predicted for introduction. If he was reelected—he had to think positively, *when* he was reelected—he was going to have to work even harder.

His senior aide in charge of his personal and constituent staff, Derrie Keller, knocked on the door and opened it all in the same motion. She was tall and pretty, with light blond hair and blue eyes and a nice smile. Everybody was kind to her because she had such a sweet nature. Clayton liked her because of her keen mind and her efficiency. She was tough when the situation called for it. She oversaw his personal staff in both district offices.

"Ah, Derrie," he said with a long-suffering sigh. "Are you going to bury me in paperwork again?"

She grinned. "Want to lie down, first, so we can do it properly?"

"If I lie down, three senators and a newspaperman will come in and stand on me," he assured her. He sat upright in his chair. He was good-looking; tall, dark-haired and blue-eyed, with a charismatic personality and a perfect smile.

Women loved him, Derrie thought; particularly a highly paid Washington lawyer named Bett Watts. The woman was forever in and out of the office. She was polite and friendly to just about everyone in the office except Derrie, whom Bett saw as too influential with Clayton.

"Are you going to stand there all day?" he prompted impatiently.

"Sorry." She put the letters on his desk. "Want coffee?"

"You can't bring me coffee," he said absently. "You're an overpaid public official with administrative duties. If you bring me coffee, secretarial unions will storm the office and sacrifice me on the White House lawn."

She knew this speech by heart. She just smiled. "Cream and sugar?"

"Yes, please," he replied with a grin.

"Here you go," she said a minute later, reappearing with two steaming cups. She put hers down and sat in the chair beside his desk with her pad and pen in hand.

"Thanks." He was studying another piece of legislation on which a vote would shortly be taken. "New stuff on the agenda today, Derrie. I'll need you to direct one of the interns to do some legwork for me."

"Is that piece of legislation connected to the old growth forest bill and the renewal of the Endangered Species Act?" she asked, eyeing the paper in his lean hands.

"Yes," he said with resignation.

"You told the media you were in favor of logging the old forests and against renewing the Endangered Species Act."

He sighed as he lifted his cup of coffee, fixed with cream just as he liked it, and looked at her while he sipped it gingerly. "That's right," he said firmly.

She glared at him. "The spotted owl's habitat is in the old growth forest. If you vote to timber it . . . ."

"It will preserve jobs for loggers," he concluded for her.

"It's an old forest," she persisted. "One of the oldest untouched forests in the world."

"Derrie, we can't sacrifice jobs because of an owl," he said, exasperated. "Listen, why don't you meet with all those lobbyists who represent the lumberjacks and the timber industry? Maybe you can explain your position to them better than I could. We need the timber industry."

"How long do you think there's going to be a timber industry if you start letting people destroy old habitats?"

"For God's sake!" he exclaimed. He sat forward in his chair. "Hasn't anybody ever explained basic economics to you? Ecology is wonderful, I'm all for it. In fact, I have a very enviable record in South Carolina for my stand against toxic waste dumps and industrial polluters. However, this is another issue entirely. We're being asked to set aside thousands of acres of viable timber to save one owl, when people are jobless while logging is prohibited in spotted owl habitats—which is, by the way, going to impact taxpayers all the way from Oregon to D.C."

"I know all that," she grumbled. "But we're cutting down all the trees we have and we're not replacing them fast enough. In fact, how can you replace something that old?"

"You can't replace it," he agreed. "But old things, even trees, die naturally. You can't replace people, either, Derrie."

"There are things you're overlooking," she persisted. "Have you read all the background literature on that bill?"

"When do I have time?" he exploded. "My God, you of all people should know how fast they throw legislation at me! If I read every word of every bill . . ."

"I can read it for you. If you'll listen I'll tell you why the bill is a good idea."

"I have legislative counsel to advise me," he said tersely, glaring at her. "My executive legislative counsel is a Harvard graduate."

Derrie knew that. She also liked Mary Tanner, an elegant black woman whose Harvard law degree often surprised people who mistook her for a model. Mary was beautiful.

"Yes, she is," she agreed. "Which is why you should listen to her when she advises you to vote in favor of a piece of legislation!"

"The people elected me, not my staff," he reminded her with a cold stare. "And this is a complex issue; very complex."

She almost challenged that look. But he'd been under a lot of pressure, and there was time before the issue came to a vote to work on him. She backed down. "All right." *For now,* she said to herself.

"I'll work my fingers to the bone for you, but I won't quit sharing my opinions on the old forest legislation," she warned. "I don't believe in profit at the expense of the environment."

"Then you aren't living in the real world."

She gave him a killing glare and walked out of the room. It was to her credit that she didn't slam the door behind her.

Clayton watched her retreat with mixed emotions. Usually, Derrie agreed with him on issues. This time, she was fighting tooth and nail. It always amused him to see her ready to scratch and claw because generally her nature was so easygoing.

The telephone rang and a minute later, Derrie's arctic voice informed him that Ms. Watts was on the line.

"Hello, Bett," he said to the caller. "How are you?"

"Worn," came the teasing reply. "I can't see you tonight. I've got a board meeting, followed by a cocktail party, followed by a brief meeting with one of the senior senators, all of which I really must get through."

"Don't you ever get tired of practicing corporate law and long for something different?" he probed.

"Something like lobbying for the environmental people who are fighting to save a few acres of forest for a near extinct owl?" Bett asked.

Clayton felt himself going rigid. "You've been talking to Miles again," he said irritably.

She laughed. "Miles is Secretary of the Interior. He likes trees. He likes owls, too. He's very unhappy with you for going against him on television."

"People need jobs, Bett," he replied.

"There won't be any when they cut all the trees down . . ."

"Have to go, Bett. I'll talk to you later." He put the phone down on another nippy comment.

Derrie buzzed him. "Yes?" he asked furiously.

"Excuse me," she said placatingly, "but it's Miles Townshend on the phone."

"Oh. Sorry. I had a disagreement with Bett," he felt drawn to explain.

"Really? Does she like little owls, too?"

He slammed the phone down on Derrie and took Miles's call.

"Don't you say one word about owls and old forests to me!" Clayton dared the former South Carolina senator.

"All right," Miles drawled. "I guess you've heard enough about them from everybody else."

"I did what I thought was best," Clayton said gruffly.

"You need to talk to your constituents before you go doing things on your own. I told you that when you won the seat. You can't do what you please in office. Not if you want to get reelected; and listen, you've got some pretty stiff opposition this time."

"I know," Clayton said heavily. "I'm not worried about the primary. There's nobody running against me on the Democratic opposition that has me nervous."

"I know. Sam Hewett has a good record in the state senate and plenty of rich backers, not the least of whom is Kane Lombard, the automotive magnate. In fact, Lombard's brother is his campaign manager. Now that Kane Lombard is living right in your lap in Charleston, you won't be able to avoid them."

"The man's got a real attitude problem, and he's an outsider. Not good South Carolina stock, for sure!"

Miles chuckled. "I hear you. Now listen, I called to offer you somebody real special for the election. He volunteered. Came to see me this morning and took a real interest in getting you reelected . . . which I wouldn't mind either if you'd stop trying to leave my owls homeless!" he added.

Clayton twisted the telephone cord unusually hard, but Miles didn't sound as if he might be strangling. "Okay. Who is he?"

"John Haralson. You remember what a mess I got into with that mudslinging opponent of mine last election? Well, it was Haralson who got me enough leverage to make him withdraw. He's savvy and he's studied law. No degree, but you wouldn't know it."

"Is he honest?" Clayton asked, because he considered that the most necessary characteristic in his people. Honest men generally had integrity.

"Well . . . I guess so. I mean, I don't know why he wouldn't be."

"You say he's good."

"He's the best. No question."

"Then suppose you send him over to see me and we'll talk."

"He's on his way now." He laughed. "I figured you'd want him. This is going to be a hot campaign."

"How are you?" Clayton asked pointedly.

There was a pause. "I get by. It's going to be a new political climate up here pretty soon, and my life might get a little easier." There was another pause. "How's Nikki?"

Clayton sighed. "She's managing."

"Your father and I should have been shot for what we maneuvered her into," he said after a minute. "I panicked. I'm sorry Nikki had to pay such a high price."

"She never blamed you."

"I did."

"It's over."

Miles didn't reply. "Let me know how Haralson works out, will you?"

"Sure thing. Thanks."

Derrie was so surprised to see John Haralson that it took her a minute to get her breath before she announced him to Clayton. The small-eyed man had curly black hair, sprinkled with gray, and the look of a con man. Derrie wondered what he wanted here.

Clayton greeted Haralson and invited him into the office, oblivious to Derrie's look of concern.

They talked quietly for several minutes and Haralson was charming and intelligent. Clayton was impressed. Not only had Miles recommended him, but Haralson had a handful of references from several newly-elected politicians for whom he'd won elections.

"I'd like you to work with me on the campaign," Clayton said finally. "I'll give you a free hand as reelection coordinator." He named a salary and Haralson grinned.

"I had a hunch you'd want me," Haralson said with

a crafty smile, "so I started the ball rolling back in Charleston a couple of weeks ago. I know exactly what to do to get you reelected, so you just sit back, do your job, and let me worry about the election."

Clayton laughed. "You sound very confident. I like that."

"I have plenty of reason to be confident. Oh, I think we'll get along very well," Haralson said. He stood up, much shorter and stockier than Clayton, and shook hands. "Leave it all to me."

Clayton remembered thinking that the man had unusually sweaty palms. Odd, but then, it was summer.

"What did he want?" Derrie asked when Haralson left. Her tone was challenging.

Clayton gave her a hard glare. "He's my new reelection campaign manager."

"Haralson?!"

He scowled. "Miles recommended him."

She knew Miles was a gentleman, but if the vicious rumors about Haralson were to be believed, the man Miles had recommended was a weasel.

"Listen, did you check him out?" she began, not wanting to start another fight.

"Yes, I checked him out!" he said, exasperated. "Do you have to question every decision I make lately?"

"Only the bad ones, boss," she said, grinning.

He groaned and went back into his office.

Derrie chuckled to herself. But the first thing she did was to make a quick telephone call and arrange to meet a man she knew in law enforcement circles in Washington. She was certain he could tell her anything she wanted to know about Haralson.

Clayton phoned Nikki that evening. He didn't mention his discussion with Derrie, which had resulted in her leaving early. He sat in his office alone with cold coffee and hot bills. He had to depend on his district director for coffee, and Stan made really lousy coffee.

"I'm not going to be able to turn loose for at least two weeks," he said sadly. "I'd love to spend some time with you before we get our feet good and wet in this campaign, but I've got too much on my plate."

"Take some time off. Congress won't be in session much longer."

"I know that. I am a U.S. representative," he reminded her dryly. "Which is all the more reason for me to push these so-and-so's into getting down here to vote when our bill comes up. I can't leave."

"In that case, don't expect me to wait for you."

"Would I? Anyway, you need the rest more than I do," he said with a laugh. "How's everything going?"

"Fine," she said. "Nothing exciting. A big fish washed up on the beach . . ."

"I hope you didn't try to save it," he muttered. "You're hell to take on a fishing trip, with your overstimulated protective instincts."

"I let this one go," she said, feeling vaguely guilty that she was keeping a secret from him. It was the first time, too. "It wasn't hurt very badly. It swam away and I'll never see it again." That much was probably true.

"Well, stay out of trouble, can't you?"

"Clay, I'll do my very best," she promised.

"Get some rest. You'll need it when autumn comes and the campaigning begins in earnest."

"Don't I know it," she chuckled.

"I landed a new campaign manager today," he said. "Someone Miles recommended."

There was a pause. "He'll be a good man, then," she said quietly.

"Sorry, Sis," he said, wincing. "I didn't mean to . . ."

"It's all right. Really. Goodnight, Clay."

"Goodnight." He hung up, cursing his own insensitivity.

Nikki hung up the phone and went to lounge on the deck, watching the whitecaps curl rhythmically into the white beach. The moon shone on them and as she sipped white wine, she thought that she'd never felt quite so alone.

In many ways Miles was still an open wound. Oddly, though, it hurt less tonight than it would have even a few days earlier.

She looked out over the ocean and suddenly she wondered what Mr. Lombard was doing.

CHAPTER
THREE

Kane Lombard was sitting on his own deck with a highball contemplating the moonlit sparkle of the ocean. He felt unfulfilled.

He was thirty-eight years old. He'd had a wife, and a son. His ten-year marriage, while not perfect, had given him a sense of security. Now he was among the ranks of the single men again, but without the youth and idealism that made marriage a viable prospect. He was jaded, and somewhere along the way he'd lost all his illusions about people. About life. He was like those waves, he thought, being aimlessly thrown onto the beach and then forgotten. When he died, there would be nothing to leave behind, nothing to show that Kane Lombard had lived on this planet.

That wasn't totally true, he chided himself as he swallowed a sip of his stinging cocktail. He had the company to leave behind. The name would probably be changed somewhere down the line, though. Names didn't last long. Men lasted least of all.

He leaned back on the chaise longue and closed his eyes. Nikki. Her name was Nikki, and she had black hair and green eyes and the face of an angel. He liked the way she looked, the way she laughed, as if life still had wonderful things to offer. He knew better, but she made him optimistic. He needed someone like that.

Not permanently, of course, he told himself. He needed an affair. Just an affair. Would she be willing? She seemed to find him attractive enough. She was a divorced woman, so she knew the rules. If he took her out and bided his time, would she be receptive? He sloshed the liquid in the glass, listening to the soft chink of the ice cubes against the watery roar of the ocean. Perhaps she was lonely, too. God knew, there was no monopoly on loneliness. Like the air itself, it permeated everything. His eyelids felt heavy. He closed them, just for a minute . . .

It was dawn when he awoke, still lying on the chaise longue, with the chill morning air in his face. The glass, long since forgotten, had fallen gently to the deck and was dry now, the ice and whiskey melted and evaporated on the wooden boards. He got up, stretching with faint soreness. His head was much better, but there were still vestiges of a headache. He stared out over the ocean, distracted. Before he had time to contemplate the pain over his eyes too much, the telephone rang loudly.

His housekeeper's strident voice called out to him.

"Telephone, Mr. Lombard!"

"I'll take it out here," he returned gruffly.

She handed him the freedom phone and he nodded curtly as he took it, waving her away. "Yes?" he asked.

"I'm Todd Sanders, Mr. Lombard," a deep voice replied. "I work for your father and brothers in New York at the *Weekly Voice*," he prompted when there was a long pause on the other end of the line.

Kane recognized the name. Sanders was his father's star reporter, if a man who was better at creating news than gathering it could be called a journalist.

"Yes, I know you," Kane said. "What do you want?"

"Your father sent me to Charleston to do a little prospecting. Since your brother is now the campaign manager for Sam Hewett, your father wants me to do a little investigating on the Democratic U.S. Representative incumbent, Seymour. Nothing that isn't routine," he was quick to add. "I'm not looking for sensational stories, just for anything we can use in the campaign, you see. I've just checked into a hotel here. Any ideas about a good place to start looking for skeletons?"

"I can't help you. I haven't lived in Charleston long enough to know many people. I only know Seymour's reputation," he added curtly. "If I put a step wrong, he'll be over me like tarpaper, I know that. We had a sewage leak a couple of weeks ago—accidental, of course—and he's been after my neck ever since. On television he pointed his finger at me saying I was the perfect example of a money-hungry anticonservationist." He shook his head. "He's gung-ho on this industrial pollution issue. It's his number one priority."

"Interesting that he's fighting for the timber companies in the northwest," Sanders murmured, tongue-in-cheek.

"The habitat of an owl out west apparently doesn't do him as much political good as digging out industrial polluters on his doorstep."

"You said it."

"Keep me posted, will you?"

"You bet."

He put down the receiver. Seymour was an odd bird, he thought. The man had little material wealth, but his old Charleston heritage had helped put him in office. The quiet backing of the Secretary of the Interior, Miles Townshend, hadn't hurt, either. The former junior U.S. senator from South Carolina was a personable man with an equally impeccable reputation, even if he had a failed marriage behind him. Miles's marriage had been very brief, Kane understood, and rather secretive, but that had been because of his bride's tender age. He couldn't quite remember, but it seemed that there had been some connection between Miles and the Seymours before that. He'd have to remember and tell Sanders the next time they spoke.

In the campaign headquarters of Sam Hewett, candidate for the Republican nomination to the U.S. House of Representatives for the district that included Charleston,

South Carolina, a heated discussion was taking place between Hewett and his advisers.

"You can't risk a personal attack on Seymour at this point," Norman Lombard muttered. His dark eyes lanced the candidate, who was tall and thin and rather nervous. "We'll take care of that later. My father owns the biggest tabloid in America and my brothers and I are solidly behind you, financially and every other way. You just shake hands and make friends. For now, worry about nothing more than the Republican nomination. When the time comes, we'll have enough to slide you past Seymour at the polls."

"What if I can't gather enough support?" Hewett asked uneasily. "I'm not that well known, and I don't have the background Seymour has."

"You'll have the name identification when we get through with you," Norman said, chuckling. "My dad knows how to get the publicity. You'll get the votes. We guarantee it."

"You won't do anything illegal?" the candidate asked.

The question seemed to be perennial in Hewett's mind. Lombard sighed angrily. His brother Kane had the same reservations any time the tabloid let its reporters loose on a story. They'd cautioned Sanders about telling Kane too much when hunting for leads in Charleston.

"We won't have to do anything illegal," Norman assured the other man for the tenth time. "A little gossip here, a little doubt there, and we'll have the seat in our grasp. Just relax, Sam. You're a shoe-in. Enjoy the ride.''

"I want to win honestly."

"The last person who won honestly was George Washington," Lombard joked cynically. "But never mind, we'll do our best to keep your conscience quiet. Now, get out there and campaign, Sam. And stop worrying, will you? I promise you, it will all work out for the best."

Hewett wasn't as certain as his adviser appeared to be, but he was a newcomer to politics. He was learning more than he wanted to about the election process every day. He'd been idealistic and enthusiastic at the outset. Now, he was losing his illusions by the minute. He couldn't help but wonder if this was what the founding fathers had in mind when they outlined the electoral process. It seemed a real shame that qualifications meant nothing at all in the race; it was a contest of personalities and high-tech advertising and money, not issues. But on that foundation, the election rested. He did want to win, he told himself. But for the first time, he wasn't sure why.

It had thrilled him when the Lombards had decided to back him as a candidate. It had been Kane Lombard's idea initially. Kane liked Sam because they were both yachtsmen, and because Sam supported tax cuts and other incentives that would help his fledgling automobile manufacturing industry in Charleston. Mainly, Sam thought, it was because Clayton Seymour had taken an instant dislike to Kane and had done everything possible to put obstacles in his path when the auto manufacturing firm had first located in Charleston. The antagonism had been mutual. Now, with Kane's latest bad luck in having a sewage spill into the river, Seymour had attacked him from every angle.

When Norman Lombard had offered to act as his campaign manager, Sam had been elated and jumped at the chance. But although Sam wanted to win, he wanted to do so honestly.

He worried about the national reputation of the tabloid Kane's father and brothers owned in New York. It focused increasingly on politics and it had published some nasty exposés on pet projects of Interior Secretary Miles Townshend lately; any projects, in fact, that favored environmental interests over industrial ones. The Lombards were publicly opposed to lobbying by any environmental group, and it was well known that Townshend had once been a member of the Sierra Club. The Lombards had been giving him some bad press lately.

In fact, their tabloid had made some veiled threats about going on a witchhunt to drag out scandals among high members of the president's cabinet. That had been about the time Clayton Seymour announced his bid for reelection.

Nicole had driven her small used red sports car into the village market near the medical center to get milk and bread—the eternal necessities—and fresh fruit. She had just arrived home and stepped onto her porch when she heard the sound of a car pulling to a stop behind her.

She turned, and found Kane Lombard climbing out of a ramshackle old jeep. She wondered just for an instant where he'd borrowed such a dilapidated vehicle before the sight of him in jeans and a white knit shirt made her heart start beating faster.

He smiled at the picture she made in cutoff denim shorts and a pink tank top. A dark tan gave her an almost continental look.

"You tan well," he remarked.

"Our ancestors were French Huguenots, who came to Charleston in the late seventeenth century to escape religious persecution in Europe," she told him. "I'm told that our olive complexion comes from them."

"I brought back the things you loaned me." He handed her a bundle. "Washed and pressed," he added.

"With your own two hands?" she teased.

He liked the way her eyes sparkled when she smiled. She made him feel young again. "Not quite." He stuck his hands in his pockets and studied her closely, with pursed lips. "Come for a ride."

Her heart skipped. She couldn't afford to get mixed up with her brother's political enemy, she told herself firmly. Really she couldn't. Her heart persuaded her otherwise.

"Just let me put these things up," she said.

He followed her inside and wandered around the living room while she put everything away.

"I should change . . ." she began.

"Why?" He turned, smiling at her. "You look fine to me."

"In that case, I'm ready."

She locked the door, grateful that she hadn't any photographs sitting around that might clue him in to her relationship with Clayton. Nor was there anything expensive or antique in the beach house. She and Clayton didn't keep valuables here.

He unlocked the passenger door and helped her inside. "It's not very neat in here," he said, apologizing. "I use this old rattle-trap for fishing trips, mostly. I take my father and my brothers angling for bass down on the Santee-Cooper River."

"You don't look like a fisherman," she remarked. She clipped her seat belt into place, idly watching his hard, dark face and wondering at the lines in it, the silvery hair at his temples. He was older than she'd first thought.

"I hate fishing, as a rule," he replied. He cranked the jeep and reversed it neatly, wheeling around before he sped off down the beach highway. The sun was shining. It was a glorious morning, with seagulls and pelicans scrounging for fish in the surf while a handful of residents walked in the surf and watched the ocean.

"Then, why do it?" she asked absently.

"My father loves it. He and I have very little in common, otherwise. I go fishing with him because it gives me an excuse to see him occasionally—and my younger brothers."

"How many do you have?"

"Two. No sisters, either. There are just the three of us. We drove my mother crazy when we were kids." He glanced at her. "Do you have family?"

"My parents are both dead," she said, her voice very quiet and distant, and she didn't add that she had a brother.

"I'm sorry. It must be lonely for you."

"It's not bad," she replied. "I have friends."

"Like the one who lets you share the beach house with him?" he asked pointedly.

She smiled at him, unconcerned. "Yes. Like him."

Kane made a mental note to find out who owned that beach house. He wanted to know the name of the man with whom Nikki was involved. It didn't occur to him then that his very curiosity betrayed his growing involvement with her.

All along the beach, people were beginning to set up lawn chairs and spread towels in the sun. It was a warm spring day, with nothing but a sprinkling of clouds overhead.

"I love the ocean," Nikki said softly, smiling as her wide green eyes took in her surroundings. "I could never live inland. Even the freighters and fishing boats fascinate me."

"I know what you mean," he agreed. "I've lived in port cities all my life. You get addicted to the sight and sound of big ships."

He must mean Houston, but she couldn't admit that

she knew where he was from. "Do you live here?" she asked.

"I'm on holiday," he said, which was true enough. "Do you stay here, all the time?"

"No," she confessed. "I live farther up the coast."

"In Charleston?" he probed.

"Sort of."

"What does sort of mean?"

"I live on the beach itself." She did. She lived in one of the graceful old homes on the Battery, which was listed in the National Register of Historic Places and which was open to tourists two weeks a year.

He could imagine in what kind of house she normally lived. He hadn't seen her in anything so far that didn't look as if she'd found it in a yard sale. He felt vaguely sorry for her. She had no one of her own except her indifferent lover, and her material possessions were obviously very few. He'd noticed that she drove a very dilapidated red MG Midget, the kind that was popular back in the sixties.

"Feel like a cup of coffee?" he asked, nodding toward a small fast-food joint near the beach, with tables outside covered by faded yellow umbrellas.

"Yes, I do, thanks," she told him.

He parked the jeep and they got out. Nikki strolled to the beachside table and sat down while Kane ordered coffee. He hadn't needed to be told how Nikki took hers. He brought it with cream and sugar, smiling mischievously at her surprise.

"I have a more or less photographic memory," he told her as he slid onto the seat across from her.

"I'll remember that," she said with a grin.

He lifted his head and closed his eyes, letting the sea breeze drift over his darkly tanned face. It had a faintly leonine look, broad and definite, with a straight nose that was just short of oversized, a jutting brow with thick eyebrows, and a wide, thin-lipped mouth that managed to be sexy and masculine all at once. His eyes were large and brown, his pupils edged in black. They were staring at her with faint amusement.

"You look Spanish," she blurted out, embarrassed at having been caught looking at him so blatantly.

He frowned slightly, smiling. "My great-grandmother was an adventuress, the descendant of a high-born Spanish lady," he replied. "She was visiting friends near Houston, where my great-grandfather was a ranch foreman. As the story goes, they survived a raging scandal when they moved up to Beaumont to prospect for oil."

"How interesting! And did they find any? Oil, I mean?"

"My great-grandfather was on hand when Spindletop blew its stack in 1901," he told her. "He made and lost a fortune in two months' time." He didn't add that his great-grandfather had quickly recouped his losses and gone on to found an oil company.

"Poor man." She looked up from the coffee she was sipping. "His wife didn't leave him because he lost everything, did she?"

"She wasn't the type. She stuck by him, all the way."

"That doesn't happen very often anymore, does it? Women sticking by men, I mean," she added wistfully, "or even men sticking by women. Marriages aren't for keeps anymore."

He scowled. "You're very cynical for someone so young."

"I'm twenty-four," she told him. "Not young at all for this day and age." She studied her brightly polished fingernails, curled around the styrofoam cup. "For the rest, it's a cynical world. Profit even takes precedence over human life. I'm told that in the Amazon jungles, they kill the natives without compunction to get them off land the government wants to let big international corporations develop."

He stared at her. "Do you really think that with all the people this planet has to support, we can afford to allow primitive cultures to sit on that much arable land?"

Her green eyes began to glitter. "I think that if we develop all the arable land, we're going to have to eat concrete and steel a few years down the line."

He was delighted. Absolutely delighted. For all her beauty, there was a brain under that black hair. He moved his coffee cup around on the scarred surface of the table and smiled at her. "Progress costs," he countered.

"It's going to cost us the planet at the rate we're destroying our natural resources," she said sweetly.

"Or aren't you aware that about one percent of us is feeding the other ninety-nine percent? You have to have flat, rich land to plant on. Unfortunately, the same sort of land that is best suited to agriculture is also best suited to building sites."

"On the other hand," he pointed out, "without jobs, people won't be able to afford seed to plant. A new business means new jobs, a better standard of living for the people in the community. Better nutrition for nursing mothers, for young children."

"That's all true," she agreed, leaning forward earnestly. "But what about the price people pay for that better standard of living? When farm mechanization came along, farmers had to grow more food in order to afford the equipment to make planting and harvesting less time-consuming. That raised the price of food. The pesticides and fertilizers they had to use, to increase production, caused the toxic by-products to leach into the ground and pollute the water table. We produced more food, surely, but the more food you raise, the more the population grows. That increases the amount of food you *have* to raise to feed the increasing numbers of people! It's a vicious circle."

"I didn't know you were an economist," he said.

"I studied it in college."

He grinned at her. "What did you take your degree in?"

"I didn't finish," she said sadly. "I dropped out after three years, totally burned out. I'll go back and finish one day, though. I only lack thirty semester hours for a major in history and a minor in sociology.''

''God help the world when you do,'' he murmured. ''You could go into politics if you keep debating like that.''

She was flattered and amused, but she didn't let him see the latter. He mustn't know how wrapped up she already was in politics.

''You're pretty astute yourself.''

''I took my degree in business administration,'' he said. ''I did a double minor in economics and history.''

''Do you work in business?'' she asked with deliberate innocence.

''You might say so,'' he said carelessly.

''Is it exciting?''

''Sometimes,'' he dodged. He finished his coffee. ''Do you like to walk on the beach?'' he asked. ''I enjoy it early in the morning and late in the afternoon. It helps me clear my mind so that I can think.''

''Me, too,'' she said.

''Kindred spirits,'' he said almost to himself, and she smiled.

He put the garbage in the receptacle and impulsively slid his hand into Nikki's.

It was the first deliberate physical contact between them, and as his strong fingers linked sensuously between her slender ones, she felt a tingling all through her body. She hadn't felt that way in years.

She caught her breath and looked up at him.

"What is it, Nikki?" he asked gently.

His deep voice stirred her even more than the touch of his hand. She felt him, as if they were standing locked together. Her eyes looked into his and she could almost taste him.

"Nothing," she choked after a minute. She pulled her fingers from his grasp firmly, but hesitantly. "Shall we go?"

He watched her move off ahead of him, her hands suddenly in her pockets, the small fanny pack around her waist drooping over one rounded hip. She looked frightened. That was an odd sort of behavior from a woman who'd let him share her home for a night, he thought idly.

She paused when he caught up with her, feeling guilty and not quite herself. She looked up at him with a rueful, embarrassed smile.

"I'm sorry. It's not personal," she confessed. "I think I told you I was married once."

He nodded. "A bad marriage?"

Her eyes were wistful; sad. "He wasn't cruel to me," she said finally. "He never hit me or drank to excess or ran around with other . . . women." She hunched her shoulders. "It just couldn't work out, that's all, and I'm wary." She looked at him, smiling slightly. "Aren't you?"

"I'm a widower," he said finally. He took a steadying breath, because it still hurt to talk about it. "I lost my wife and son in an accident a year ago."

"I'm very sorry."

"So was I. It's been rough, dealing with it. Sometimes, I don't think I have yet." He put his hands in his pockets and looked down at her while they strolled along the white sand. Whitecaps rolled, foaming, onto the nearby shore, and overhead the seagulls danced on the wind with black-tipped white wings spread to the sun.

"You're very big," she remarked.

He chuckled. "Tall. Not big."

"You are," she argued. "I'm five foot five and you tower over me."

"I'm barely six foot two," he told her. "You're a shrimp, that's why I seem big to you."

"Watch your mouth, buster, I'm not through growing yet," she said pertly, cutting her sparkling eyes up at him.

He chuckled. "Smart mouth."

"Smart, period, thank you so much."

"Now that we've both admitted that we're wary of getting involved, can we hold hands? Mine are cold."

"I might have suspected there would be an ulterior motive," she mentioned. But all the same, she took her left hand out of her pocket and let him fold it under his warm fingers.

"You aren't cold," she protested.

"Sure I am. You just can't tell." His fingers tightened, and he smiled at the faint flush on her cheeks as the exercise began to tell on her. "You ninety-seven-pound-weakling," he chided. "Can't you keep up with me?"

"Normally, I could run rings around you," she said heavily. "But I'm still getting over the pneumonia."

He stopped abruptly, scowling. "How could I have forgotten, when I heard the doctor warning you not to get chilled. Idiot! You don't need to be out in this early morning air! Why didn't you say something?"

His concern made her heart lift. "It's been a week since I got out of bed," she assured him. "And I haven't been sitting home idle all that time."

"You haven't been overdoing it, have you?"

"Not really," she admitted. Her obligations with the Spoleto Festival had included lots of telephone calls and paperwork, which she did sitting down. Nevertheless, her strength was still lagging behind her will.

"What a waif and stray it is, and it hasn't much of a mind at times, either," he murmured softly.

She started to take offense, when he moved suddenly and swept her completely off the beach into his warm, strong arms. He turned and started walking back the way they'd come.

Nikki was breathless with surprised delight. It was the first time in her life that she'd experienced a man's strength in this way. She wasn't sure she liked the feeling of vulnerability it gave her, and that doubt was in her eyes when they met his.

"I can see the words right there on the tip of your tongue," he said softly, his deep voice faintly accented and very tender as he smiled at her. "But don't say them. Put your arms around me and lie close to my chest while I carry you."

Shades of a romantic movie, she thought wildly. But the odd thing was that she obeyed him without question, without hesitation. A breathy little sigh escaped her lips. She dropped her eyes to his throat, where thick hair showed in the opening, and she felt a sweet swelling in her body as he drew her closer. Her face ended up in the hot curve of his throat, her arms close around his neck.

"Nikki," he said in a rough, husky voice, and his arms suddenly contracted, crushing her soft breasts against the wall of his chest as he turned toward the car.

It was no longer a teasing or tender embrace. Her nails were biting into his shoulders as he walked, and she felt the closeness in every pore of her body. Her breasts had gone hard-tipped, her heart was throbbing. Low in her belly, she felt a heat and hunger that was without precedent.

"Oh, baby," he whispered suddenly, and she felt his open mouth quite suddenly on the softness of her throat where her tank top left it bare to her collarbone.

She closed her eyes with a shaky gasp. The wind blew her hair around her face and cooled the heat in her cheeks. He was warm and strong and he smelled of spices. She wanted him to strip her out of her clothes and put his warm, hard mouth on her breasts and her belly and the inside of her thighs. She wanted him to put her down on the beach and make love to her under the sky.

With a total disregard for safety and sanity, her hand tangled in the thick, wavy hair at the back of his head and she pulled his mouth down to the soft curve under her collarbone.

CHAPTER
FOUR

Kane's head was spinning, but when Nikki coaxed his mouth down, he came to his senses with a jolt. He jerked his face up and put her down abruptly. Stepping back, he tried not to show how shaken he was. He looked into her dazed, misty, half-closed green eyes.

She was shaken, too, and unable to hide it. His lips had almost been touching her bare skin when he'd withdrawn them. She felt as if she'd been left in limbo, but she had to keep her head.

"Thank you," she said. "I knew that you could save me from myself," she managed with irrepressible spirit.

He smiled in spite of himself. "I suppose I did. But I'd never have believed it of myself. I'm not one to throw away opportunities, and you have a mouth like a ripe apple."

"I'm thrilled that you think so."

He laughed at his own reaction to her. It had been a long time since he'd felt anything so powerful, yet this woman absolutely delighted him. "In that case, don't you want to come with me to a quiet, deserted place?"

"Of course I do." She pushed back her disheveled hair. "But it really wouldn't be sensible. I don't even know if you like opera, for heaven's sake! I could never become involved with a man who didn't like opera, no matter how wickedly attractive he was."

He chuckled. "Is that so? As it happens, I love opera."

She was having trouble with her legs. They didn't want to move. And the throbbing need in her body was getting worse, not better.

"Stop tempting me to do sordid and licentious things," she told him firmly. She pushed back her disheveled hair. "I'll have you know that until I met you, I was determined to be a virtuous woman."

He grinned. "I'm delighted with the wording. But your virtue may become endangered if you spend much time around me. So how about going sailing with me?"

Her hand poised above her hair. "Sailing?"

"Your eyes lit up. Do you like sailing?" he asked.

"I love it!"

He chuckled. "I'll pick you up early tomorrow." He paused. "If you're free?"

She knew he was wondering if the lover she'd led him to believe she had would mind.

"He isn't jealous," she said with a slow smile.

"Isn't he?"

His dark eyes sketched her face and he began to worry. He knew he was losing his grasp on reality, to take this sort of chance. She appealed to him physically. That was all. There was an added threat. What if she found out who he was?

His own apprehension amused him. What if she did, for God's sake? What could she do, blackmail him because they'd spent an innocent night together?

She burst out laughing. "I live with my brother," she said.

"Your what?!" he burst out.

"My brother," she said. "I didn't know you from an ax murderer, so I let you think I had a live-in lover to protect myself—one who came home every Friday night."

He saw the light. His eyes began to sparkle and then he, too, laughed. "And he didn't come home—I never noticed!"

"That doesn't mean that I want a lover, however," she said gently. "I'm not ready, yet. Not at all."

The taut little remark hurt him. He'd just had her in his arms, warm and willing, and had had an exciting glimpse of how she'd be with a man.

"That's just as well," he said slowly. "Because I already do have a lover."

Why should that shock her? She shifted a little and averted her eyes to the beach. She really wasn't shopping for a lover, so wasn't it just as well that he already had one?

"I'm glad," she replied absently, though she felt anything but happiness. "I wouldn't mind a friend, though," she added suddenly, her blue eyes linking with his as she smiled. "I have very few of those."

"I doubt if anyone can boast more than one true friend," he said cynically. "Okay. Friends it is."

"And no funny stuff on the sailboat," she said, returning to her former mood with mercurial rapidity. "You can't lash me to the mast and ravish me, or strip me naked and use me to troll for sharks. You have to promise."

He grinned. "Fair enough."

"Then I'll see you tomorrow."

He studied her face, perceiving pain behind the gaiety. That hurt him more than the remark that she didn't want a lover. "Yes," he agreed. "Come on. I'll take you home."

That evening, sitting alone on the deck, she argued with her conscience. It didn't help that Clayton telephoned to tell her about the progress he was making.

"I've won over a new ally," he told her, and mentioned the congressman's name. "How's that for a day's work?!"

"Great!" she said, laughing. "Uh, how's the owl controversy?"

"It's a real hoot," he muttered. "Derrie and I aren't speaking because of it, and Bett's mad at me, too. Here I am a conservation candidate, voting against a little owl and a bunch of old trees just because it will mean new jobs and economic prosperity. The women in my life think I'm a lunatic.''

"I'll remind you that we can't replace that owl, nor trees that are primary growth trees and more than a hundred years old . . .''

"Cut it out!'' he wailed.

She laughed. "Okay. Blood is thicker than water.''

"If you say so. How are you? Getting some rest?''

"Enough.'' She hesitated. "I . . . met someone.''

"Someone? A man? A real, honest to God man?''

"He looks like one. He's taking me sailing.''

"Nikki, I'm delighted! Who is he?''

She crossed her fingers on her lap. "Just an ordinary man,'' she lied. "He's into . . . cars.''

"Oh. A mechanic? Well, there's nothing wrong with being a mechanic, I guess. Can he sail well enough not to drown you?''

"I think he could do anything he set his mind to,'' she murmured dreamily.

"Is this really you?'' he teased. "You were off men for life, the last time we spoke.''

"Oh, I am,'' she agreed readily. "It's just that this one is so different,'' she added. "I haven't ever met anyone quite like him.''

"Is he a ladies' man?''

"I don't know. Perhaps.''

"Nikki,'' he began, hesitating. She'd had a rough experience at an early age. She was vulnerable. "Listen, suppose I come down for a few days?''

"No!" She cleared her throat and lowered her voice. "I mean, there's no need to do that."

"You're worrying me," he said.

"You can't protect me from the world, you know. I have to stand on my own two feet sometime."

"I guess you do," he said, sounding resigned and not too happy. "Okay, sis. Have it your way. But I'm as close as the telephone if you need me. Will you remember that?"

"You can bet on it."

"Then I'll speak to you soon."

When he hung up, Nikki let out the breath she'd been holding. That was all she needed now, to have Clayton come wandering up to the house and run head-on into Kane. Things were getting complicated and she was certain that she needed to cut off the impossible relationship before it began. But she couldn't quite manage it. Kane had already gotten close to her heart. She hoped that it wouldn't break completely in the end.

She wondered how Kane was going to keep her in the dark about his wealth. If he took her sailing in a yacht, even a moron would notice that it meant he had money. He solved the problem adroitly by mentioning that he couldn't rent the sailboat he'd planned to take her out in, so they were going riding in a motorboat instead. It was a very nice motorboat, but nothing like the yacht he usually took onto the ocean.

Nikki smiled to herself and accepted the change of conveyance without noticeable effect.

"I know I said I'd take you out on a sailboat," he explained as he helped her into the boat, "but they're not very safe in high winds. It's pretty windy today."

It was, but she hardly thought a yacht would be very much affected. On the other hand, she knew why her supposed house guest didn't want to arrive with a million dollar plus sailing ship.

"Oh, I like motorboats," she said honestly, her eyes lighting up with excitement as Kane eased into the driver's seat and turned the key. The motor cranked right up and ran like a purring cat.

He glanced at her with a wry smile. "Are you a good sailor?"

"I guess we'll find out together," she returned.

He chuckled and pulled away from the pier.

The boat had a smooth glide on the water's surface, and the engine wasn't overly loud. Nikki put up a hand to her windblown hair, laughing as the faint spray of water teased her nose.

"Aren't you ever gloomy?" he asked with genuine curiosity.

"Oh, why bother being pessimistic?" she replied. "Life is so short. It's a crime to waste it, when every day is like Christmas, bringing something new."

She loved life. He'd forgotten how. His dark eyes turned toward the distant horizon and he tried not to think about how short life really was, or how tragically he'd learned the lesson.

"Where are we going?" Nikki asked.

"No place in particular," he said. He glanced at her with faint amusement. "Unless," he added, "you like to fish."

"I don't mind it. But you hate it!" she laughed.

"Of course I do. But I have to keep my hand in," he added. "So that I don't disgrace the rest of my family. The gear and tackle are under that tarp. I thought we'd ease up the river a bit and settle in a likely spot. I brought an ice chest and lunch."

"You really are full of surprises," she commented.

His dark eyes twinkled. "You don't know the half of it," he murmured, turning his concentration back to navigation.

He found a leafy glade and tied the boat up next to shore. He and Nikki sat lazily on the bank and watched their corks rise and fall and occasionally bob. They ate cold cut sandwiches and potato chips and sipped soft drinks, and Nikki marveled at the tycoon who was a great fishing companion. Not since her childhood, when she'd gone fishing with her late grandfather, had she enjoyed anything so much. She'd forgotten how much fun it was to sit on the river with a fishing pole.

"Do you do this often?" she wanted to know.

"With my brothers and my father. Not ever with a woman." His broad shoulders lifted and fell. "Most of them that I know don't care for worms and hooks," he mused. "You're not squeamish, are you?"

"Not really. About some things, maybe," she added

quietly. "But unless you're shooting the fish in a barrel, they have a sporting chance. And I do love fried bass!"

"Can you clean a fish?"

"You bet!"

He chuckled with unashamed delight. "In that case, if we catch anything, I'm inviting myself to supper." His eyes narrowed. "If you have no other plans."

"Not for a few weeks, I haven't," she said.

He seemed to relax. His powerful legs stretched out in front of him and he tugged on the fishing pole to test the hook. "Nothing's striking at my bait," he grumbled. "I haven't had a bite yet. We'll give it ten more minutes and then we're moving to a better spot."

"The minute we move, a hundred big fish will feel safe to vacation here," she pointed out.

"You're probably right. It just may not be a good day for fishing."

"That depends on what you're fishing for," she said, concentrating on the sudden bob of her cork. "Watch this—!"

She pulled suddenly on the pole, snaring something at the end of the line, and scrambled to her feet. Whatever she'd hooked was giving her a run for her money. She pulled and released, pulled and released, worked the pole, moved up the bank, muttered and clicked her tongue until finally her prey began to tire. She watched Kane watching her and laughed at his dismal expression.

"You're hoping I'll drop him, aren't you? Aren't you?" she challenged. "Well, I won't. Supper, here you come!"

She gave a hard jerk on the line and the fish, a large bass, flipped up onto the bank. While Kane dealt with it, she baited her hook again. "I've got mine," she told him. "I don't know what you'll eat, of course."

He sat down beside her and picked up his own pole. "We'll just see about that," he returned.

Two hours later, they had three large bass. Nikki had caught two of them. Kane lifted the garbage and then the cooler with the fish into the boat. Nikki forgave herself for feeling vaguely superior, just for a few minutes.

Kane had forgotten his tragedies, his business dealings, his worries in the carefree morning he was sharing with Nikki. Her company had liberated him from the business that occupied more and more of his time. Since the death of his family, he'd substituted making money for relationships. Food tasted like cardboard to him. Sleep was infrequent and an irritating necessity. He hadn't taken a vacation or even a day off since the business trip he'd taken with his wife and son that had ended so tragically.

Exhaustion had caused the carelessness that had led to his swimming accident. But looking at Nikki, so relaxed and happy beside him, he couldn't be sorry about that. She was an experience to treasure, even though he knew he'd only be with her for a brief time. After a few weeks apart, he wouldn't even be able to recall her name. The thought made him restless.

Nikki noticed his unease. She wondered if he was as attracted to her emotionally as he seemed to be physically. It had worried her when he'd admitted that he had a lover. She wondered if he were important to the woman because he was becoming just that to Nikki. She trembled inside at the thought.

Although she had once been married, her husband had never been able to bring himself to make love to her. Miles had touched her lightly and without passion, and she had been so young and desperate to please her father when she married that she had questioned her husband's indifference at first. Because she'd been infatuated with Miles initially, his coldness when she tried to coax him into intimacy had left scars. She now knew the pain that rushing into intimacy could bring; she would never rush into any relationship again. And she certainly didn't want the extra complication of Kane's lover. No matter how much she might desire him, Nikki was determined to resist temptation.

Throughout the trip home she forced herself to think about the fishing. This had been one of the most carefree days of her life. When they arrived at her house she could tell Kane's mind was no longer on fish—nor was it on her. She wondered what had him so preoccupied.

"I have to make a few telephone calls, or I'd help you clean the fish," he said when he left her at the front door of her beach house with the cooler. "I'll be back in a bit."

"Business?" she asked.

His face showed nothing. "You might call it that." He didn't say anything else. He smiled at her distractedly and left with a careless wave of his hand.

Nikki went in to clean the fish, disturbed by his sudden remoteness. What kind of business could he have meant?

Kane listened patiently while the angry voice at the other end of the telephone ranted and railed at him.

"But you promised that we could go to the Waltons' party tonight! All my friends will be there, and at least two art critics are coming down from New York!" Christy sounded like a disappointed child. "How can you do this to me? What sort of deal are you working on that demands a whole evening of your time?"

"I told you, I've got other plans, Christy," he said in a very quiet voice. She was an artist, and was becoming very well known. He couldn't fault her intellect. But their mutual need for safe intimacy had been their only common ground. He didn't like her friends, and they certainly didn't like him. Christy wanted a man who could fit into her bohemian life-style. Kane wasn't cut out for it on any permanent basis. Now that Nikki had come into his life, he was sorry he hadn't ended it with Christy months ago. By now, she'd probably have been involved with someone else; perhaps that psychologist friend of hers who seemed to fascinate her lately.

"Will you phone me, then?" Christy asked with a long sigh.

"As soon as I have time. But it might be better if we don't see as much of each other in the future," he added, as gently as he could.

There was a hesitation, then she said sadly, "Perhaps you're right. You're a wonderful lover, Kane, but I always have the feeling that you're thinking about cost overruns when we're together."

"I'm a businessman," he reminded her.

"You're a business," she said, laughing softly. "A walking, talking industry, and I still say you should be in therapy. You haven't been the same since . . ."

He didn't want to hear any more. Christy swore by therapy. He didn't. "I'll phone you. Good night."

He put the receiver down before she could say anything else. He'd had enough of her amateur psychoanalysis. She did it all the time, even when she was in bed with him.

He got up and changed from jeans and a jersey into dress slacks and a comfortable yellow knit shirt. Fried fish with Nikki was more enticing than a prime rib and cocktails with Christy and her friends.

He selected a bottle of wine from the supply he'd imported and carried it along with him. He wondered if Nikki knew anything about fine white wine. She was an intelligent girl, but she hadn't the advantages of wealth. She probably wouldn't know a Chardonnay from a Johannesburg Riesling. That was something he could teach her. He didn't dare think about tutoring her in anything else just yet. She could become even more addicting than alcohol if he let her.

Nikki had cleaned and fried the fish and was making a fruit salad and a poppyseed dressing to go with it when Kane knocked briefly and let himself into the cottage.

She glanced over her shoulder and smiled at him. "Come on in," she invited. She was wearing a frilly floral sundress that left most of her pretty, tanned back bare while it discreetly covered her breasts in front. She was barefoot at the kitchen table and Kane felt his body surge at the picture of feminine beauty she presented. Nikki dressed the way he liked to see a woman dress, not flaunting her sex but not denying it, either.

"I've just finished the salad and dressing. Want to set the table?" she asked brightly.

He hesitated. He couldn't remember ever doing that in his life. Even as a child, there had always been maids who worked in the kitchen.

"The plates are there," she nodded toward a cupboard with her head. "You'll find utensils in the second drawer. Placemats and napkins are in the third drawer." She noticed his expression and his hesitation with faint amusement. "You do know how to set a table?"

"Not really," he admitted.

"Then it's high time you learned," she said. "Someday you may get married again, and think how much more desirable you'll be if you know your way around a kitchen."

He didn't react to the teasing with a smile. He stared at her with a curious remoteness and she remembered belatedly the dead wife he'd told her about.

"I don't want to marry anyone," he said unexpectedly. "Especially a woman I've only just met," he added without being unkind.

"Well, certainly you don't want to marry me right now," she agreed. "After all, you don't even know me. Sadly, once you discover my worthy traits and my earthy longings, you'll be clamoring to put a ring on my finger. But I'll have to turn you down. I'm holding out for Tom Selleck."

"Are you, really?" he mused and his eyes twinkled. He turned away from her and began searching in drawers. He began to put things on the table in strange and mysterious order, and she couldn't resist one more jibe.

"You really should pay more attention to the place settings in restaurants," she remarked, noting that he had the forks and the knives in the wrong place.

"I don't want to make a career of it."

"Suit yourself," she said. "Just don't blame me if you're never able to get a job as a busboy in one of the better hotels. Heaven knows, I tried to teach you the basics."

He chuckled faintly. She turned and began to put the food on the table. Afterwards, she rearranged the place settings until they were as they should be.

"Show-off," he accused.

She curtsied, grinning at him. "Do sit down."

He held the chair out for her, watching when she hesitated. "I am prepared to stand here until winter," he observed.

With a long sigh, she allowed him to seat her. "Archaic custom."

"Courtesy is not archaic, and I have no plans to abandon it." He sat down across from her. "I also say grace before meals; another custom which I have no plans to abandon.''

With a twinkle in her eyes that she didn't let him see, she obediently bowed her head.

Halfway through the meal, they wound up in a discussion of politics and she didn't pull her punches.

"I think it's criminal to kill an old forest and sacrifice a species of owl to stave up the timber industry," she announced.

His thick eyebrows lifted. "So you should," he said matter-of-factly.

She put down her fork. "You're a conservationist?"

"Not exclusively, but I do believe in preservation of natural resources. Why are you surprised?" he added suspiciously.

That was an answer she had to avoid at all costs. She forced a bright, innocent smile to her face. "Most men are in favor of progress."

He studied her very intently for a moment, before he let the idea pass. "I do favor it, but not above conservation, and it depends on what's being threatened. Some species are going to become extinct despite all our best efforts, you do realize that?"

"Yes," she said. "But it seems to me that we're paving everything these days. And there have been some pretty spectacular incidents involving the hard-heartedness of developers in developing nations."

"I know. I read, too."

"Do we really have the right—we who belong to industrial nations, I mean—to deprive other cultures of their heritage and religion and life-styles just because we believe that we're superior?"

"Of course not," he returned. "But it's happening, just the same. Most cultures consider their own superior to any other. But we have technology on our side. That makes our destructive abilities just as formidable as our constructive ones. It's hard for any primitive or undeveloped culture to fight that."

"Some do."

"Indeed. I've even heard of projects that were stopped because of the right sort of intervention by concerned parties. But it isn't a frequent occurrence."

"I hate a world that equates might with right."

"Nevertheless, that's how the system works. The people with the most money and power make the rules. It's always been that way, Nikki. Since the beginning of civilization, one class leads and other classes serve."

"At the turn of the century, industrialists used to trot out Scientific Darwinism to excuse the injustices they practiced to further their interests," she observed.

"Scientific Darwinism," he said, surprised. "Yes, the theory of survival of the fittest extended from nature to business." He shook his head. "Incredible."

"It's still done," she pointed out. "Big fish eat little fish, companies that can't compete go under . . ."

"And now we can quote Adam Smith and all the dangers of interfering in business. Let the sinking sink. No government intervention."

She stared at him curiously. "Are you by any chance a closet economist?" she queried with a smile.

"I took Western Civ in college, back in the dark ages," he chuckled. "History fascinates me."

"Me, too," she enthused. "I wish I knew more about it."

"You could go back to school and finish your degree," he suggested. "Or, failing that, you could take some extension courses."

She hesitated. "That would be nice."

But she didn't have the time, much less the financial means. She didn't have to say it. He knew already. She'd ducked her head as she spoke, and she looked faintly embarrassed.

She had to stop spouting off, she told herself firmly. Her tongue would run too far one day and betray her brother to this man. She hadn't lied about college, though. One of the terms of her settlement with Miles Townshend at their divorce was that he would help pay for her to go to college. He had contributed half of her tuition, and she'd worked very hard toward her degree. The pain she'd felt at her bad experience had spurred her to great heights, but she hadn't been able to finish. She'd had to drop out just after her junior year to help Clayton campaign.

"What do you do for a living?" he asked suddenly.

She couldn't decide how to answer him. She couldn't very well say that she hostessed for her brother. On the other hand, she did keep house for him.

"I told you. I sculpt," she said brightly, and smiled.

He'd hoped she might have some secret skill that she hadn't shared with him. She seemed intelligent enough. But apparently she had no ambition past sculpting. That disappointed him because he liked outgoing, capable women who had lives of their own. He disliked women whom he could dominate too easily or overwhelm. He wondered if, like Christy's, her friends were all artists.

"I see," he said quietly.

He looked disappointed. Nikki didn't add anything to what she'd said. It was just as well that he lose interest in her before things got complicated, she told herself. After all, she could hardly tell him who she really was. But the sting was there, just the same.

CHAPTER FIVE

Nikki put the dishes away while Kane wandered around the living room, looking at the meager stock of books on the shelves. She sounded like a great reader, but the only books, he noted, were rather weathered ones on law.

"They were my father's," she told him. "He wanted to be a lawyer, but he couldn't afford the sacrifice of his time once he was established in his profession."

He probably didn't have the money, either, Kane thought silently. He glanced at her. "Don't you have books of your own?"

"Plenty. They're not here, though. Dad had the house built so close on the beach that it tends to flood during storms and squalls, so we don't leave anything really valuable here."

As if she probably had anything valuable. His dark

eyes slid over her body quietly, enjoying its soft curves but without blatant sexual messages.

"I like the way you look at me," she said hesitantly. His eyebrows arched and she laughed a little self-consciously. "I mean," she amended, "that you don't make me feel inferior or cheap. Women are rather defensive when men wolf whistle and make catcalls. Perhaps men don't realize how threatening that can be to a woman when she's by herself. Or perhaps they do."

"You're very attractive. I suppose a man who lacks verbal skills uses the only weapons he has."

She made a face. "They are, aren't they? Weapons."

He moved closer. "You're destroying my illusions," he told her. "I was just thinking that you were unique; a woman comfortable in her femininity."

"Oh, I am," she said. "I enjoy being a woman. But there are looks and words that make me uncomfortable. I dislike harrassment."

He smiled gently. "Would you believe that men can be made just as uncomfortable by aggressive women?" he asked softly.

She laughed. "One doesn't think of women making men uncomfortable."

"Really?" he teased.

She looked at him with open curiosity. "Do you have to fight off aggressive women?"

His smile faded. "Fishing, Nikki?" he asked, and the tone of his voice disturbed her.

"You're very attractive. It's reasonable to assume that you haven't been a monk."

His broad shoulders moved restlessly. "As I told you, my wife and son died . . . violently . . . a year ago," he said, without elaborating about the circumstances. "But she and I had grown apart long before that." He hesitated. "Afterward, I took a mistress."

Nikki felt a fool. She turned away jerkily. "I shouldn't have pried."

"It's not like that," he said angrily. "Not now. I mean, it was a casual thing from the beginning. I needed someone. She was loving and sweet."

Her eyes closed on a wave of unexpected wounding. She didn't dare consider why it should hurt to know that he was intimate with another woman.

"I see."

"No, you don't," he said shortly. "I've broken it off with her."

Her eyebrows went up. "Because of me?" she blurted out without thinking first.

"Because the feelings were gone, for both of us. I was honest with her from the outset." His eyes narrowed. "I'll be just as honest with you, right up front. I don't want to get married again."

She didn't allow her expression to waver. "Neither do I. But friendship is all I can offer you," she added quietly.

His eyebrows arched. "Why?"

She could hardly tell him it was because he and her brother were enemies. She shrugged carelessly and turned away. "I don't want an affair with you, that's all."

"How do you know, until you try it?" he challenged, and there was a sudden, wicked smile on his face to punctuate the question. "I'm good in bed, Nikki. There would be no risk with me; no consequences."

Except my heart and my brother's career, she thought. Her head turned just enough to glance back at him. "Do you like banging your head against brick walls?" she asked pleasantly.

She made her point. He sighed and jammed his hands deep into his pockets. "I must," he mused. "All right. I'll leave it alone." He hesitated, and his frown was thoughtful. "Nikki, you must have had a terrible experience."

"In a manner of speaking," she agreed finally. "And I don't know you well enough to discuss it with you," she added when he opened his mouth to question her. "Be a nice man and stop poking and prodding at my past."

His eyebrows lifted. "Do I get a reward if I do?"

She smiled. "Apple pie, with ice cream."

He pursed his lips, and his eyes twinkled. "Okay."

"I knew your stomach would be your weak spot," she said smugly.

After they finished the pie, amicably, they sat on the deck and sipped freshly made piña coladas and listened to Respighi's *Pines of Rome*. Nikki had been surprised to discover that Kane liked it as much as she did. It was a moody piece, and when she closed her eyes, she could almost see Roman legions marching off to battle.

"Not that I'm complaining," Kane mentioned, "but isn't this music a bit somber?"

"Melancholy, perhaps," she agreed. "I like Debussy, too."

"So do I."

"Are you melancholy?"

His eyes were briefly haunted. He threw down the rest of his drink. "All of us have bad memories, Nikki."

She knew why he might. She wished she could tell him. That she knew how his family died. Her eyes sought his hard face and lingered there, watching the taut muscles work as he stared out to sea. Was he remembering his little boy? His wife?

"Kane?" she called softly.

He took a steadying breath, but the pain was grinding into him. His son. His son . . . !

She saw his fingers contract around the half-empty glass, going white. She got up and went to him, easing down into his lap, curling up against him.

He shivered. His powerful body froze for an instant, as if her warmth had locked it up. Then he became aware of her and his eyes slid down to meet hers.

"You looked as if you needed to be held," she said quietly. "If I'm wrong, you can always dump me on the floor."

"That would be ungrateful." He put the glass on the table beside the chair and wrapped her up in his arms. They were warm against the chill of the night air. She closed her eyes as her cheek rested against the warm throb of his heart. The breeze brushed her hair against his face and the sound of the surf was loud and soothing.

"Life hurts," he said after a minute, and his hand began absently caressing the short hair at her nape.

She was remembering her own wounds. She heard Miles's deep voice apologizing for letting himself be panicked into marrying her, for encouraging her to care for him when he couldn't give her a normal physical relationship. There had been tears in his eyes, and she had comforted him. But she had cried, too, because she had thought herself in love with him.

"They were killed a year ago this week. I miss my son," he said suddenly.

Her fingers flattened on his shirt and smoothed it over the hard, warm muscles. "I'm sorry," she said simply.

His cheek eased down on her hair and rested there. He couldn't remember when he'd felt such peace with another human being. He hadn't allowed himself to stop working, driving himself, because the memories had been torment. But Nikki eased his pain.

She knew it, too. She shifted a little closer to him, the movement trusting and very arousing.

"You know better than that," he murmured dryly, staying her with a big hand at her waist.

Actually, she hadn't until just now. But there was no need to let him know it. Playfully, she punched him in the ribs to divert his attention, and he jumped.

Delighted, she sat up on his lap and looked at the stillness of his expression. "Are you ticklish?" she taunted, and her hands moved quickly down toward his ribs.

He caught them both, wrestling her beside him in the chair. He was laughing, and his voice was deep and happy in the darkness.

She laughed, too. It was new to be so open and happy with someone. There would be no deep, dark secrets with Kane, no unpleasant surprises. In many ways he was an open book. Certainly, he was heterosexual without any doubt. He made her curious. . . .

"Pixie," he drawled when he had her temporarily helpless. There was just enough light to allow him to see her eyes beneath his.

"Pirate," she whispered back. And he looked like one, with his dark hair falling rakishly across his broad forehead, and a devilish light in his dark eyes.

There was a growing tension in their bodies as he held her there in the windy darkness, with the surf crashing on the beach beyond the house.

He moved, just barely, but enough to let her feel the muscular length of his legs curling around hers as her feet rested beside his on the hassock. His hand slid behind her back and gathered her up against him with gentle insistence.

"You smell of roses," he whispered as he bent his head. "I want to kiss you breathless."

"Is that a threat or a promise?" she whispered as his mouth eased down over hers.

"You tell me . . ."

She lifted herself closer to him, and fell headlong into pleasure. Her body trembled softly as he deepened the kiss. She liked the way his tongue stabbed into her mouth, she liked the coconutty taste of the piña colada that adhered to his lips. He had a careless confidence that stopped just short of arrogance. But behind the experienced touch was the same wonder that she was feeling.

When he lifted his head, her lips followed. He laughed a little breathlessly and pulled away.

"Stop that," he chided. "I'm trying to be the gentleman my mother raised me to be."

She smiled warmly. "A real man can survive temptation."

"Not this much," he said bluntly. He put her aside and stood up abruptly, but he was grinning. "I'm going home before you compromise me."

"Oh, I feel so dangerous," she murmured, and deliberately stretched.

He groaned. "I'm leaving. Right now."

Nikki chuckled as she got to her feet, too. "I'll walk you to the door, like a good hostess." She took his arm and clung to it on the way. "Is this goodbye, then?" she asked, but she was only half-teasing.

He opened the door and looked down at her. "I like being held when I hurt," he said unexpectedly. "I could do the same for you, when you need it."

"Thanks. I'll remember that."

He leaned against the door jamb, with one hand in his pocket. "Listen, Christy and I were through long before tonight. I don't want you to get the idea that I think of women as disposable.''

''I knew better.''

He reached out and touched her face with gentle curiosity. ''Magnolia Gardens is the prettiest place this side of heaven. Have you seen it?''

''Yes. Half a dozen times. But I'll enjoy seeing it again.''

''Tomorrow?''

She nodded.

He bent and kissed her tenderly. ''This is all wrong,'' he said heavily. ''I don't want to get involved with you.''

She reached up and linked her arms around his neck, stepping into his body. ''I don't want to get involved with you, either.''

His hands met and passed behind her. ''It's the wrong time,'' he said against her mouth.

She parted her lips and pushed upward. ''Oh, yes . . . !''

He kissed her hungrily, again and again, until his body made him stop. He groaned and forced himself to take a step backward. Her arms fell to her sides. She smiled wickedly, and he laughed.

''I'm leaving,'' he said.

She put her hands behind her to lessen temptation. ''What time tomorrow?''

''Is five too early?'' he asked ruefully.

''No. But you'll get breakfast if you wait until six,'' she assured him.

He nodded. His dark eyes were still hungry when he went out the door.

Nikki cleaned up the house and went back out to sit on the deck. She knew she couldn't afford to become addicted to Kane. She knew, too, that Kane would be furious if he knew the deception she was practicing by not telling him who she was. But right now, nothing seemed to matter except being with him.

The next day, he took her to Magnolia Gardens, and she clung to his big hand and intercepted the envious looks of other women. He watched her just as covetously as she watched him, and the kiss he gave her when they parted that night was more expressive than any words. If she was falling in love—and she was—then he must be, too. As they spent more and more time together, Nikki knew that they were headed for the point of no return. She cared for Kane so much that she knew she wouldn't be able to refuse him anything he wanted. For the first time since her marriage, she was letting her emotions guide her actions.

The bar in downtown Washington was a very nice one, in a part of town that was relatively safe. Derrie had a pistol, and a permit for it, but she never carried it. Her self-defense training would have to suffice if she got into trouble. Meanwhile, she needed some information that she couldn't get anywhere else.

A striking dark man with his long hair in a ponytail looked up from a booth by the window when she entered. She went straight to him and sat down across from him in the booth.

"What's your poison?" he asked in an accentless voice, and with a smile that was even reflected in his large, dark eyes.

"Irish coffee," she said.

"The caffeine won't counteract the whiskey," he reminded her.

She laughed. "In that case, you can take me home when we're through talking."

"No problem. I would have, anyway." He placed the order with the waitress and then stared at Derrie with dark, quiet eyes and waited patiently for her to speak. She knew that the patience wouldn't deteriorate if she took a half hour. It was Cortez's one virtue.

"What do you know about John Haralson?" she asked, keeping her voice down.

His eyebrows shot up. "Why do you want to know?" he asked warily.

"Will you try to stop sounding like a government agent?"

"Force of habit. Sorry." The waitress brought their drinks. He paid her for his and Derrie fished a bill out of her pocket for the waitress and waved away the change.

"Haralson is going to work for my boss," Derrie said after she'd sampled the coffee.

Cortez rattled the ice in his whiskey and soda and

stared into it thoughtfully. "Interesting. I thought your boss had more sense."

"He's got reelection on his mind. Miles Townshend recommended Haralson to him. He helped put Miles back in office before he got the cabinet position."

"Oh, Haralson's good at what he does, no question," Cortez said, nodding. "But you don't want him working for your boss."

"Then how do I convince my boss to get rid of him?"

Cortez looked up. "You can't. Get rid of him, that is."

"Yes, I can, if I know . . ."

He leaned forward. "You can't get rid of him because he's finally in a position where I can reach him. Keep out of this. Let me take him down."

Derrie scowled. "You aren't going to tell me anything, are you?"

He smiled. "No."

She glowered at him. "He could ruin my boss's career. Mary Tanner was Miles's senior legal counsel when he was a senator, and she knew all about Haralson's methods. She's the one who told me he'd been involved with something illegal. She won't tell me what. I was hoping you would."

"Mary has one of the finest legal minds of the century," he said. "She'll be a judge one of these days."

"I hope so," she agreed, reflecting on the expertise of her friend, who was a descendant of the Gullah slaves who inhabited the islands off the South Carolina coast.

"But what about Haralson? Why won't anybody tell me anything?"

"Too risky at this point. Say nothing. Do nothing. I'll be in Charleston for a couple of weeks, apparently on vacation. I'll be in touch."

She wanted to argue with him. She knew better than to try. "All right." She sipped her coffee and liked the bite of the whiskey. "Phoebe's going to be home for a few weeks," she added with a sly grin. "She'd love to meet you."

He glowered at her. "I'm not a museum exhibit for junior archaeology majors."

"Minors," she corrected. "Her major is anthropology. And you're Comanche; a descendant of Mongoloid people from Asia. An indigenous aborigine."

His eyes narrowed. "Which makes you a Caucasoid interloper. No. I don't want to meet Phoebe."

"She's blond and blue-eyed and tomboyish and she loves to dig up things."

"For God's sake, don't you have any idea how Native Americans feel about archaeology?" he burst out.

"Sorry! But she doesn't dig up people. Only old pots."

"Which could be sacred relics . . ."

She shoved a bowl under his nose. "Have some peanuts," she invited.

He gave her a hard glare, which she returned with a smile. "If you won't tell me anything about Haralson, I'm leaving."

"I can't tell you anything," he replied. "You'll have to trust me."

Since the day she'd met him, at an exclusive Washington banquet, Derrie had been drawn to the tall, brooding man. They were friends. She found him intelligent and a refreshing change from some of the more aggressive business types who wanted to date her. Cortez knew that she was stuck on her boss. If there was a woman in Cortez's life, he was very quiet about it. All the same, she'd never been able to get him to meet her niece, Phoebe.

Cortez drove her back to her apartment in the nondescript car he used for work.

"Why don't you buy a sports car?" she asked when she got out of it.

"Wouldn't I be a picture, with my hair flowing in the wind?" he mused.

"Your hair never flows in the wind. You never let it down."

"Too risky," he said with a straight face. Only the twinkle in his dark eyes betrayed him. "I might revert."

"Not you. Not with a Harvard degree."

"Thanks for the testimonial. I'll see you in Charleston. Stop worrying."

"That'll be the day," she sighed.

On the following Friday, Clayton flew back to Charleston for the weekend, taking a sulky Derrie with him. She'd said that she had a date with a promising Washington politician for a play and Clayton had deliberately conned her into this trip and out of D.C.

They'd already had one minor disagreement about his hiring of John Haralson, but as they entered the airport Derrie drew back from any blatant argument because of Cortez's warning. She only hoped that Haralson wouldn't destroy Clayton politically before Cortez could do what he planned. She wondered just how dirty Haralson was, and about what. Was it the way he conducted political campaigns, or something more?

"Couldn't you stop glaring at me?" Clayton asked with a hopeful smile. "Your eyebrows are going to grow in that position and you'll look like a wrestler."

She tossed back her blond hair. "Good! I could get a job throwing men around." She gave him a meaningful look.

"And give up fighting me?" he mused. "You'd be miserable."

"I don't know. I might adopt one of those poor little spotted owls whose houses you're going to help cut down!"

Now he was glaring back. "I'm not personally going to evict one single feathered resident of the northwest forest."

"You're going to vote for a bill that does," she returned.

"I want to protect jobs for loggers. Do you know how many of them are out of work because of these lawsuits by environmental groups?" he asked.

"Do you know that logging jobs have actually increased in the past few years and still loggers are out of work?'' she persisted. ''If the owl's habitat is sacrificed, what's next? Ours? Another thing: The government provides and maintains roads into the national forests, and the timber industry uses them. Those forests are maintained through taxes! And who do you think is footing the bill for it all? The American taxpayer, that's who.''

''Wood benefits us all,'' he said, unconvinced.

''Yes. But at what cost?''

''You're thinking only with your emotions, Derrie,'' he argued. ''Forests are replanted constantly. My God, woman, everything from the apartment you live in to the paper you write on comes from trees! Do you honestly think our culture can survive without the timber industry?!''

''Before you vote on whether or not to renew the Endangered Species Act or allow logging in the old growth forests, it might be just as well if you talked to a few people besides the timber lobby about it. I know you like Duke Brannigan. But he isn't being paid to tell you both sides of the issue; he works for the timber companies.''

''Duke and I are friends,'' he began stiffly.

''Friends are people who don't try to coerce you into voting in their favor on the floor of the House,'' she pointed out.

''One day, so help me, Derrie . . . !'' he burst out furiously.

She made him a bow and walked out. Clayton left the bags for his assistant and started toward the steps.

But he didn't hurry. He wasn't anxious to catch up with her until he cooled down.

The investigative reporter from the *Weekly Voice* frowned over a tidbit of information that he'd extracted from a representative of the biggest and best of the local waste disposal companies. The Coastal Waste Company executive had told him that Kane Lombard had, without reason, suddenly dissolved his contract with the solid waste disposal group and replaced CWC with a little-known local company.

The CWC representative was still fuming about the incident, which had been inexplicable; his company had an impeccable reputation all over the southeast for its handling of dangerous waste disposal. CWC had drivers who were specially trained for the work. They used vehicles designated for only the purpose of handling toxic materials, and the vehicles were double insulated for safety. The drivers were trained in how to handle an accident, what to do in case of leakage. The company had even been spotlighted on the national news for the excellence of its work. And now, without reason, Kane Lombard had fired them. The damage to their reputation was their chief concern.

Had they tried to contact Lombard to find out his reason? Sanders had asked. Of course they had, the CWC representative replied. But Lombard hadn't answered their call at his beach house. His housekeeper had insisted that he couldn't be reached. That, too, was

SUSAN KYLE

odd. Lombard wasn't known for dodging controversy or arguments.

His choice for a new solid waste contractor was curious. A local company called Burke's had been sued only a year earlier for dumping chemicals from an electroplating company directly into a vacant field instead of at the small town's landfill.

Sanders had been sent south to try to find something that might help the Republican congressional candidate, Sam Hewett, in his campaign. He wasn't specifically told to dig up dirt on the Seymours, but he was certain that some scandal concerning them would help. However, what he'd found was certainly not going to hurt the Seymours.

He tried to phone Kane, without success. His employer's eldest son was apparently out of the beach house every time Sanders called, according to the housekeeper, or he was refusing to answer the telephone.

Failing to connect there, Sanders had spoken to Kane's father in New York. Mr. Lombard was worried when Sanders mentioned that he hadn't been able to get past Kane's housekeeper to speak with him.

"Go down there, then," Lombard told him. "Make him aware of what's going on before it's too late. Funny, it isn't like Kane to absent himself from business," he murmured curiously.

"So I've heard. Seymour will use anything he can find to hurt Sam Hewett's campaign," he added. "Your son Norman is Hewett's campaign manager and Kane

106

is his brother. A scandal that includes one Lombard could conceivably hurt Hewett."

"I know that. Have you found anything that we can use?" he added.

"If you mean about the Seymours, no. They have an impeccable reputation in Charleston . . ."

"Don't hand me that. The best families always have some dark secret. Find theirs."

"Mudslinging . . ."

"I don't pay you to have a conscience, Mr. Sanders. Go and see Kane. And dig deeper. I'll tell Norman what's going on." The line went dead.

It was too late to do that today. Sanders kicked off his shoes, put his glass on the bedside table, and sprawled on the bed. His dreams of a literary career as a novelist were long dead. He wrote what he was told to write and drew a good salary, but he felt like a vulture feeding on the waste dump of humanity.

Haralson was making a phone call of his own. It was Friday night and Clayton Seymour was very predictable in one way; he was always home in Charleston by seven on a Friday evening.

He'd expected the candidate to sound tired, but Seymour actually snapped at him when he answered the telephone. "What is it that couldn't wait until Monday?" he added tersely.

"I thought you'd like to know that Kane Lombard has

contracted with a fly-by-night waste disposal company that's suspected of dumping toxic waste somewhere in the coastal marshes.''

"What?!?"

Haralson grinned. "He's been so careful in every other area not to antagonize anyone about conservation issues. Now here he goes and hires a local man with a really bad reputation to dump his toxic waste. And he fires a company with the best reputation in the business to do it!''

"Facts, Haralson, facts.''

"I've got them. Give me a few days and I'll prove it.''

"Remind me to give you a raise. Several raises.''

Haralson laughed out loud. "In that case, you can have the videotapes in stereo with subtitles.''

"Good man. I knew I made the best choice when I hired you. Don't cross the line, though,'' he cautioned. "Don't give him any ammunition to use against us.''

"He won't get any from me.''

"Thanks.''

Clayton hung up, his former bad humor gone in a flash of delight. Lombard had publicly announced his intention to fund Sam Hewett's campaign and Norman Lombard, one of Kane Lombard's brothers, was the Republican candidate's campaign manager. Not only that, Lombard had been making some nasty, snide comments about Seymour having the background but not the brains and know-how to do the job.

This might be a little on the shady side, to tell the

world in the election, but he was going to use it. He'd been bested too many times by people without scruples.

At least he didn't take money under the table, he thought, rationalizing his use of what Nikki would call gutter tactics. No doubt Nikki would disapprove, if she knew. But then, he added, he would be doing the city a service, wouldn't he? An industrial polluter deserved every legal hassle he got!

In the meantime, there was no reason for Nikki to know anything yet. She needed her vacation. There would be plenty of time to fill her in later.

He couldn't help but wonder how Haralson had managed to dig up such a tasty scandal for him. He really would have to give the man credit. He was a definite asset.

Derrie unpacked her bags in her small apartment. She had enough clothes for the few weeks that Clayton had just informed her they'd be in Charleston working on the reelection campaign while Congress wasn't in session. Then she lamented about the argument she'd had with Clayton. It had surprised her that he'd insisted on her accompanying him to Charleston tonight even though he never worked on Saturday. He'd convinced her that tomorrow was going to be the exception and he couldn't work without her.

She wished that he couldn't live without her. But she was hardly much competition for Bett Watts, who was smart and beautiful.

Who am I kidding, she asked her reflection in the mirror. She had two new gray hairs among the thick blond ones. She also had wrinkles at the corners of her big dark blue eyes, and dark circles beneath them from lack of sleep. She'd worked for Clayton for years and he never noticed her at all. He was too busy enjoying the flashier companionship that his political standing gave him.

He was very discreet, but there were women in his life. Or there had been, until he and Bett had become an item. Derrie stood on the sidelines handing him letters to sign and reminding him of appointments, and he never did more than tease her about her deprived social life. Which was his fault, of course, since she didn't want to go out with anyone except her stupid boss.

He was really getting out of hand, she asserted as she got ready for bed. The newly elected congressman who'd taken her with him to Washington three years ago was changing before her eyes. He'd run for the office on a conservation platform, but it was eroding these days. His lack of defense for the forests was just the latest in a line of uncharacteristic actions lately. And add his hiring of John Haralson to that . . .

He'd had angry letters from any number of constituents about his voting record during the present session of Congress. He'd voted against several environmental issues. And he was suddenly going against his ex-brother-in-law, Miles Townshend, an active conservation advocate. Miles was only in his early forties now, but he was smart about politics. He'd tried to caution

Clayton about taking votes for granted. Clayton hadn't been listening lately.

Derrie wondered if Nikki had noticed the changes in Clayton's personality. Nikki hadn't been well, and Clayton had spent more time in Washington than ever during the past six months.

She climbed into bed and pulled up the covers, heartsick and demoralized. She'd never before argued so much with Clayton. Now it seemed she was fated never to do anything else. She desperately wanted to talk with Nikki about him.

Bett Watts was going over more legal briefs than she'd ever wanted to see in her life. Sometimes she thought it would be wonderful to just marry Clayton Seymour and chuck this career business. But then she'd stop and realize that she couldn't stay at home all the time and give up the challenge and excitement of her work. Once in a while, she actually did some good.

But what she wanted most of all was to be a lobbyist. It was a high-paying job and it carried a lot of prestige. She could pick and choose her causes and argue for them. Arguing in court was one of her greatest skills.

The drawback was her relationship with Clayton. She couldn't go on seeing him once she took a lobbying job with any group. It would mean a conflict of interest for him, and it could cost him his career.

She thought it hardly fair that she had to give up her dreams because they might threaten his. She had tried to sort out the conflict in her mind for days, and she was no closer to an alternative.

After the campaign was over—and Clayton would win, she was certain—they would have to talk about the problem and face it. She was very fond of Clayton. But she'd worked hard all her life, first to earn enough to get her through law school, and then to keep her head above water with the most prestigious law firm in Washington. All those years of sacrifice and study were worth more than a footnote in her life story. Clayton had to understand that she was too vital, too intelligent to be only an extension of a man—even though she loved him to distraction. She would have a hard choice. She dreaded it.

CHAPTER
SIX

It had been so simple at first, Kane told himself as he piloted his yacht out into the Atlantic. All he had to do was spend a lot of time with Nikki and eventually he'd tire of her. But he hadn't. He and Nikki had been inseparable for the better part of two weeks and he was more consciously aware of his own loneliness than he could remember being since the death of his wife and son. When he wasn't with Nikki, he felt like only half a man.

He lifted his dark face into the fresh breeze. One of his forebears had been Italian, another Spanish, and even another one Greek. He had the blood of the Mediterranean in his veins, so perhaps that explained why he loved sailing so much.

He glanced over his shoulder at his crew. They were working furiously to put up the spinnaker, and as it set, his heart skipped a beat. The wind slid in behind it, caressed it, then suddenly filled it like a passionate lover and the sailboat jerked and plowed ahead through the water.

The wind tore through his hair like mad fingers. Kane laughed at the sheer joy of being alive. It was always like this when he sailed. He loved the danger, the speed, the uncertainty of the winds and the channels. He was sure that in colonial days he would have been a pirate. At the very least, he'd have been a sailing man. There was nothing else that gave him such a glorious high. Not even sex.

He spun the wheel to avoid collision with a lunatic in a high-powered motor boat. He mumbled obscenities under his breath as the big yacht slid easily through the wake of the other boat.

"Damned fools," he muttered.

Jake, his rigger, only laughed. "It's a big ocean. Plenty of room for all sorts of lunatics."

The older man was wiry and tough. He had red hair, going gray, and a weatherbeaten sort of leathery skin. Jake had crewed for the yacht "Stars and Stripes" with Dennis Conner in the America's Cup trials the year she won the race. Like the other tough seamen who survived that grueling sport, Jake had a freedom of spirit that gave him a kinship with Kane. From the time Kane was a boy, he had looked to Jake for advice and support in hard times. The older man was in many ways more his father than the tabloid owner in New York who shared his name.

"You're troubled," Jake observed as they traveled

seaward amid the creaking of the lines and the flap of the spinnaker as Kane tacked.

"Yes."

"Bad memories?" Jake probed.

Kane took a slow breath. "Complications. I seem to be acquiring them in bunches like bananas lately. Especially one slender brunette one."

"Another woman?"

Kane chuckled. "Not just another woman this time. I can't get her out of my system. I don't want to get married, but she won't have an affair with me."

"I see. Well, it's probably better to avoid entanglements," the older man agreed easily. He glanced up at the ballooned sail and smiled as he admired the set of it. "We're making good time. We really ought to enter this baby in the Cup trials."

"I don't want to sail in the Cup."

"Why not?"

"For one reason, because I don't have the time."

Jake shrugged philosophically. "I can't argue with that. But you're missing the thrill of a lifetime."

"No, I'm not. Look out there," he said, gesturing toward the horizon. "This is the thrill of a lifetime, every minute I spend on this deck. I don't have to prove anything to the world, least of all that I'm the best sailor in the water."

"Nice to feel that way. Most of us feel we have to live up to some invisible, indefinable goal."

"Why bother? You can't please most people. Please yourself instead."

Jake leaned against the rail and stared at him, hard. "That's selfish."

"I'm a selfish man. I don't know how to give." He met Jake's eyes, and his own were cold, leaden. "Like the rest of the minnows in this icy pond we call life, I'm just trying to stay alive in a society that rewards mediocrity and punishes accomplishment and intelligence."

"Cynic."

"Who wouldn't be? My God, man, look around you! How many people do you know who wouldn't cut your throat to get ahead or make a profit?"

"One. Me."

Kane smiled. "Yeah. You."

"You're restless. Isn't it about time we went back to Charleston and you did what you do best?"

"What do I do best," he asked absently, "run the company or make waves for the local politicians?"

"Both. I don't run a major business, but I know one thing. It's damned risky to leave others in charge for too long, no matter how competent they are. Things go wrong."

Kane turned to study his friend. "Something you know from experience, right?"

Jake chuckled. "Yeah. I sat out half a race and we lost the Cup."

"Not your fault."

"Tell me that every day. I might believe it." He glanced out over the sea toward the horizon. "Storm blowing up. We're in for some weather. It might be a good idea to head back, before you get caught up in the joy of fighting the sea again," he added with a dark look.

Kane had cause to remember the last time he'd been in a battle with the ocean during a gale. He'd laughed and brought the boat in, but Jake hadn't enjoyed the ride. He'd been sick.

"Go ahead, laugh," Jake muttered.

"Sorry. I need a challenge now and again, that's all," he said apologetically. "Something to fight, someone to fight. I guess the world sits on me sometimes and I have to get it out of my system."

"The world sits on us all, and you've more reason to chafe than most. It's just a year today, isn't it?"

"A year." Kane didn't like remembering the anniversary of the violence that had killed his family. He scowled and turned the wheel, tacking suddenly and sharply, so that the yacht balanced precariously over on its keel.

"Watch it!" Jake cautioned. "We could capsize, even as big as we are."

"I hate anniversaries," Kane said, heat and hurt in his deep voice. "I hate them!"

Jake laid a heavy, warm hand on the broad, husky shoulder of his friend. "Peace, compadre," he said gently. "Peace. Give it time. You'll get through it."

Kane felt sick inside. The wounds opened from time to time, but today was the worst. The sea spray hit him in the face, and the wind chilled it where it was wettest. He stared ahead and tried not to notice that there were warm tracks running down his cheeks.

When he got back to the house, his housekeeper was giving Sanders hell because he was drinking up Kane's Scotch whiskey.

What, he wondered, was Sanders doing here?

He walked in, interrupting the argument. They both turned toward him. Sanders was tall, just over six feet, very blond and craggy-faced. He was an ex-war correspondent and had the scars to prove it.

Kane dismissed the housekeeper and went to the bar. He poured himself two fingers of scotch, adding an ice cube to the mixture.

"What do you want?" he asked his family's star reporter.

"To tell you what I've uncovered."

Kane's hand stilled with the glass of scotch held gingerly in it. "Well?"

"You take your scotch neat," Sanders remarked, moving closer. "I suppose you can take your bad news the same way. Seymour is after you. The rumor is that he's got something he can use to get you on environmental charges, something to punctuate the raw sewage leak at your plant last month."

"That incident was an accidental spill into the river," Kane said curtly. "We weren't charged."

"Not for that, no. But it put you on the Environmental

Protection Agency's watch list and evidently Seymour thinks where there's one violation there are bound to be others. They say he's found one.''

Kane ran his hand through his windblown hair. He knew there would be problems with his plant manager away so long. His replacement wasn't as experienced, but he was capable. That's what he told Sanders. He didn't tell him that Jurkins had a child with leukemia. That was why Kane had bent over backwards to help him. He had a soft spot for children. Now more than ever. And Jurkins had made a point of telling him the child's condition.

"New or not, he's clumsy. You can't afford to let this go without looking into it.''

"Why is Seymour on my tail?''

"Because your family's tabloid is crucifying him over his support for the spotted owl, because your brother Norman is Sam Hewett's new campaign manager, and because your whole family is endorsing Hewett, his major Republican opponent.''

"None of that is news.''

"It's relevant, though.'' He sipped his drink. "Did you know that the brand new secretary of the interior is Seymour's ex-brother-in-law?''

Kane frowned. "Is he?'' he asked absently.

"He's having his own problems. He's under fire from industry over the spotted owl; he likes owls.''

"Seymour mustn't like them much: his position has hurt him at home,'' Sanders said cynically. "However, a few well-placed and well-timed blows at industrial pollution in his home district could kindle a lot of public opinion in his favor and put him back in Washington. I don't know what he's found, but he's got something. You can bet if John Haralson is helping him—and he is—he's got something.''

"Haralson.''

"Townshend's former campaign director—Mr. Sleaze,'' he added curtly. "The original dirty tricks man.''

"Working for Seymour? That doesn't sound like Seymour. From what I've read about him, he's never been a politician who tried to smear anybody for personal gain. He's an idealist.''

"Perhaps he's learned that idealism is a euphemism for naiveté in politics. You can't change the world.''

"That doesn't stop people from trying, does it?''

"Seymour is going to concentrate on you. Your family news tabloid has been making his stand on the owl issue his major embarrassment since this spotted owl thing began, and the press coverage he's getting because of it has cost him points in the polls. If he can connect you with anything shady, the inference is that he can cost your family some credibility. That will also hurt Hewett—because your brother is his campaign manager. In other words, if you get known as a polluter and your brother is working for Hewett, some people will think Hewett is guilty by association. That's what your father thinks, anyway,'' he added.

"You're his star reporter,'' Kane said. "What do you think?''

Sanders put his empty glass down. "I think you'd better make sure there's nothing to connect your company with any more environmental damage."

"I told you, that sewage leak was purely accidental. I don't have anything shady to worry about."

"You sound very sure of yourself," Sanders said quietly. "But you've been away from work over two weeks."

"I have reliable managers," Kane said, getting more irritated by the minute. He didn't want to admit that Nikki was the main reason for his sudden reluctance to return to work. Every second he spent with her had become precious, fragile. He was obsessed with her, to the point of forgetting the work that had been so necessary to him. Only a few more days, he told himself. He'd have her out of his system soon, then he could concentrate on his plant again.

"Do you trust your manager to keep you out of court, when he's working half-days from a computer at home since his kidney stone operation?" Sanders straightened. He was almost Kane's own height. "Then why have you turned out a reputable company like CWC?"

"CWC." Kane nodded. "Oh, yes, I remember. I had a talk with Jurkins, my new solid waste manager. He said that CWC had done a sloppy job at enormous cost. He wanted permission to replace the company and get someone more efficient, and a little less expensive."

"That's very interesting. CWC has a very good reputation. One of the national news magazines recently did a piece on them. They're very efficient and high-tech."

Lombard pursed his lips and scowled. "Are they? Well, perhaps they've fallen down on the job. Jurkins faxed me some paperwork that pretty much proved his position. But I'll look into it when I get back to Charleston. Meanwhile, what have you found out about Seymour?"

"Nothing yet. But I've got a few rumors to check out."

Kane laughed coldly. "Any hint of corruption will do. I may need some leverage if Seymour finds anything I don't know about. Good God, I take a few days off and everything falls apart. I'd better telephone the plant and talk to that new man again."

"I wouldn't," the other man advised. "Let me check around first."

"Why?"

"If there's any under-the-table dealing going on, the fewer people who know we suspect, the better."

"It won't do me any good to wait if Seymour's people find anything illegal going on."

"That's what worries us," Sanders said. "I think Seymour has found something. Worse, there may be some deliberate evidence." He stressed the words.

Kane rubbed the back of his neck, wincing as he touched a sunburned area. *When it rains, it pours,* he said to himself.

Sanders put down his glass. "Well, all I have are suspicions right now, mainly because of Haralson's involvement. I've heard some things about him locally, from the underworld element. I'll let you know if anything surfaces.''

Kane nodded, wondering dimly why Haralson's name sounded so familiar. But his mind was already away from the small problem of waste disposal and back on Nikki.

John Haralson was talking to Clayton Seymour, grinning from ear to ear while he puffed on a cigar.

"Want to know how we're doing?" Haralson asked merrily.

Clayton nodded. "I hope you've got something pleasant to report," he said, "and that it's not about trees or owls!"

The older man laughed. "No, it's not. Lombard's company kicked out CWC in favor of Burke. Remember him? He was charged with dumping toxic waste in a swamp a year or more ago and he weaseled out of the charge."

Clayton's smile faded. "How do you know?" he asked curiously.

Haralson pretended innocence. "Contacts. I have all sorts of contacts."

"Go on."

"Well, Burke ordinarily charges about one-fifteenth of what Lombard was paying CWC for hauling off the waste. Now he gets what CWC used to get, and he doesn't have their overhead."

Clayton paused. "That puts the onus on Lombard's hired man, not on Lombard himself. He's not getting anything out of it."

"It will look as if he is," Haralson said smugly. "We don't have to mention the kickbacks to his janitorial man. We can say that Lombard was cutting costs. It's a well-known fact that he's just recently laid off some employees because of the recession."

Clayton stiffened. "You're talking about concealing facts."

"Not permanently," Haralson said smoothly. "Just long enough for the news media to pick up the story and run it a few times. They love dealing with industrial polluters. Save the planet, you know."

"But . . ."

Haralson's eyes narrowed and he leaned forward intently. "If you don't get Lombard's neck in a noose and squeeze, his man is going to eventually uncover the truth about your sister Nikki and her marriage to Miles Townshend. Can you think what that will do to you, and to them, if the press gets wind of it?" he added suddenly, pressing an advantage that he didn't even have. Then he held his breath, waiting for the shot in the dark to register.

He wasn't disappointed. "Oh, my God," Clayton said, shaken.

Haralson was jubilant. That meant that there was some scandal in the family; he might need to know that one day. Haralson always tried to have something on everybody with whom he did business. Sometimes that came in handy. It had worked out very well with Jurkins, whom he knew from a certain clinic where his business associates peddled their wares. Jurkins had come in very handy indeed. So had his brother-in-law . . .

"A big scandal could cost you the election, couldn't it?" Haralson pressed his advantage. "And Townshend could lose his cabinet position. The press would crucify you all. Think what Lombard's brothers could do with that little secret in the *Weekly Voice*."

Clayton was sweating. It was the first time he'd compromised his ideals to save his career. He had no choice. "All right. Go ahead and do what you have to." He glanced up. "But make sure that no one knows how you're doing it."

"You can count on me. In fact, I've got a man in mind who's going to do a little undercover work for me, to see where Lombard's company is putting that illegal waste."

"Who?" Clayton was feeling sicker by the minute.

"A man I know. He's in town and contacted me. He's on vacation, but he jumped at the chance when I mentioned I had a small problem that needed investigating."

"Can he keep a confidence?"

"He's a Comanche Indian. You tell me."

Clayton nodded. "Like one of those people in 'Dances with Wolves,' " he said.

"No. The Indians in that movie were supposed to be Sioux, although the actual book really was written about the Comanche. He doesn't wear feathers and beads on the job. And if you call him chief, you'd better be standing on the other side of a wall. He's touchy about racial slurs.''

"Does he have a name?''

"Sure. It's Cortez.''

Clayton found himself grinning, the fear subsiding a little. Haralson wasn't going to do anything really illegal. Of course not. "You're kidding me.''

"I'm not. One of his great-grandfathers was a Spaniard. He calls it the only bad blood in his family tree. His sense of irony is pretty keen, which is why he uses the name of the Spanish conqueror of Mexico. He spends his free time on the Oklahoma homeplace. On it, you couldn't pronounce his name.''

"You say he's a good investigator.''

"One of the best.''

"There won't be a conflict of interest involved?''

"Only if we tell anyone he's helping us,'' Haralson said innocently.

He got a glare in return for his helpful comment.

"It was a joke! There's no problem,'' Haralson chuckled. "When he's on vacation, what he does with his free time is his own business. We're not asking him to do anything illegal. In fact, we're asking him to help us catch a polluter, aren't we?''

Clayton wasn't so sure about that, but he wasn't going to allow himself to dwell on it. Surely the thing was to win the election, not worry about how to do it. And he had no finer feelings for Kane Lombard. If the man was polluting, he should be caught.

"No, we aren't doing anything illegal," Clayton said, speaking from years of hands-on experience with the law. "In essence, we're asking him to look for a violation of the EPA codes."

"That's right. So just pretend I never said a word. I'll do what's necessary to save your bacon."

Clayton's light eyes narrowed. "I have great respect for the law. Don't sweep anything under the carpet," he said.

"Not unless I have to," Haralson promised.

Clayton had to be satisfied with that. But he wasn't. He just hoped Miles Townshend knew what he was doing when he suggested Haralson.

Cortez was enjoying himself. Haralson was a master manipulator, and he thought he had the key to unlock Cortez's baser instincts. He was going to be in for a surprise one day soon. Just now, Cortez was playing along. He'd deliberately sought Haralson out, and had mentioned that he was in Charleston on a long vacation. He had actually watched the wheels turning in the other man's mind as Haralson first remembered Cortez's expertise as an investigator and then suddenly saw the best way to further his own ends. Haralson had explained his problem briefly and enlisted Cortez's help.

"You want me to save the hide of a Texan?" Cortez had mused.

"Not at all . . ." Haralson had said quickly. He took the remark seriously, and he was trying to pacify Cortez.

For a Comanche, Cortez was unusually tall and lean. He was powerfully muscled, scar-faced, with deep-set large black eyes and a rawboned face that seemed to be all sharp angles. As dark as he was, he looked much too light for a Comanche. Haralson wasn't going to remark on it, though. He'd heard some hair-raising stories about Cortez, some of which were probably true.

His record since he'd left the reservation police for college and afterward started working for government agencies was impressive. But right now, his job was a little shadowy. He'd been an FBI agent, but whether or not he still was, Haralson couldn't find out. For all he knew, the other man could have gone with some independent agency. Like the Company. A cold chill grabbed him, and then he chided himself for being so silly. Cortez was just a man, and any man had a price. He had Cortez's in his pocket right now.

"I hate Texans," Cortez was saying. He didn't blink. It was one of the more disconcerting things about him. "They forced my people completely out of the state back in the 1800s, off our ancestral lands and into Oklahoma."

"If I remember my history, Texans weren't too fond of Comanches, either. But I'm not asking you to help a Texan. I'm asking you to help put one out of business."

"Ah," Cortez said smoothly. "Is that so?"

"It is, indeed. I need some help. A little detective work . . ."

Cortez studied the other man with unwavering intensity. "I'm on an extended vacation. Do your own detective work."

"You promised, Cortez," Haralson reminded him. "And just to show you that my heart's in the right place . . ." He held out an object on his palm.

The other man hesitated. His brow furrowed. "What is that?"

"You know what it is. I hear you've been looking everywhere for one. Help me out on this," he added, "and I'll sell it to you at the market price."

Cortez pursed his lips. "That's right, hit me in my weakest spot!"

"Always know a man's weaknesses when you plan to trade with him," Haralson chuckled. "Well?"

Cortez's long fingers settled on his raven-black ponytail. He eyed Haralson with something approaching admiration for an instant. The man certainly knew how to exploit people. Only a few people knew that Cortez was a numismatist. Coin collecting was his only hobby. Haralson was thorough. "All right," he agreed. "But only because I'm a certified collector."

"Which I already knew." Haralson handed him the coin, a 19th-century two-and-a-half-dollar gold piece.

"I'll write you a check. You can't imagine," Cortez murmured, handling the coin with something akin to reverence, "how many years I've been looking for one of these."

"Sure, I can."

Cortez gave him a speculative look. "You'll get your

pint of blood. I'll see if I can connect Lombard's larcenous employee to Burke's with something concrete. But if I find anything illegal going on, I'll inform the appropriate people at once."

"Would I expect anything less from you?" Haralson asked with a wicked smile. "Trust me." He put his hand over his heart. "I have a soul."

"If you do, you keep it in your wallet," Cortez agreed. "You had knowledge of a crime and didn't report it."

Haralson stared at him uncomfortably. He hadn't thought things through that far. He and Cortez were acquaintances, not really friends, and the Comanche made a bad enemy.

"I suspect," Haralson said quickly. "I don't know for sure. But if Lombard is polluting, shouldn't he be caught?" His eyes went narrow. "Caught and hung. He's such a judgmental man, it's only fair that he should be judged, you know." He was speaking without really choosing his words. "He should pay for his sins."

Cortez frowned, watching him. Haralson looked oddly uncontrolled. "Do you know Lombard?" Cortez asked quietly.

That brought Haralson back, and he blinked. "Know him? How could I?"

"You spend a lot of time in Charleston these days; even since before Lombard started the auto plant here," he pointed out.

"I like the coast," Haralson said nervously.

Cortez knew why. But he wasn't going to risk giving

away that information. "So do I. That's why I decided to vacation here," he added.

He turned away, coin in hand, and went to pick up his jacket. "Okay, I'll snoop around Burke's for you. I'll be in touch as soon as I've checked out a few people and places."

Haralson watched him go with actual discomfort. He'd thought he had Cortez right where he wanted him. But there was something mysterious in the other man's manner that puzzled him, and he wondered if, for the first time in memory, his instincts about people had let him down. Most people could be exploited if you knew their weaknesses. But the shadowy man remained as mysterious to Haralson as he was to most other people, and he'd trusted him with a secret. What if Cortez started asking questions? He had plenty to hide. But surely that crack about the time he spent on the coast hadn't meant anything. Cortez didn't know anything about it. How could he? Haralson had been very careful. Well, except for Jurkins. But he could keep that naive fellow in line. All it needed was a little white powder. He chuckled. He stuck his hands in his pockets and started walking back to his car.

He was on his way. He'd have Lombard skinned, and Clayton Seymour back in office owing him favors, in no time. In his line of work, it was necessary to have a few politicians on his payroll. Seymour couldn't be bought, but he'd tie the congressman to him first with assistance and then by blackmail. He'd get whatever he wanted in the way of protection. It had worked with everyone else he'd ever known. It was why he was still in business. Townshend had been his one loss, but then, he couldn't get much on Townshend. The man had been very secretive. But Seymour had given him away. If he played his cards right, Haralson thought, he might discover the secret that would put a cabinet member in his pocket, too.

Nikki lay in Kane's arms on the sofa at her beach house, watching the stars come out on the horizon out the picture window. It was dark, and he had come over, as he usually did, to have supper with her. They'd just finished.

"Happy?" he asked at her temple.

"Oh, yes." She curled closer into his big body, enjoying the feel of him. This tender touching had become an integral part of their relationship, and while it had made her apprehensive at first, now she looked forward to being held by him. When he kissed her with such slow hunger, she could feel the desire pulsing through him. She liked that. It proved to her that she wasn't falling twice into the same trap.

She looked up at him, savoring the hard masculinity of his features. She smiled and touched his long, sexy mouth.

He smiled back, accepting the wordless invitation. He kissed her slowly, hungrily. His hand went between them to open his shirt and draw her hand inside, so that she could caress the muscles under the thick pelt of curling hair that covered his chest. He liked it when she touched him this way. He liked her mouth, her smile, everything about her. But especially he liked the sharp passion she kindled in him. He'd never known such liberating pleasure before.

They had done very little kissing, despite their attraction to each other. Companionship, teasing, laughter had hallmarked their relationship so far. Trips to tourist spots like Magnolia Gardens with its exquisite floral grounds had combined with dancing and eating out to give them time to explore all the things they had in common—and there were many. But the more they were together, the worse the hunger to touch became. Tonight, it reached flash point.

He groaned suddenly and his hand went between them again, this time to search for the buttons that secured her soft knit shirt. Usually, she protested when he got this far. But this time, she didn't stop him. She shifted, in fact, to give him better access.

Blood rushed to his head as his big, callused hand found its way gently under the lacy bit of nothing that concealed her soft skin under the loose shirt. She was soft, like thistledown, and he felt her breath catch under his mouth as he caressed the nipple to hardness.

He felt her begin to tremble and when she gasped and lifted closer, he sat up.

"Don't stop," she whispered, mindlessly seeking to prolong the first real passion she'd ever experienced.

He looked down at her misty eyes, her swollen, parted lips. "I'm not going to stop," he assured her softly. "I just want to look at you."

The words didn't quite register until his big hands pulled her up so that he could remove the shirt and the lacy bra under it.

"Kane," she began uncertainly.

He pulled her to him, inside his own loosened shirt, and groaned as he felt the silky softness of her bare breasts settling against his hot skin. "Oh, God," he whispered reverently.

Nikki stopped breathing. She had never been held like this. She exploded with sensation, and she moaned as she reached up to hold him, moving her body against his to prolong the delight.

His hands held her slender waist, keeping her close; his face was pressed into her neck. He shivered and so did she.

"Three weeks is long enough," he said, his deep voice faintly strained. "I want to love you, Nikki."

She pushed away from him just a little, trying to regain her sanity, but her motion drew his eyes down to her tip-tilted breasts, and he looked at her as if he'd never seen a woman.

"They look like apples," he said roughly. "Pert little apples . . ." His head bent suddenly and his mouth fastened over her breast with expertise and unconcealed hunger.

The moist heat of his mouth was at first shocking, and then violently arousing. Nikki felt a burst of warmth in her lower abdomen that brought a husky cry from her lips. She arched backward, lost, totally lost, her whole body pleading for more.

She didn't realize that he'd picked her up, or that he was walking out to the deck. She had long since forgotten who her brother was, why she shouldn't permit Kane any intimacies. She could barely recall her own name.

He put her down on the biggest of the lounges, under the stars, with the surf crashing beyond the high rails of the deck.

His mouth was on her waist, her lower belly, her thighs. She felt the irritating fabric that separated her from his hungry mouth being pulled away, and her only thought was one of relief. The night air and his mouth were relief itself.

"No!" she choked when he drew away.

"Only for a minute," he promised roughly, bending to kiss her with aching hunger. "Just for one minute, Nikki."

He stripped off his clothing with a total lack of concern for buttons and fasteners, pausing only long enough to search in his wallet for a small object that his shaking hands produced.

Nikki wanted to avoid this. Her mind filled with reasons against what was going to happen, but her body refused to cooperate. It arched and moved sinuously on the lounge while she moaned helplessly, almost sobbing in the flash of hunger in her as she looked at the perfection of his body.

"Please," she whispered, holding out her arms to him. "Please, please . . ."

He rolled over her, pulling her with him, on top now so that she could feel the cushion of hair that ran down his chest, to his manhood, to his powerful legs. He was big and warm, and the feel of him in her arms was everything she'd dreamed it would be.

She clung to him while he kissed every soft inch of her in the darkness. The surf was barely audible above the feverish beat of her own heart. She was being foolish, but she didn't care. Nothing mattered except to have Kane fill the aching emptiness inside her.

He was as helpless against the white heat as she was. He kissed her until kissing was no longer enough. His mouth fitted itself perfectly to hers and he moved between the long silky length of her legs and felt them curl around him. He shuddered as he searched for admittance . . . and found it.

She stiffened a little, but that didn't surprise him. He was better endowed than most other men.

"I won't hurt you, I promise," he whispered into her mouth. His tongue teased around her lips as he caressed her inner thigh and felt her begin to relax. He managed a smile when he pushed and recognized the warm, eager acceptance of her body. "Better now?" he asked as he began to move.

Nikki's heart was beating so rapidly that she couldn't find words. Her eyes met his above her and found so much more than desire in them. Her hands trembled as they clung to his big arms, and the rhythm of his body was audible as the cushions moved under them. It had hurt, but he hadn't seemed to wonder why. She felt the beginning of pleasure and her eyes reflected her surprise.

"Prevention can make it uncomfortable," he said softly. "But I think I can compensate for that. Here, Nikki. Like this."

He moved her, just a little, and the shock of pleasure she felt the next time he shifted made her cry out.

"Now, we'll ride the wind," he whispered, laughing huskily as his hips enforced his possession of her in quick, deep movements that dilated her wide green eyes with pleasure and made her gasp in jerky rhythms. "That's it. Help me, Nikki. Help me!"

She lifted to him, shivering, clinging. He was her world. She refused to think of anything else tonight. Her teeth bit gently into his broad shoulder as it moved. "I love you," she sobbed. "Kane, I love you, I love you . . . !"

There was an ominous creak in the wood of the lounger. "The chaise . . . !" she whispered. But her sharp movements had taken him too far over the edge.

His hand had gripped her upper thigh and his teeth ground together in a feverish drive for satisfaction. "Damn the chaise," he bit off. His eyes closed. "Oh, God, Nikki, make me . . . feel it . . . Make me feel it, honey, make me feel it!"

The sudden violence of his movement gave her one sweet glimpse of the ecstasy she didn't quite experience before he arched up and convulsed, a long, hoarse groan tearing out of his throat as he shuddered.

Nikki watched him without embarrassment, fascinated with her first intimacy. She'd only seen that look on a man's face once, when she'd found Miles in bed with another man.

Miles. Clayton. She felt Kane collapse heavily on her soft body and she knew sudden panic. What had she done? Kane had no idea who she was, he knew nothing about her life. Now they were suddenly lovers, and what was he going to do when he found out about her past?!

"God, that was good, it was so good," he whispered, shaken. He pulled away from her and rolled her back into his arms, his mouth slow and tender against her startled lips. His hand gathered her close to his hips and one big leg hooked over her hips, holding her there while he played gently with her mouth.

She melted under his kiss, still hungry, still unfulfilled, all the moral and ethical issues sliding away as he kindled her latent hunger all over again.

"You didn't have time. I can give you what you need now. Just ease over me," he whispered, softly joining her body to his, "and let me do the rest. Nikki, I want to give you the moon. I want to give you everything. You're part of me, you belong to me, you're my heart, Nikki. You're my whole heart . . ."

The tenderly whispered words were part of the magic, too, and she succumbed without a protest, even though she realized that this time, there was no protection. This was irresponsible, it was . . . delicious! Unbearable!

She gasped and pulled him closer, wanting him so close that even the air couldn't manage to get between them. She whispered it to him while he rocked her in that incredible intimacy, his big hands under her thighs, his voice whispering intimate things, praising, teaching. He nibbled at her mouth while his body pleasured hers until the pleasure caught like a fire and she cried out and began to plead with her whole body for what he was going to give her.

"Are you ready?" he whispered unsteadily. "Are you ready, Nikki? Now?"

"Yes. Yes, please . . . !"

He made her look at him when it happened, so that he could see her eyes for the briefest instant before pleasure convulsed her, humbled her, took her out of his arms and out of the world for one golden split second.

She couldn't stop crying. Apparently it was natural, because he made no apologies. In fact, he acknowledged the lack of control for exactly what it was, the first in a series of pinnacles that seemed to rise and crest like the sea itself. He kept pace with her until she was exhausted and incapable of even one more shiver of ecstasy.

They were both bathed in sweat, their hair drenched as if they'd been swimming.

"Come," he said quietly. He took her hand and led

her down to the beach, nude, and into the surf. They stayed just in the shallows, gently bathing each other. Then he picked her up and carried her back up the beach and into the house.

He showered them both and then carried her to bed. He climbed in beside her, cradling her against him, and turned out the lights.

"Kane, we shouldn't have," she said in pleased exhaustion.

"It was inevitable," he replied quietly. "And it won't be the last time. Now that we've had each other, we won't be able to stop. It was too good."

"You didn't use anything the last time."

"I know." He sounded odd. He felt odd. He was a fanatic about prevention. Or he had been, until tonight. He looked down at Nikki's face with wonder. "Suppose I told you that I took no precautions the last time because I was out of my mind with loving you?" he said softly.

But she was sound asleep. He pushed her hair back from her forehead and bent to kiss her pale face. He'd never known anything like loving Nikki. He smiled as he contemplated all the long, sweet times that lay ahead of them. A man was no good living alone. She was quick, and intelligent, and she made him whole. He rolled over onto his back, grimacing a little and then laughing with delight at the soreness. A lifetime with a woman like this would be too short. Entirely too short. If a baby came of that incredible night they'd shared, Nikki would love it as much as he would. All his scars, and hers, would heal as they built a life together. He gathered her close against his side and fell asleep. There would be plenty of time for talking.

CHAPTER
SEVEN

Kane had made breakfast by the time Nikki was awake. She rose with a scratchy throat and a slight cough, and in a subdued mood. She was keenly aware of the deception she'd practiced on Kane, and the incredible passion that she'd shared with him. If she'd loved him before, it was nothing to the way she loved him now. But she'd deceived him. She had to tell him the truth. But, how?

He smiled when she came into the kitchen. He was fully dressed, too, and he looked more vital than she'd ever seen him. There was no embarrassment or shyness in the way he was looking at her. Nikki wondered if that was how it was between lovers. She had a lot to learn. She was happy to be learning it with him.

She smiled back, and lifted her face for his gentle kiss.

"Good morning." He pulled her close and held her with aching tenderness, his lips against her hair. "I was half afraid that I dreamed it," he whispered, and bent to brush his mouth softly over her own. He lifted his head and searched her warm, tired eyes. "You haven't had much sleep," he said.

"Neither have you." Her heart was almost bursting as she looked at him. She felt wrapped in the heady glow of love, and it radiated from her eyes. Was she imagining it, or was the same look in his?

He touched her face as if he'd never seen anything so beautiful. "You're mine now," he said seriously, and he didn't smile.

Her heart skipped. "And you're mine," she replied with wonder.

He nodded. He'd said that it was much too soon to be serious, he'd told himself that he could let go of her once he'd worked her out of his system. All lies. He looked at her and melted inside. She was in his bloodstream. After last night, he knew that his heart would starve to death if he ever lost her.

She saw the faint fear in his dark eyes and at some subconscious level, she understood it. He'd lost his family. He must be apprehensive of any emotional involvement at all.

"It's too soon for you," she began softly.

He put his finger across her lips. He didn't smile. His eyes were dark with tenderness. "No, it's not," he said huskily. "I had to let go of the past eventually, and so did you. I won't ever let you go, now." He took her hand and pressed it hard against his chest. "You're right here, Nikki," he said roughly, as if the words were being dragged past his lips.

She was ready to believe in miracles. Her joy knew no bounds. She reached up and kissed him, too touched for mere words, and felt him envelop her, lift her, to share a kiss so profound that it left them both trembling.

"I love you," she whispered at his lips.

"I didn't notice, of course . . ." He was laughing, now, but not in any cruel way. His eyes were soft; mysterious.

She bit his lower lip, clinging to him. Her eyes searched his and her hands smoothed over the cool, thick hair at his nape. "Kane," she said in a bare whisper, "you don't know me . . ."

His mouth covered hers briefly. "I know all I need to know," he murmured. He smiled. "But I have some things to tell you, eventually," he added, and wondered why she stopped smiling. He let her go reluctantly, lost in the radiance of her pretty face. "Here, you must be starved. Sit down and have your breakfast."

"I hate to tell you, after you've gone to all this trouble. But I'm not very hungry." In fact, the sight of food made her nauseous. Her throat was scratchy and her chest felt very tight. She'd been chilled in the ocean last night. Chad had warned her about that.

Kane frowned as he looked at her wan face. She coughed a little and moved uneasily in the chair.

He grimaced. "How's your chest, Nikki?"

"It's a little tight . . ."

"Drink some coffee. Then it's off to the doctor. I'm not risking you. Not now."

She was delighted by his protectiveness. She lost her fear of losing him when she saw the look on his face. It was going to be all right, she thought, amazed. He really did care.

"Come on, come on," he said, digging into his eggs and toast. "Drink up. I have to take proper care of you."

She laughed. She felt terrible, but her spirits were sky high. "Are you going to be a bully?"

"Solely where your health is concerned," he promised.

Derrie's niece Phoebe had just wandered in, with a stack of library books.

"I'm researching an area in the Southwest for my first unsupervised dig," she told her aunt with great excitement. Actually Phoebe was twenty-two and Derrie only a couple of years older, but Phoebe's sister had married a man (who soon died) with a young daughter. The relationship seemed to baffle strangers who assumed they were sisters.

"Another dig," Derrie moaned. "You're going to turn into an artifact yourself if you don't do more dating and less digging."

"Archaeology is more exciting than men." She pushed back wisps of blond hair that had come down from the bun she wore it in. She'd been persuaded by

Derrie to trade her spectacles for contact lenses, but she hated them. Her face was still too heart-shaped, her forehead too wide, her mouth too long. She wasn't pretty and she knew it, and was defensive about it.

"You've never been around one long enough to find out. I know a man who would fascinate you," Derrie mentioned. "He's unattached and intelligent . . ."

"The last man you brought home to me was a construction worker whose vocabulary consisted of 'sweetie,' 'baby' and 'let's get it *on*,' " she emphasized the last word, with an appropriate stance.

Derrie chuckled. "He was a nice, uncomplicated man. I liked him."

"Then you can go out with him," Phoebe said with a grin. "I have better things to do with my life. Did you know that the Hohokam culture in Arizona had one of the largest and most efficient irrigation systems in the world, at a time when the rest of it was largely uncivilized?" she murmured, her nose in a book again. "And that the Anasazi vanished without a trace?"

Phoebe was a slender woman of medium height with pretty hair and pale blue eyes, and even a sense of humor, but she was going to die an old maid because she'd rather dig up old cultures than live in the one that had spawned her. Derrie sighed and went back to the notes she was compiling for Clayton.

Chad was out of town, but Kane took Nikki to a local doctor, who discovered that she had a fever and the beginnings of chest congestion. With her recent medical history, he decided that he couldn't take any chances. He prescribed antibiotics and a day in bed.

Kane took her straight home to his beach house. It seemed that he was no longer concerned with hiding his wealth from her, and she smiled at the opulence of the place but made no comment. He didn't comment on it, either. There was plenty of time to let her know what he did for a living, and just how wealthy he was.

He asked his housekeeper to show her to the guest bedroom, which would have suited any visiting dignitary right up to the president of the country. Kane went off to his office to conduct business and Nikki slept.

When she awoke, it was dark and she was lying in an unfamiliar bed. It was king-sized, with a white and brown and green color scheme that was repeated in the curtains and the bed clothes. The furniture was dark Mediterranean and as sturdy-looking as the man who obviously lived here.

She stirred, trying to raise herself, but it was just too much of an effort.

Kane opened the door and came in, wearing a black and white toweling robe and nothing else. His dark hair was damp, if neat. He smelled of soap.

"This isn't where I went to sleep," she pointed out.

He chuckled. "No, it isn't. I want you with me at night, in case you need anything."

"I might be contagious," she pointed out with an impish smile. "I might infect you."

"It's much too late to worry about that," he said, and his eyes were tender. "Need anything?" he asked softly.

"I need to get to the bathroom."

"No problem there." He pulled back the covers, revealing Nikki in a pale blue silk gown, and lifted her gently free.

"I can walk," she protested.

"No, you can't," he teased. He liked carrying her. She didn't seem to mind too much, because she curled comfortably into his chest. "I hope you like the gown," he remarked. "I had my housekeeper go out and buy a couple of these for you."

"I like it," she said. "Thank you." She was relieved that it wasn't a used gown; one of his former lover's, perhaps.

He noticed her frown. "I wouldn't give you castoffs," he said irritably.

"Are you reading my mind?" she teased. "I'm sorry. I thought about your lover and it made me jealous."

He hesitated at the bathroom door and bent to kiss her forehead with whispery tenderness. "That's over. You'll never have a reason to be jealous again. You're the only woman who'll live with me from now on."

Live with him. Live with him. "You said you didn't believe in marriage," she pointed out.

"I wasn't ready." He hesitated. He felt himself backing away. Last night had been delightful madness. But in broad daylight, all his uncertainties had returned.

Nikki's expression was revealing. "Give me a little time, Nikki," he said softly. "We'll go slow and easy, okay?"

He put her down and opened the bathroom door for her. Several minutes later, her face washed if haphazardly, she opened the door and he returned her to bed.

He sat down beside her, disturbing the tie of his robe to reveal a portion of his broad, hairy chest. "Here, swallow this," he said, producing a pill from a small vial. "Doctor's orders," he added when she hesitated.

She took it from his big hand and managed to swallow it past her sore, tight throat. She grimaced as she handed back the glass of water he'd given her. Her eyes lingered on what she could see of his bare skin and as she dragged them away, he glanced down and chuckled at his state of undress.

"Was I giving you a floor show?" he mused. "Does it matter? You know what I look like."

His dark eyes slid down to the clinging fabric of her gown. Only spaghetti straps held the bodice in place, and he'd already dislodged one. His hand moved, slowly tugging it the rest of the way down until he bared her breast to the mauve rise of her nipple. Her eyes widened on his face, as if she couldn't believe what was happening.

"What's wrong?" he whispered deeply.

Her nails bit into his wrist. She couldn't hide her pleasure from him. He knew too much about her.

"Yes," he murmured, completing the slow descent of the silk, and his eyes found her, enjoyed her, took pleasure from the exquisite creamy firmness of her breast in the sudden silence of the room.

No one had ever made her feel that she might die if he didn't do more than look. Not even in her younger days, before Miles destroyed her confidence in her femininity, had she known such a primitive need.

"You have a little fever, still," he said, letting his fingertips touch her, trace her, worship her. "Your skin is hot to the touch. Especially here, Nikki, where it's hardest. It makes you tremble when I caress it, doesn't it? It makes you want to pull me down and wrap your legs around my hips and pull me into you, because after last night, you know that's the only thing that's going to make the aching stop."

"Damn . . . you!" she choked.

"You don't want it any less than I do," he whispered. "Look, Nikki. Let me show you."

He stood up, his body vibrating with the same fever that held her captive. His hands loosened the single knot that held his robe in place. He pushed it aside and dropped it, and stood before her with magnificent pride in his aroused masculinity, in the perfection of his tall, hard-muscled body without a single white line to mar the even tan that covered it.

Nikki's face colored, but she couldn't look away. He was beautiful. Her eyes traced him with the same rapt fascination an artist would bend on a work of art. He was a work of art.

"You are utter perfection," she whispered.

"So are you." His legs held a faint tremor as he

looked and wanted her just short of the point of madness. With a groan, he pulled the robe back on and wandered to the window, taking deep breaths until he could get himself under control again. She did drive every sane thought out of his mind. It was unbelievable how badly he wanted her. But she was sick and he had to take care of her. He repeated that to himself until he felt better.

When he came back to the bed, she was sitting up against the headboard with the covers around her, looking guilty. He chuckled. "I'm all right. But that could become addictive," he mused, watching the confusion his dark eyes were causing.

"What could?"

"Letting you look at me," he said with a grin.

She made a face at him. Her hands tangled on the covers. "What now, Kane?" she asked.

He sat down beside her, his expression one of reluctant resignation. "Nikki, I told you that a year ago my wife and son died, but not how. They were killed in an outbreak of gunfire overseas, and I feel responsible for it," he said bluntly. "I'm not coping very well. Sometimes the nightmares keep me awake for days," he concluded roughly. "It isn't that I don't feel anything for you. I do. I feel so much." His big shoulders rose and fell. "I denied it before, but I guess it is a little too soon to be thinking about a permanent arrangement."

She bit her lip in silent misery. "I think I knew that," she said. "You must miss them terribly."

"I do." He put his head in his hands and leaned his

elbows on his knees. "I miss my son every day of my life. God, I'm so tired."

"Why don't you climb in here with me," she said.

He looked down at her blankly. "Why?"

She managed a weak smile. "Because I think you need holding again." She pulled her arms free of the covers and held them up to him.

He was still wondering two hours later why he'd gone so eagerly into those outstretched arms a second time. She made him vulnerable. Even his wife hadn't had that effect on him. Nikki made him feel protected, safe. He'd rolled over with her, cradling the length of her over-warm body to his, holding her as he tried to cope with his uncertainties.

She'd smoothed his dark hair, whispering soft incoherences, and after a time, the edge of the pain had been dulled and blunted and he had felt a sigh of peace ease out of his broad chest.

"It's all right to be alive, even if they can't be," she whispered at his ear. "They love you, too, and miss you, and know where you are. In some sense or other, they know."

His big hands flattened on her back, feeling the warmth of her seep into him, making him stronger. It was an incredible sensation, as if they were touching inside somehow, mind and heart and spirit. He wasn't sure he wanted to. On the other hand, the wonder of it overshadowed his doubts and fears, and suddenly all he could think about was how sweet it was to hold her. But it wasn't close enough.

"No," he whispered when she softly protested the sweep of his hands carrying away her gown. "No, let me. I want to be as close to you as we were last night. I won't take you. Let me hold you like this."

While he spoke, he shouldered out of his robe, and seconds later she was lying nude against his equally bare body. She shivered at the now familiar contact.

"You're hungry," he whispered, and his voice was both surprised and tender. "So am I. But you're an invalid and I have too much conscience to take advantage of it."

"Are you sure?" she whispered back.

His hands swept down her spine and he groaned pleasurably as he felt her soft skin in exquisite detail, her breasts on his chest, her belly against the helpless thrust of his body.

"No, I'm not sure, but I can't let you go," he murmured roughly. His hands pressed gently at the base of her spine and moved her, his long leg trespassing between her thighs.

He pulled her close and adjusted the covers. "Lay your cheek on my chest and go to sleep," he murmured.

There was no more argument left in her. She closed her eyes and her body seemed to melt into his. Only seconds passed before she was asleep.

In the morning, she awoke in her gown and alone. Mrs. Beale brought her breakfast and pumped up the pillows for her. The woman was pleasant enough, but Nikki wondered why Kane had left her. Perhaps he had wanted to spare her the embarrassment of having Mrs. Beale find them together in bed. He didn't know it, but Nikki wouldn't have been embarrassed. She loved him too much to let anyone else's opinion matter. Even Clayton's, though it was going to be difficult to tell Kane the truth about her brother.

When Kane stopped in the doorway later to check on her, he looked somber and weary. In fact, he'd awoken early and all the doubts that Nikki's arms had erased had returned. His mind was clear this morning, and he had cold feet. He was afraid to let himself love her, he was afraid of the risk. He hated the look on her face that told him she didn't understand his sudden coolness after the physical delight they'd shared.

"Feeling any better?" he asked.

She nodded and smiled warmly, without embarrassment. "How are you?"

"Harassed by business," he said. His eyes narrowed. "I have to make a few telephone calls, but I'll share lunch with you. Can I have Mrs. Beale bring you anything?"

"No, thanks. I still have some of the juice she brought me at breakfast."

"Okay."

He smiled, letting his dark eyes slide over her pretty face. Even sick, she was lovely to look at.

"You've got a little more color than you had yesterday. How's the chest?"

"It's better," she assured him. "Kane, thank you for bringing me here and taking care of me."

"You trusted yourself to me," he reminded her quietly. "You looked after me when I couldn't. Now it's my turn. Besides, who else have you got to look out for you?"

She had a brother who loved her, who wouldn't know where to look if he started searching for her right now. "Thank you anyway," she murmured while she wondered in a panic what would happen if Clayton should telephone late at night and not find her at the beach house. Would he rush up here looking for her, involve the police? She had to find a way to contact him.

Meanwhile, she looked at Kane with faint puzzlement and involuntarily, her eyes drifted to the pristine pillow beside her head.

"May I ask you something?" she said softly.

He moved into the room and paused by the bed. "What do you want to know?"

"Did you . . . love your wife very much?"

He hesitated before answering. "I felt very tender with my wife when we first married," he said finally. "I was in love with her, and she with me. We reached heights that I'd never found with anyone else. But it all went wrong when she got pregnant. After our son was born, she lived for him. I suppose I did, too. We lost each other in the art of being parents." At the mention of the little boy, something terrible flared in his eyes, in his face. The nightmares exploded, like the bullets that had wiped out the young life and all his hopes and dreams.

"Kane!"

She dragged herself up from the bed, shaky on her feet, but anguished at what she saw on his face.

"Darling, it's all right," she whispered, hugging him fiercely. "It's all right."

He swallowed and his body jerked. His hands found her shoulders, resting heavily there while he fought the terror. He'd shut it out for a whole year. Now, with her, it was all coming back. The comfort she offered was making him vulnerable. He realized, shocked, that he felt safe to talk about it because Nikki was there to hold him when the nightmares came.

"Kane, don't look back," she said, nuzzling his chest with her cheek. "You have to stop tormenting yourself."

"They died," he said in a ghostly whisper. "They were shot to pieces, lying there in the metal coffin that had been a car."

Her arms contracted. She could barely stand, but she couldn't leave him now. She smoothed her hands over his broad back through the soft knit shirt and heard his voice drone on, the painful memories spilling over from his mind to his tongue. Almost incoherently, he told her all of it, and his voice shook when he reached the end.

"I'm sorry," she whispered. "So sorry, Kane."

The words were barely audible now as his voice and his strength gave out. He hadn't talked about it until now. He couldn't seem to stop. The fears and pain were dragged from him until he felt helpless.

"They never knew," she assured him. "It was quick. At least be grateful for that small mercy. They didn't suffer."

"He was my son," he choked. "And what was left of him . . . God! God, I can't . . . think . . . can't bear to think of it . . . !"

She reached up and kissed his wet eyes, his face, gently comforting him while he relived the horror. Except that this time, he wasn't alone. He didn't have to face it by himself. His big arms pulled Nikki closer and for the first time in his life, he clung willingly to a woman for strength.

Nikki felt the moment when he came out of it, when his own will began to reassert itself.

His big hands contracted roughly on her shoulders. "I haven't spoken of it to anyone. Not even to Jake."

"It's good to talk about the things that hurt most," she said quietly.

"So they say," he said, angry at himself for pouring out his pain twice in less than twenty-four hours, and especially angry at Nikki for being here, for listening, for seeing his weakness. But he couldn't allow himself the weakness of totally falling in love with her, he thought.

"I can't make you promises of forever or commitment, Nikki."

Her eyebrows lifted in astonishment at his blatant remark.

He held up a hand. "I'm talking about marriage." He studied her mutinous expression. "You're a fighter,

Nikki, and I like your mind as much as I enjoy your delightful body. But I can't . . . handle this."

And with that enigmatic statement, he turned and left the room. Nikki stared at the closed door for a long time, counting her regrets and heartache.

Kane had made it plain that he didn't want her for a wife, that he was resentful of her influence over his emotions. It would only go downhill from here, and he was growing less likely to commit himself by the minute. And it hurt.

She had to get well quickly and get out of here. She only hoped that Clayton didn't decide to telephone the beach house in her absence. Things could get very, very complicated if he did. As if, she added silently, they could actually get any worse than they already were!

CHAPTER
EIGHT

Cortez hated being stared at. In many big cities, he went unnoticed, but Charleston had a small-town atmosphere and he was a stranger. He even looked alien with his dark bronze skin and long hair in its neat ponytail. Even the sunglasses he wore with his gray suit made him conspicuous, especially since he seemed to be the only person on the streets wearing a suit.

Posing as a small businessman who might need to hire Burke's if he moved his factory to Charleston, he'd followed a trail of rumors about illegal dumping. In the process he had learned a lot about Burke's latest deal with Lombard.

"Cherokee, aren't you?" his informant had asked. "I been up to Cherokee myself. Pretty impressive, seeing them chiefs stand out there in them pretty war bonnets. Must have had to kill a lot of eagles to get all them eagle feathers.''

Cortez had almost bitten through his tongue while he tried to smile nonchalantly. He wanted to tell the man that Cherokees never wore war bonnets except for the tourists, that war bonnets were limited to the Plains Indians. He wanted to add that the Cherokees had been a very civilized people who had their own newspaper in their own language in the 1820s, and that their capital of New Echota was in no way dissimilar to a white town of the same period. He could also have told the man that killing eagles was an offense for which one could go to prison these days.

But he didn't. Over the years he'd come to accept that many people stereotyped Indians and that those old attitudes were as constant as the summer sun. It wasn't the last time he'd have to cope with such misconceptions.

As he ate a sandwich and sipped coffee in the small café Derrie had recommended, he considered all that his informant had told him. After some time, he noticed a pair of pale blue eyes coolly appraising him. He turned his head and stared back without blinking. Usually that intimidated the curious. But it didn't work this time. The young girl's head tilted a little and the light caught her blond hair. She couldn't be much more than a teenager, he thought. She was slight and not especially pretty except for that hair. Wrapped up in a huge, dirt-stained denim jacket, she didn't look like the fastidious sort. His eyes dropped. She was wearing Western boots, but not pretty city ones. Hers were hard-used boots, caked with mud and full of scratches. He liked that.

His black eyes returned to hers. She smiled almost apologetically, as if she realized that he didn't want her attention, and went back to sipping her coffee.

Figuring she'd seen enough, he laughed to himself and left a tip for the waitress before he went to the counter to pay his check. He was off to find a local marsh. Burke's idiot employee had let something slip that he shouldn't have, and Cortez was going to check out the area.

He started to leave the cafe, but the young blond was watching him. On impulse, he walked to her table and stood next to her, his sunglasses dangling from one lean, dark hand.

She looked up and grinned. "I know. I was staring. I'm sorry if I made you uncomfortable."

Both eyebrows lifted. That was forthright enough. "Why were you staring?" he asked bluntly.

"There's something I've been dying to ask you, but I thought I'd already irritated you enough."

"What?"

She hesitated. "Do you have shovel-shaped incisors?" she asked earnestly.

Instantly he realized who this was and why Derrie had recommended this café. The mud-caked boots, the dirt-stained clothing. It all made sense. She'd been on a dig. It was Derrie's niece, Phoebe.

"I'm an anthropology major, doing my minor in archaeology," she explained and laughed.

"You look as if you've been digging," he said, motioning toward her boots.

"Indeed we have," she said enthusiastically. "We found part of a Woodland period cooking pot with charred acorns in it. My professor says that the design is one that Coe cites in his sourcebook on ceramic sequences and that it's over two thousand years old."

"Along a river bottom, no doubt?"

She grinned. "Why, yes!"

"Find anything else?"

"No. It wasn't a burial site, thank God," she said heavily. "I wouldn't like to dig up somebody's great-grandfather. I think you get haunted for things like that."

He liked her already. He wouldn't have minded staying to talk, but it was getting late. "To answer your original question, yes, like all Native Americans and Asians and other members of the Mongoloid classification, my incisors are shovel-shaped," he said, smiling at her. "Now," he added, leaning down menacingly, "are you going to ask how many scalps I carry on my war lance?"

Her eyes twinkled. "Oh, that would be much too personal a question," she said with mock somberness.

He couldn't contain a chuckle. He turned and walked out of the café, shaking his head. If she'd been a little older, who knew what might have developed. As it was, he was a man with a mission. Derrie's niece would have to wait.

Armed with names and backgrounds, when he reached his hotel room he removed his laptop computer from its padded briefcase, hooked it into the modem, and plugged it in. He accessed the mainframe in Washington, D.C., at FBI headquarters, with his password and called up the information he needed.

The unit was attached to a small printer. He printed out hard copy of the data and disengaged the modem. Now he knew not only that Burke had indeed violated EPD regulations, but he'd actually been charged twice already. The witnesses had never shown up to testify and Burke had gotten off. But this time, Burke and his brother-in-law had left a trail. Who better to follow it, Cortez reasoned dryly, than a Native American?

He changed into jeans and boots and a blue checked shirt and let his hair down. He was going tracking.

The rental car he was driving was nice without being flashy. He enjoyed driving. Back on the reservation he had a banged-up pickup with a straight shift. He thought of it longingly.

As he started out of the city, on an impulse he drove past the café where he'd had lunch. He wasn't altogether surprised to see Phoebe, standing beside a muddied old Bronco parked near the café. Her face was red and her hair was askew. She was kicking the flat rear tire repeatedly while asking God to do some pretty strange things to her vehicle.

Cortez pulled in behind her and cut off the engine. She hadn't even slowed down when he reached her.

"Flat tire, huh?" he asked, nodding. "I saw one of those once."

She pushed back her tangled, windblown hair and looked up at him in disbelief. He looked so different with his hair down and wearing jeans that she didn't quite recognize him at first.

He took off his sunglasses. "You busy?" he asked.

She was catching her breath from the exertion. "Why? Are you going to offer to kick it," she indicated the flat tire, "while I rest?"

"No. I thought you might come with me and help me track a truck. Then I might offer to fix the flat for you."

She nodded slowly. "Right. I'm having a panic attack and you're in it."

He caught her by the hand. Nice, he thought as he led her toward his car, she had nice hands. They were strong but soft. He opened the passenger door, but she hesitated.

With exaggerated patience, he pulled out his wallet and flipped it open, holding it under her eyes. He watched her expression change. His credentials always seemed to either impress or intimidate people.

"FBI," she stammered. Her face paled. "You can't be serious. You're going to arrest me for assaulting a Bronco?!"

"Unprovoked assault on a horse," he agreed.

Her lower jaw fell.

He pursed his lips. "Okay. I'm deputizing you to assist me in an investigation. Better?"

"Me?"

"You."

She shrugged. "All right, but I'm not shooting anybody."

"Deal." He put away his wallet and helped her into the passenger seat. "I have to find a place called Pirate's Marsh. Do you know it?"

As he'd guessed, she did. "Why, yes, it's just a few miles down the road. Turn right at the next intersection."

He grinned, glad that he'd followed his intuition. An archaeology student would know all the isolated spots. Or, most of them. Minutes later, they were on their way out of town.

He followed her directions easily to a large area near the sea with huge live oaks dripping moss dotted around the shore. Two or three were uprooted.

"That's from Hurricane Hugo," she told him when he stared at the felled giants. "Amazing how powerful wind can be."

"Wind, rain, all of nature," he murmured.

"What tribe are you, anyway?"

He folded his arms across his chest. "Take a guess."

Her eyes narrowed. "You can't be Apache because you're too tall—although Cochise was well over six feet. You aren't light enough to be a Crow, or dark enough to be an Apache, and you don't have the look of a Sioux. Cherokee, maybe, or even Choctaw."

His eyebrows lifted. "Not Comanche?"

"You're not dark enough, and you're too tall," she repeated, "and you don't have a blocky build and a square, heavy face and a flattened nose."

"My parents do."

She stilled. "Comanche?"

He nodded.

"But . . ."

"Apaches are short, but Cochise was over six feet tall," he reminded her. "And there was a Spaniard in my ancestry," he added coldly.

"Spaniards are notoriously short . . ."

"Cesar Romero isn't."

She threw up her hands. "I give up."

"Good. Be quiet and let me look."

He started walking, his eyes on the ground. His little sojourn at Burke's had given him a good look at the sort of tires the man used on his dilapidated vehicles. They had an odd tread that he'd memorized. Plaster casts would be better, but he could do that later. He had some plaster in the car, and a jug of water. All he had to do now was find something in this bog and a tire track that he could link to Burke.

He needed to identify a chain of evidence if he planned to prove an infraction of federal law. It might not be his jurisdiction, but he knew a couple of the EPA boys. He'd had quite enough of people polluting the earth with their industrial waste.

"What are you looking for?" she asked. "Maybe I could help."

He glanced at her. "Tire tracks. Something nasty in the water."

"Okay." She started walking.

"Do you have a name?" he asked suddenly.

She looked up. "Of course I do," she said, and kept walking.

His lips tugged up. "What is it?"

"Phoebe."

He smiled.

"Well, it is," she muttered, glaring at him. "What's wrong with being called Phoebe?"

"It's unusual, that's all."

"What are you called?"

"Wouldn't you like to know?" he challenged. He knelt and his eyes narrowed on a tire tread. Close, he thought, but not the right one. Not by a long shot.

"What are you called?" she persisted.

He got up, his eyes still on the ground. He pronounced a set of syllables with odd stops and a high tone. He glanced at her perplexed expression and smiled.

"It doesn't translate very well," he told her. "My mother saw a red-tailed hawk the morning I was born. If you translate it, it means something like "he who came on the wings of the red-tailed hawk.""

"That's beautiful."

"Sure." He knelt again to examine a print. This one was right on the money. "Bingo," he murmured to himself. He got up, ignoring the girl, and followed the tracks. When he came to a boggy place, he stopped and his keen eyes swept the expanse until he found what he was looking for: the rusty edge of a barrel.

"Well, well," he said to himself. "Some days it all comes together."

"Did you find what you were looking for?" she asked, joining him.

"Yes. Thanks for your help."

She grinned. "Do I get a badge now?"

He laughed out loud. "No."

She sighed. "It was fun while it lasted."

He reached out and caught a strand of her hair, fingering it gently. "Is it naturally this color?"

"Yes. Both my parents are very dark. They say that I'm a throwback to a Norwegian ancestor."

He let the hair go reluctantly. It was very soft, and he looked at her for a long moment, aware of some regrets. "How old are you?" he asked.

"Twenty-two. I was a late starter in college," she confessed.

"Not that late." His dark eyes slid over her body in the concealing thick coat and he wished that he had time to get to know her properly. "I'm thirty-six," he said. "The name I use with whites is Cortez."

She held out her hand. "It was nice to meet you."

"Same here. Thanks for the help."

Her fingers contracted briefly around his and he smiled down at her. Since Phoebe didn't recognize his name, Derrie must not have mentioned him. That was just as well for the moment. "We live in two different worlds," he remarked quietly.

"I was thinking the same thing," she confessed shyly.

His fingers gently caressed hers. "Where do you go to school?"

"University of Tennessee at Knoxville," she said. "But I'm off this summer, so I've been hanging around with some friends who study archaeology locally. I'm a senior at the university. I graduate next spring."

"Then maybe I'll see you at graduation, college girl," he said unexpectedly.

Her expression was very still, and he dropped her hand.

His face hardened and his dark eyes glittered with anger. "No, you wouldn't like that. I'd stand out too much, wouldn't I?" he asked curtly, turning on his heel.

"Why, you bigot!" she exclaimed, picking up a small dead limb and heaving it at his back. She ignored his shocked expression. "You inverted bigot! You take offense without any provocation whatsoever, you bristle before you even ask questions, you . . . you . . . !" She looked down and found another limb.

He moved suddenly then and gripped her wrist before she could throw the limb. "Not nice," he chided. "Don't throw things."

"It isn't a thing, it's a tree limb," she pointed out, struggling against his strength. "Let go of my wrist!"

171

"Not on your life." He took the limb away effort-lessly, but he didn't release her arm.

She stared up into his eyes with resignation and faint excitement. He was very strong, but his grip wasn't in the least painful. "I would be honored if you came to my graduation, even if you came dressed just as you are now," she said curtly.

"Do you always kick vehicles with flat tires? Any other bad habits aside from that nasty mouth?"

"It takes a few bad words to show a flat tire you mean business!"

He smiled. "Does it, really?"

"You don't curse. Not in your own tongue," she said smugly, surprising him. "I haven't come across a Native American language yet that contains nasty words."

"We don't need them to express ourselves," he said with a superior smile.

"Well, stand me in the rain and call me an umbrella!" she said, tongue-in-cheek.

"No time," he returned. He let go of her wrist and turned. "I'll drop you off at a garage. You'll need help changing that tire."

"You said you'd do it."

"I said I'd see that it got done. I can't change a tire," he said matter-of-factly. "I was one of the last guys to serve in Vietnam, when they were evacuating refugees. I caught a burst of shrapnel in the shoulder. It did some damage. It doesn't slow me down, but I can't lift much."

She winced. "Oh, I'm sorry, I didn't mean to sound that way," she said miserably. "I keep putting my foot in my mouth."

"Pretty little feet," he mused, staring down at them. "Boots suit them."

She smiled. "You aren't angry?"

He shook his head. "Come on."

He drove her to the garage nearest her Bronco and waited until she came around to his side of the car to tell him she was going back out with the mechanic.

"Thanks a lot," she told him.

He shrugged. "My pleasure."

She hesitated, but there wasn't really anything else to say. With a funny little smile, she waved and ran back to the waiting mechanic. Cortez forced his eyes away from her and drove on without a backward glance. He was already working on the proof he'd need to have Lombard and his company cited for violation of environmental law.

Nikki was sitting in the living room when Kane's friend Jake came to see him. She and Kane were walking cautiously around each other after three days of cold civility and she was ready to go home. His indifference was killing her.

Jake's eyebrows lifted, and there was brief shock on his face. But he smiled politely when Kane introduced her only as "Nikki."

"Nice to meet you," Jake said politely. He glanced

at his friend. "Uh, Kane, I need to see you for a minute outside. Boat business," he added quickly.

"Sure. Excuse me, Nikki." Kane left her on the sofa. She was dressed in her jeans and a tank top. It was hot outside and both men wore shorts, although Kane's legs were much better suited to them than Jake's. Nikki didn't have any shorts with her and Kane hadn't encouraged her to ask for them. She tempted him enough in jeans and he was doing his best not to make matters worse. He was worrying himself sick over the fact that he'd gone off his head and not taken precautions the second time he'd made love to her. In the heat of the moment, he'd been too impatient for pleasure to fish around for protection. Now he regretted it—too late.

"Well, what is it?" Kane asked.

"I've got to replace the radio in the yacht," the older man told him. "It's almost gone. I had an estimate on repairing it, but it's going to be less expensive in the long run just to replace it. Is it all right if I order that one we looked at and have it expressed down here?"

"Go ahead," Kane invited. "I have plans for her weekend after next." He glanced back toward the house, his face quiet and not much happier than Jake had seen it lately. "I thought I might put in a new plant manager in the Charleston plant and sail down to the Caribbean when she goes home."

Jake cleared his throat. "I guess you know your own mind, and I'm not one to interfere. But is this wise?"

Kane scowled. "What do you mean?"

"I wouldn't have thought that you'd want to give Clayton Seymour any intimate glimpses into your life."

A big hand shot out and caught Jake's upper arm with bruising strength. "What the hell do you mean, Seymour?!"

Jake nodded. "That's Nicole Seymour, Clayton's sister, in there. My daughter is married to a senator from Virginia, remember. She and Nikki are casual friends. I recognized her immediately from photos I've seen. She's a dish, isn't she?"

Kane was shocked, and he instantly felt his stomach tighten. He felt betrayed. He hadn't had a clue who Nikki was. His mind was racing. If he knew her identity now . . . did she know his? He needed to find out. Afterward, whether she did or not, he had to get her out of his life and fast. He couldn't afford to pass out any free tickets into his business to Clayton Seymour!

Jake saw how upset Kane was. "Sorry to give you the bad news, but you had to know sometime."

"Yes. I did." A hollow feeling claimed Kane as he dismissed Jake and walked back into the house. Nikki sat watching him with wide, curious eyes. His own were blazing with white-hot fury. She knew before he spoke that Jake had recognized her and told Kane who she was. All her hopes and dreams were incinerating in those hate-filled eyes.

She girded herself for battle and stood up. It gave her the only advantage she was likely to get.

"You know," she said.

"I know, all right," he replied, his fists clenched by his side. "Your brother and his head-hunting associate are looking for ways to bring me down. Are you one of their ideas?"

She wanted to hit him. "Does it look like I am?" she returned with flashing eyes. "Do you think I could make a jet ski hit you so that you could wash up on my beach and pass out!"

"That wasn't all that happened."

"That's right, we seduced each other," she said it without inflection. "How would knowing that help my brother bring you down? If anything . . ." She stopped. That last statement had been a big mistake.

"Candidate's sister plays fast and loose with opponent's largest campaign contributor?" he asked with soft venom. "How would that look on the front page of my father's tabloid?"

She turned green. This couldn't be happening. She couldn't have cost Clayton the election.

His chin lifted. "I've heard all about you, over the years. They say you're one of the brightest young hostesses in politics. I might have recognized you in one of those designer gowns you wear. Insiders say that you're the brains and drive behind Seymour. But you don't look so tough to me."

"Pneumonia will make the toughest of us mellow, just briefly," she said, inclining her head. "So it's war, is it?"

He nodded slowly.

"No holds barred?"

"That's how I fight," he returned, ramming his hands deep into his pockets.

"Fair enough. But there's one condition. No mudslinging."

He lifted an eyebrow. "You know better."

She felt her face color with bad temper and her own hands clenched. "No mudslinging about what we did together," she said, forcing the words out.

He wanted to hit her where it hurt most. She'd made a fool of him, and she still might use it to her own advantage. His face set into unfamiliar lines.

"We had a one-night stand," he said. "And I'm not running for public office. If I were, you might actually worry me."

Which told her how much purpose she served in his life. Mary Tanner had warned her once about giving in too soon to a man's ardor. "Men love in the darkness and are indifferent in the dawn," she'd said dryly. "Keep your eyes open and your heart closed until you're sure that it's more than a passing fancy."

At the time, the advice had been unnecessary, because Nikki wanted nothing to do with men. Now it came back at her with vivid force.

"Meaning that I couldn't possibly worry *you*, Mr. Lombard?" she said, reverting to her old spirit. "Why don't you reserve judgment until after your candidate loses the election?"

He admired her spirit. But there was nothing in her face to tell him that she cared one way or the other about the loss of their relationship.

"We'll see about who loses." He paused. "You knew who I was, didn't you?"

"Not until the day after your accident," she said. "It was your name that rang bells, then I connected it with the Rolex."

His face was hard, and she saw the storms in his eyes with regret. "I seem to recall that the Seymours are one of the better families; but pretty penniless."

She lifted her chin proudly and smiled. "Then you are uninformed. I told you that I sculpt. My busts command a high price, and my brother makes a substantial living. We don't have a yacht, of course. But we get by."

The barb found a target. He glared at her.

"I'll leave now. Thank you for taking care of me. I don't imagine you'd have let me in the front door if you'd known who I was."

"Not a chance," he said pleasantly. There was nothing pleasant either in his smile or in his eyes.

"That's the difference between us," she said, turning at the door to the hall. "I'd have taken care of you even if I had known your name."

She went to pack and forced herself not to let one scrap of emotion show. She was going to get through this. After all, she'd survived Miles.

Kane was gone when the cab arrived to take her back to her beach house. Mrs. Beale saw her off with a curious expression. Kane had left no note, but he had said to wish Miss Seymour a pleasant journey. Nikki told herself he should save such sentiment for himself. He'd need it when she and Clayton got through with his candidate in the polls.

If her heart was breaking, she was the only person who needed to know it.

CHAPTER
NINE

John Haralson drove out to Pirate's Marsh in his BMW at the tail end of a convoy that included local media, a team of EPA investigators, Cortez, and a shocked public health official.

"This marsh is practically in the Edisto River," the public health official gasped. "What is that?" he persisted as the investigators pulled a barrel out of the marsh and began to inspect it.

"Paint solvent," one said curtly, rubbing his gloved hand over the muck to read the legend stenciled on it in bright orange. "Lombard, Incorporated," he added shortly. "Here's another one: antifreeze. And another, full of motor oil . . . all leaking. Of all the cheap . . . there are provisions for disposal of substances like this at the Pinetree Site landfill. Why, why, would he pay someone to dump it here instead?!"

"To cut costs, of course. A man with a truck is plenty cheaper than an outfit qualified to handle toxic waste. Hold it right there and let me get a shot of it," a newspaper photographer called. He snapped the picture, incorporated with two dead water birds floating on the surface, waited for the film to advance automatically, and took three more. The broadcast journalists were rolling their own videocameras furiously. "That should do it. Do you think this will make a case?" he asked the EPA people.

"Indeed it will," one commented.

Haralson dragged Cortez aside. "Busybody," he hissed at his friend. "I didn't want to release this to EPA and the local newspapers and TV people yet! You shouldn't have told all these people!"

Cortez knew why. A press release from Seymour to go with this revelation would give him a boost in the polls. But he'd pulled one on Haralson, and he wasn't sorry. He wanted to panic the man into making a stupid move. Just one.

"I didn't. I told the state Department of Health and Environmental Control. The man turning purple over there, and giving many details to the media, is their chief field rep. He hates polluters."

"Furthermore, this is a clear-cut violation of the Clean Water Act, the Resource Conservation and Recovery Act, the Comprehensive Environmental Response Compensation and Liability Act, the Hazardous Materials Transportation Act . . . !" the field representative for DHEC broke in furiously.

"Slow down!" a tall, sandy-haired reporter called. "Can you give us that again?"

Haralson recognized Todd Sanders. He worked for the Lombards' tabloid. God alone knew why he was collecting information, when old man Lombard was hardly likcly to nail his own son to the masthead of the news tabloid. His presence here was disturbing. Like Haralson, Sanders had a reputation for digging deep.

"You shouldn't have donc this," Haralson repeated absently.

"I work for the federal government," Cortez reminded him. He produced his wallet. "See? I have identification." And he did. It said FBI. He closed the wallet. Haralson had been too preoccupied to look at the date on the ID. People usually were.

Haralson was thinking ahead. "This will be all over the state by morning."

"I do hope so," Cortez said easily. "A man who dumps this sort of garbage in a wildlife area should be drawn and quartered by the media, along with the people who hired him to do it!"

Haralson gave him a quick glance, but Cortez didn't seem to notice. Haralson whipped out his pad and began to take down what he was going to say. This was a heaven-sent opportunity, and it was going to stand Clayton Seymour in excellent stead with local voters. He began to smile.

"Did you find proof of a connection?" he asked with careful indifference. "More than just stenciled letters on oil drums, I mean?"

"I wouldn't have called in all these people if I hadn't," Cortez said, gesturing as the EPA people pulled yet another drum out of the marsh. "I can tie these tire treads to one of Burke's trucks. One of the field reps is getting casts of them over there," he gestured to the man with the plaster. "And one of Burke's own employees told me about the site."

"This is one excellent piece of investigation."

"Of course it is. I work for the . . ."

"Government!" Haralson chuckled. "Yes, I know. You eat, drink, and sleep the job. How could I have forgotten? But do remember who put you on to Burke's in the first place. I'm not such a bad investigator myself."

Cortez didn't say a word.

"Think how well this is going to work out. Sam Hewett will lose the attention of his senior aide with Lombard fighting the environmental people. Seymour will win the election, Lombard will be prosecuted for environmental homicide, and Burke will be spending years as someone's girlfriend at Leavenworth."

"Sure. Now we've got Lombard on the run."

"What was that?" Cortez asked curiously.

"Nothing," Haralson said. "Nothing at all. Thanks for your help."

"Thanks for selling me the gold piece. See you back in D.C."

"Yeah. Sure. Think nothing of it." Haralson was already walking away, grinning like a Cheshire cat as he bent his head to light a cigar. Cortez, watching him, wondered how Haralson had survived so far. Maybe he thought keeping Seymour in office was worth risking his freedom.

Sanders had been led to Pirate's Marsh by his scanner. He'd overheard the traffic on the CB radio receiver he always carried with him.

God knew he'd tried to warn Kane. It was going to be hard to tell him that Seymour held all the aces this time. He phoned Kane at the office.

Breaking the news wasn't quite as bad as Sanders had expected; it was worse. Kane ran out of foul language after the first five minutes of yelling. Then he got nasty.

"My God, why didn't you know before now? How did you ever get to be an investigative reporter in the first place?!" Kane snarled.

"I tried. I just couldn't get any doors to open for me," Sanders said quietly. It wouldn't be politic to remind Lombard that he'd tried to warn him about the risk of letting that new employee remain in his position of solid waste manager. It would do no good to remind the man after the fact. "It was really bad out there," he added involuntarily. "They ran some footage on a local station a few minutes ago. There are dozens of dead birds strewn around the marsh, and Congressman Seymour called a press conference to denounce you and promise retribution. Secretary of the Interior Miles Townshend has also denounced you to anyone who would listen—and plenty have . . ."

"Sweet Jesus," Kane exploded with something akin to reverence. "I'll kill Burke with my bare hands!"

"Get in line. Yours isn't the only company logo they found out there, although it certainly was the most prominent. Orange stencils, for God's sake! Listen, call a press conference of your own while there's still time. Give a statement. Tell people where you were when the solid waste manager changed waste disposal companies."

Kane hesitated. He suddenly realized that if he did that, he would have to tell the world that he'd stupidly let himself be nearly killed by a jet ski. And that Congressman Seymour's sister had kept him occupied day and night for three weeks while his throat was being cut back home.

He could have wrung her neck for that. She might not have caused the accident, but she'd kept him so involved that he couldn't be bothered to think about his business until it was under the gun. And that was her fault, whether or not it had been a deliberate ploy.

That fact might give him some leverage later with Seymour if he needed it. He'd keep Nikki's dark secret, for now.

"I won't do that," Kane told Sanders.

"Why not?!"

"Because there's a woman involved," Kane mused. "And I might need that little tidbit later on. So I won't mention it now."

"Seymour is going to hound you to death over that

marsh,'' Sanders pointed out. ''You can't sit down and let him crucify you! You could go to jail, for God's sake, don't you know the penalties for those violations? Under RCRA alone, you could face a fine of $50,000 and two years in prison!''

Kane stared blankly at the other man. ''Don't be absurd. I'll have to pay a fine, but it won't amount to more than that. It wasn't deliberate.''

''When Congressman Seymour gets through, it will certainly sound as if it were,'' Sanders said doggedly. He stared at the floor. ''Look, let me poke around and see if I can turn up anything more on this, before Seymour gets on a bandwagon.''

''Go for it,'' Kane said heavily. ''And while you're at it, keep digging on Seymour's background . . . . And Sanders . . . I shouldn't have flown off the handle like that. It's been a hard week.''

''Things will get better. I'll phone you in a couple of days.''

He hung up. Kane stared down at the telephone, barely seeing it at all.

He was shaken. He knew that indiscriminate dumping was a long-standing problem. Many companies had been charged with it. He would probably face a large fine, and not much more. But he hoped Sanders would turn up something he could use aginst Seymour, just the same. He didn't relish the thought of having to use Nikki's presence in his life as a weapon against her brother.

* * *

Derrie was cheerful the next morning, having just heard the news. She greeted Clayton with a smile.

"Well, I'll bet you feel good. That toxic dump will be a feather in your cap. How did you find out about it?"

"From Haralson and his investigator," Clayton returned, smiling at her as he put down his briefcase in the small office he kept for constituents in Charleston. He rented space in a suite of law offices where everything was tastefully furnished and very sedate.

"Was he personally responsible, do you think?" Derrie asked. "Mr. Lombard, I mean."

"What does that matter?" he asked, puzzled.

She frowned. "That doesn't sound like you."

Clayton sat down and stared at her. "I'm fighting for my political life," he said slowly. "If I don't get Lombard's back to the wall, his family may dig deep enough to find something scandalous to print." He didn't mention that the reason for Nikki's divorce from Miles contained a bombshell. It had been fortunate that there had been a much juicier political scandal going at the time of the divorce. No one had paid much attention to Miles Townshend—a very noncontroversial figure—because of the timing.

"Could he find something, if he tried?" Derrie asked. "Something that would hurt Nikki?"

Clayton stared at his thumbnail as if he'd just built it. "Yes."

She understood now. He was trying to divert the tabloid from looking into his sister's background by using Lombard's predicament as a shield. She didn't approve. But she began to understand. Clayton was fiercely protective of Nikki.

"I see now why you're using this to your advantage," Derrie said. "But it hardly seems fair to destroy a man's business on the possibility that someone might dig into Nikki's past. Mr. Lombard's wife and little boy were killed in a terrorist struggle in Lebanon just last year. He doesn't deserve to be crucified if he's not personally responsible."

"What do you mean, if he's not responsible?" he demanded.

She hesitated. "I just meant that I don't think he was responsible for the actual handling of his waste products," she said.

"Of course he's responsible. I feel . . ." He stopped as the telephone rang, picking it up. "Seymour," he said into it. "What's that? You've had them blow up some photographs of those dead birds and put them on the placards they carry? Are you sure . . . okay. Well, listen, if you pay them, it can be traced . . . Listen, I don't like this . . . !"

He hung up with a rough sigh. Haralson sounded jubilant, but Clayton felt a sense of guilt. How absurd. He had to keep Lombard off his back and protect Nikki. This was the best way.

"Maybe he's right. It will heat things up at Lombard's plant," he said to himself. He glanced at Derrie.

She seemed shocked. "Call the local television stations. Tell them we've heard that a group of environmentalists is about to start a picket line at Lombard's plant."

Derrie was staring at him, her blue eyes incredulous. "You've paid people to picket him!"

"I haven't. It's Haralson's idea," he said stiffly. "He says that by putting Lombard on the defensive, we can protect ourselves from any tabloid threat."

"And you believe him? Clay, this isn't the way!" she cried. "For heaven's sake, this is dirty. It's dirty!"

"And you don't want to soil your lily-white hands?" he chided coldly. She pricked his conscience, brought out his own doubts and fears. He didn't like it.

She had to bite her tongue not to reveal what Cortez had said about Haralson. She only had one choice left. She took it. "I won't soil my hands," she said quietly. "What you're doing is against everything I've ever believed in."

"Do you think I want to do it?" he asked, his eyes troubled. "Derrie, I'm in a corner. I have to fight my way out, with whatever it takes. Politics is not for the faint-hearted, you know that!"

"But, I don't," she said softly. "Clay, you're digging your own political grave. You're letting Haralson turn you into one of those cardboard placards. If you win, he'll own you."

"He didn't own Miles, did he? He helped Miles win."

"And collected political favors right and left, no doubt, because Miles has a reputation for helping people who help him. But even he wouldn't do anything under the table. Clay, why do you think Haralson had to approach Miles to get this job with you? There are plenty of campaigns going on. A good manager shouldn't have to look for work! And have you seen that car he drives? Yours isn't as fancy . . .''

He didn't like what he was hearing. He didn't want to think about it. "I just do the job," he said. "How I get back in doesn't matter, for God's sake! I work for my constituents. I work damned hard."

"I know that. But you're intimating that winning is worth a lessening of principles."

"I'm protecting my sister," he said, turning away. "That's all you need to know."

"No, you aren't. You're protecting yourself against the Republican challenger and trying to regain the points you lost by sacrificing the spotted owl and Kane Lombard on the altar of personal gain."

"Lombard is guilty! I didn't coax him into illegal dumping. So don't judge me!"

"Oh, I wouldn't dream of judging you," she agreed. "Your own conscience will hang you out to dry one day."

He stood up abruptly, cold with anger. "If that's how you feel, why don't you quit?" he asked tautly.

"I'd be delighted!" she said, her small hands making fists beside her slender hips. "I was offered another job just a week or more ago, with a politician who has a conscience and a little moral fiber. I daresay he'd hire me in a minute!"

"Then feel free to join him," Clayton invited. She made him hate himself. "And damn you, and damn the spotted owl," he added in that terse, correct tone.

She couldn't remember a time when he'd ever cursed her. She'd hit him where it hurt. He wasn't good at hiding things from her. She was sorry she'd had to tell him the truth about what he was doing to his reputation, but it was necessary.

Then, it suddenly dawned on her that he'd just fired her. After years of hard work and hero worship, she'd been fired, and he'd made it sound as if she were quitting. It didn't quite register all at once.

The ringing of the telephone startled them both. Automatically Derrie reached for it. She listened for a minute and in a taut voice announced, "It's Nikki." She handed him the receiver and walked out, closing the door too quietly behind her.

"Hello, Nikki, what do you want?" he asked tautly.

There was a pause. "I need you to pick me up," she said, her voice hoarse and strained.

He was immediately concerned. "What's wrong?"

"I almost had a relapse. It's just bronchitis and I'm much better," she added quickly. "I've seen a doctor and I have antibiotics, but I don't want to stay down here alone, and the car's acting up. I don't really feel like trying to drive it home, in case it breaks down."

"Don't blame me, I told you to trade it. Was it Chad who saw you?"

"No," she said quickly, hoping that he wouldn't see Chad for a while, because Chad knew that Kane had been with her at the beach house. "I went to another doctor."

"When were you diagnosed?"

She hesitated. "Three days ago."

"And you haven't called me until now?!" he raged. "Nikki, in the name of God . . . I'll be there in two hours. No. I can't be! Oh, heavens. Nikki, I'll send Derrie down for you. Don't worry."

He put down the receiver and strode into the outer office, nervously running his hands through his thick hair as he went. The path had been very clear in his mind: he'd go and get his sister. But he had a briefing with the environmental people at one o'clock, and he couldn't miss it.

When he opened the door to Derrie's office, she was standing at her desk with red eyes. Furious tears were streaming down her face. She'd already cleaned out her desk drawers and was picking up the small box that held the meager contents of her three years as his aide. All at once, he came to his senses.

"Derrie, no," Clayton said hesitantly, shocked at those tears. He'd never seen her cry. "Listen, I didn't mean it," he began slowly. "I've had a bad morning . . ."

"I've had a worse one," she said icily, her blue eyes glaring at him. "I've pulled up a list of people who've applied for jobs here recently. I gave it to Louise," she said, naming the secretary who worked in the outer office with the bookkeeper. "You can interview them at your pleasure. Meanwhile, you'll have to handle the

office on your own. I'll come back to retrain someone."
She nodded toward the appointment book. "The names
and telephone numbers of your appointments are right
there. I guess you can make a pot of coffee all by
yourself if you have to," she added with bitter sar-
casm.

"Nobody ever made it right until you took over the
job," he said with a wistful smile. It didn't help. She
was still frozen. "Derrie, you can't leave," he said.
"You're necessary here."

"You did fire me," she reminded him. She felt a cold
pleasure when he grimaced. "But even if you hadn't, I
can't work for a man who puts his political neck above
honor." Her soft eyes had gone hard, glaring at him.
"You've been around Haralson for too long already.
Whatever he's got is contagious and you've caught it."

"But, you can't leave right now!" he ground out.
Then he dashed all her illusions by adding, "Damn it,
Nikki's got bronchitis. I have an appointment at one,
and I need you to go down and get Nikki at the beach
house and drive her home. You can take my car."

He needed her to work. That was all it had ever
been, all it would ever be. She'd loved him, and he had
nothing to give her. Why had it taken so long for her to
realize it? She sighed heavily. "All right. I'll go down
and get her," she offered. "Because I like Nikki. But
I'll take my own car."

He sighed heavily. "What am I supposed to do until
I can find someone?"

"That's your problem," she said with quiet dignity.

She shifted the box in her arms. "You shouldn't have taken me for granted for so many years," she added, searching his eyes steadily, and for what might be the last time. "I'm sorry, but I can't take any more."

"All right," he said gruffly. He indicated the box. "Don't you want to leave that here?"

Her eyebrows lifted. "Why? I'm not coming back."

She turned and walked out the door, leaving it ajar because she had her hands full.

Clayton Seymour stood by the desk and stared after her with a mind that absolutely refused to register what had happened. He'd never had to worry about leaving the office before, because Derrie was so competent and capable. She could handle anything. Now she was gone. He'd fired her. He wondered if he could ever replace her. His relief over Lombard's fall was overshadowed by his emptiness at losing the best assistant he'd ever had. Why couldn't she understand that he needed Haralson? The man was proving to be a miracle worker.

Nikki was not surprised to see Derrie at the door when she answered it.

"Clayton didn't come with you?" Nikki asked weakly.

"He has to answer his own questions from the constituency and make coffee," Derrie said with forced carelessness. "You see, this is my last official act as his secretary. I've quit. No, that's not right," she said with a quizzical look. "I've been fired."

Nikki stared at her, seeing the faint swelling around her eyes and the visible pain of her decision.

"Why?"

"Because your brother is going to crucify Kane Lombard for something he may not even be guilty of."

Nikki's heart jumped wildly in her chest. "Lombard . . . what did he do?"

"You don't have television here, do you?" Derrie asked. "Well, it's all over the news. Lombard has been charged with several counts of industrial pollution of a major tributary. They say he cut costs by throwing out a reputable waste disposal company and replacing it with some local who was notorious for dumping vats of pollutants in deserted fields and marshes. There's been terrible damage to wildlife. It's a felony to dump toxic wastes illegally, you know."

"Oh, my God," Nikki said shakily.

Without registering Derrie's curiosity, she wobbled to the phone, picked it up and blindly dialed Kane's number without considering the consequences.

But his housekeeper answered it, and all she would tell Nikki was that Mr. Lombard had been called urgently back to Charleston.

Nikki put down the receiver. It had been madness to try to call him. He wouldn't speak to her, anyway. Not after the way they'd parted.

She'd never felt quite as bad. "He wouldn't," she said. "He wouldn't do such a thing."

"I know that," Derrie said. "The poor man's had so

much tragedy . . . Wait a minute, how do you know he wouldn't?''

Nikki hesitated. ''I've read about him,'' she hedged.

''Of course,'' Derrie said with an apologetic laugh. ''So have I. He seems like a decent sort of man.'' Her smile vanished. ''Your brother seems to be losing all his values since that man Haralson came to work for him. I wish I could tell you . . .'' She hesitated. ''Never mind. I'm through being his barricade and pacifier and chief coffee-maker. I'm not sacrificing my conscience for the sake of any job. I have a good brain and it's going to waste.''

Nikki managed a wan smile. ''Indeed you have, but I fear for my brother's future if you aren't in it. You were his balance wheel. He'll be lost without you.''

''I know.'' Derrie's eyes were sad as she recalled the things Clayton had said to her, but she forced the misery away. ''We have to get you back to Charleston. What can I do?''

''Help me pack,'' Nikki said. ''Then I'll dress and we'll get under way.''

''Did you borrow Clayton's Lincoln?''

''I did not. I brought my pretty little white Ford Tempo, and you'll be very comfortable in it.''

Nikki laughed. ''I wouldn't dare argue with you.''

''I was going to hire a limo,'' Derrie confessed, ''and let your brother get a migraine when he saw the bill. But in the end, my conscience wouldn't let me.''

Nikki puzzled over the things Derrie had said. She

couldn't help but wonder what Clayton had really done to make Derrie quit.

Kane Lombard met the vicious publicity head-on. He had known what was going to happen from the minute Sanders had called to tell him the news. He wasn't guilty, but by the time the media got through with him, he'd look it.

It wouldn't be a nine-day wonder, either, he realized when he saw the headlines. Seymour had jumped in feet-first with charges that Lombard was a prime example of the capitalist who put profit before conservation. He was going to make an example of Kane, and he had strong support.

Many of the same public officials who had paved Kane's way when he opened the automobile plant were now lined up visibly with the opposition.

"It's going to be a circus," Kane remarked, looking down on the mob at the gates of the plant from his sixth-story window.

Gert Yardley, his elderly executive secretary, nodded. "I'm afraid so. And the news people are clamoring for interviews. You'll have to give a statement, sir."

"I know that. What do you recommend? How about, 'I'm innocent'?" he asked, turning to face her.

"I have no doubt whatsoever about your innocence," Mrs. Yardley said, and smiled sympathetically. "Neither does Jenny," she added, naming the junior secretary who shared an office with her. "Convincing those ravenous wolves outside is going to be the problem."

He stuck his hands in his pants pockets and turned away from the furor below. "Get my father on the line, will you?"

"I can't, sir," she said. "He telephoned two hours ago and said to tell you that he's on his way."

"Great." He lifted his eyes skyward. "My father is just what I need to make a bad day worse. I can handle my own problems."

"I'm sure he knows that. He said you might need a little moral support," she added with a smile. "A man who's being publicly hanged shouldn't turn away a friend. Even a related one."

"I guess you're right." His dark eyes narrowed. "I want to see that new waste disposal man, what's his name, Jurkins. Get him up here."

"He's out sick," she returned grimly. "And Ed Nelson, who is still recuperating from his kidney stone operation, has just had a relapse. He and Mr. Jurkins both called in. They both swore that they knew nothing about Burke's true method of operation."

"They would, wouldn't they? God forbid they should try to cross the picket line. All right, call Bob Wilson and get him over here," he said, thinking that it would most likely take Bob and his entire law firm to get him out of this mess.

"I already have," she said. "He'll be here momentarily."

"Thanks, Gert," he replied.

She smiled. "No problem. I'll buzz you when Mr. Wilson arrives."

She left him, and he turned back to the window. It was threatening rain. Maybe that would dissuade some of the lesser-paid protesters, he mused. He thought about Nikki, and despite his anger at her deception, and the impossibility of their relationship, he allowed himself to miss her. She would have been the best medicine in the world to perk him up, with her high spirits and stubborn will. From what he'd learned about her since their breakup, he could easily imagine her whipping the lynch mob outside into a select committee on wildlife rehabilitation.

"As far as the company goes, you haven't got a legal leg to stand on," Bob Wilson told him an hour later. "I'm sorry, but they've got ironclad evidence linking Lombard, Inc., with Burke's and the illegal dumping site. The fact that you didn't personally make the decision to hire him doesn't negate the fact that you approved your subordinate's hiring of him. The buck stops at you. The company is in violation of several environmental laws, federal, local and state, and it will be prosecuted for at least one felony count, probably more as the investigation continues and they find more of Burke's handiwork. A fine is the least of your worries right now."

"In other words, even if I were willing to prove that

I was incapacitated at the time of the hiring, it wouldn't lessen my responsibility in the eyes of the law.''

"That's exactly right." Wilson frowned, because Kane looked momentarily relieved. "Of course, Burke will be prosecuted along with you. He's an accessory.''

"Good. I hope they hang him out to dry. I only just found out—on the news, mind you—that Burke's brother-in-law is Jurkins, my new solid waste manager. Jurkins was upset when I asked him about it earlier. He said Burke was his late wife's brother and that he wasn't getting any kickbacks from the new contract. He said Burke's had a good reputation." He ran his hand through his hair irritably. He glanced at Wilson. "Can I prosecute Jurkins for making that decision without my written approval?''

"You did approve it," Wilson said with forced patience. "Jurkins denies any wrongdoing. He said that he told you what he'd done and you said it was all right.''

"But, my God, I had no idea who Burke was or that CWC's record had been misrepresented to me!''

"Jurkins swears that he can show you on paper what CWC did to discredit themselves. If you recall, he also swears that he didn't know Burke had been in any trouble, whether or not that's true. You're still culpable, regardless of that," Wilson informed him. "I can't see any legal way out of this. You'll have to plead guilty and hope that we can negotiate a reasonable settlement.''

"While that s.o.b. gets away scot-free?''

"Which one?''

"Burke."

"We're investigating," Wilson assured him.

"Could kickbacks be involved here?" he asked suddenly, staring at his legal counsel. "If they were, there'll be proof, won't there?" Kane persisted.

"We're already exploring that possibility. So far, we can't find any evidence that anyone who works for you has had any drastic change in life-styles, but we're not finished yet. If there is anything, it will turn up."

Kane leaned back against his desk. "You mean that this whole situation was innocently arrived at?" he asked.

"I can't prove that it wasn't at this point."

"Suppose I fire Jurkins?"

"What for?" Wilson replied. "He's done nothing except make a mistake in judgment, allegedly trying to save you money on operating expenses and hiring his brother-in-law who has five kids and needs all the work he can get. He's just full of apologies and explanations and excuses."

"We could take the case to the newspapers; to my father's, in fact."

"You aren't thinking," the other man said patiently. "Jurkins may be a scalawag, but he's a working man with a daughter who has leukemia, remember? If you start persecuting him, despite what he's done, it's only going to reinforce the negative image of your company as a money-hungry exploiter of working people. People will overlook his illegal dumping because you're picking on him. In fact, the press will turn it around and make a hero of him; the little guy trying to make a buck, being persecuted by big business.''

''I don't believe this!''

''I've seen it done. Being rich is its own punishment sometimes.''

''I employ hundreds of people. I've donated thousands to civic projects, I've helped renovate depressed areas . . . doesn't any of that count?'' Kane thundered.

''When the hanging fever dies down, it probably will. You only have to live through the interim.''

''You're just full of optimism, aren't you?''

Wilson laughed. He got to his feet and went to shake hands with Kane.

''I know it must look hopeless,'' he told the other man. ''But, don't give up. It's early yet.''

Kane glowered at him. ''And when it rains, it pours. Get out there and save my neck.''

''I'll do my best,'' was the promise.

Nikki was exhausted in body and spirit when she and Derrie reached the old Victorian family home in the Battery barely an hour later.

''You'd better sack out in the downstairs bedroom until you've got more wind to climb those stairs,'' Derrie suggested.

''I guess so,'' Nikki returned, with a wistful look at the gracefully curving staircase with its sedate gray carpet. Her chest was much better, but she still got winded very easily. ''It's just that I feel safer up high.''

"Who doesn't?" Derrie said, laughing. She helped Nikki into the bedroom and then unpacked for her while Nikki got into her pajamas and climbed into bed. "Good thing Mrs. D. has been here."

"If it weren't for Mrs. D. three times a week, I couldn't keep this place," Nikki pointed out. "She was a young girl when she kept house for Dad, but even middle age hasn't slowed her down. Doesn't she do a good job?"

"Wonderful." Derrie put the last of the dirty clothes in the laundry hamper. "You said that you'd been sick for several days. However did you manage alone?"

Nikki averted her eyes. "I didn't eat much," she said, "and I had a jug of bottled water by the bed. The antibiotics worked very fast."

"Did your neighbor treat you?" Derrie asked.

"Yes, Chad Holman lives just down the road, and he's always been good to us," Nikki assured her, relieved. It was highly unlikely that Derrie would run into Dr. Chad Holman to ask about Nikki's return bout of pneumonia. Kane's intervention would never have to be mentioned.

"I told you that you were doing too much at Spoleto," Derrie chided, glancing at the other woman as she lounged in the bed.

"I'm on the mend. I got chilled, that's all." She blushed, remembering exactly how she had got chilled. "I'll be more careful."

"You should cancel that gala affair in September. It's already July. You won't be well enough . . ."

"Yes, I will," Nikki said firmly. "Stop brooding. You've stopped working for my stupid brother, so you're hardly required to worry about me."

"I'll miss your stupid brother," Derrie said sadly, as she looked at Nikki and smiled. "But it wasn't because of him that I've been your friend."

"I know that. I'm sorry Clayton ever let himself get mixed up with Haralson," Nikki said quietly. "He's going to take my brother down if he isn't very careful. This fight with Kane Lombard could be just the thing to do it, too. Mr. Lombard doesn't strike me as the kind of man who takes anything lying down, and his family owns one vicious tabloid in New York."

"Lombard is very much on the defensive right now," Derrie observed. "They say his plant is surrounded by rabid environmentalists with blown-up photos of the dead birds in that marsh."

Nikki winced. She could imagine how Kane would feel. She'd learned enough about him during their acquaintance to tell that he was a man who loved wildlife. If he wanted to preserve the little spotted owl, certainly he wouldn't do anything deliberately to kill birds.

"I think you should know," Derrie began slowly, "that some of those protesters who are picketing Mr. Lombard's plant were hired to do it."

Nikki's lips parted as she let out a sudden breath. "Does Clayton know?"

Derrie turned, uncomfortable and uneasy. "Well, you see, that's why I quit."

CHAPTER
TEN

Nikki couldn't believe what she was hearing. But she knew that Derrie wouldn't lie.

"Clayton has always been concerned for the environment—well, until the spotted owl, anyway," she said, and frowned as something occurred to her. "It's Haralson, isn't it? Since he's been around Clayton has become too involved in winning to see the methods he's using."

"I wish I knew why," Derrie replied. She couldn't let on how much she knew about Haralson's methods. Mary Tanner said the man was notorious for getting something on the people he helped—insurance, he called it. "Nikki, is there a skeleton in your family's closet that Kane's father could rattle?"

Nikki went very still. "Doesn't everyone have skeletons?" she asked uncertainly. She thought of Miles and his political position. His secret could ruin him, and eventually everyone, including Clayton and Nikki. Untold damage could be done. Miles was such a gentle man that she feared the threat of exposure could make him do something foolish. She chewed on a fingernail. "Derrie, do you know something about Haralson that you aren't telling?"

"Just gossip," she hedged. "But watch yourself, will you?"

Nikki's eyes glittered. "If Haralson tangles with me, he'll wish he hadn't," she promised her friend. "I'm no novice to political wheeling and dealing. I can pull strings, too."

"In the meantime, you might talk to Clay," Derrie suggested. "Perhaps he'll listen to you."

"I'm sorry you won't stay with him," Nikki said.

"I can't. He wanted me to call the television stations and get them over to Mr. Lombard's plant." She grimaced. "That was Haralson's suggestion, too, I'm sure, but Clayton was willing to do it."

"I see." Nikki didn't recognize these tactics. Her brother wasn't a vicious man. Even in his solitary anti-environment stance, his goal was to save jobs, to put people to work. He never worked for personal gain.

"I would have refused to call the TV stations, too," she said when Derrie appeared to be waiting for reassurance.

Derrie forced herself to smile. "It feels funny to be without a job," she said slowly.

"What will you do?"

"Something I may regret. I'm going to work for the competition. Sam Hewett asked me to work for him not long ago. He's very pro-environment and I know his family," she said, grimacing at Nikki's pained look. "He's a good man and tough, but he won't fight dirty. Not even if the Lombards try to get him to." She lowered her eyes. "I'm very sorry. I wish it hadn't come to this."

"So do I. Let me talk to Clayton before you rush into anything," Nikki pleaded.

Derrie moved closer, a hand going to her tangle of blond hair. "You don't understand, Nikki," she began. "There's more to it than just this campaign. I've finally seen the light. He's never going to love me."

Nikki knew how she felt. Her own heart was still raw from Kane's rejection. "Oh, Derrie," Nikki said miserably. "Whoever he gets as a replacement won't come close to you. You're the only long-term staff member he's kept from the old days in the state house of representatives. I know how much he respects you."

"Well, I hope you and I will still be friends."

"Don't be absurd, of course we will. Thank you for helping me get home, Derrie."

"Any time." She picked up her purse and moved to the door. It was all beginning to hit her now. "I'll call Mr. Hewett and then have a nice lazy weekend before I start back to work, if he still wants me, that is."

"I have no doubt that he will."

Nikki looked concerned and Derrie instantly knew why. "I'm not going to sell out Clayton, even if he is a rat."

"You know I'm not thinking along those lines," Nikki said with a smile. "I know you too well."

"It would be natural to wonder. But I'm not vindictive. Mostly, I'm hurt." She breathed heavily. "I'll get over it. Life happens."

"Doesn't it just?" Nikki said sadly, remembering Kane and what she'd had to sacrifice. "I want to know how things work out for you."

Derrie smiled at her. "You will, I promise."

Clayton visited Nikki that evening. He looked drawn and preoccupied.

"Worn out from learning to make coffee?" Nikki asked mockingly when he walked into the living room. She was curled up on the couch waiting for him.

"So she told you," he said. He dropped heavily into his armchair and stared at her. "You look awful."

"I feel better than I did," she replied. "I caught a chill. Stupid of me, under the circumstances, but I'm better now." She'd managed to say that without remembering Kane's part in the chill. Almost.

"I'm glad. I would have come, but I had an appointment I couldn't break. Derrie left me in an impossible situation," he said angrily.

She laughed in spite of herself. He looked as he had when they were children and someone had taken a treasured toy away from him. The two of them looked very much alike except for the darkness of Nikki's skin. He shared her dark hair but he had blue eyes, and she had green ones, a legacy from both sides of the family.

"She quit," he muttered. "Can you imagine? I asked her to do one little thing beyond her regular duties, and she walked out!"

"You fired her," Nikki reminded him. "And I know why she walked out," Nikki returned. "I'd have walked out, too. Haralson is remaking you, Clay. You've changed more than you realize."

He glared at her. "If the Lombards get hold of the real reason your marriage ended, do you have any idea what they'll do to you and Miles in that supermarket sleaze sheet they've made millions on? In his position, and under the present administration, Miles would be crucified if he were forced out of the closet!"

"Yes, I know," she agreed quietly. "And our old and hallowed family name would be tarnished. But I'd rather face that than watch you use the same tactics to get reelected."

"You have to play hardball sometimes. Haralson knows what he's doing. Maybe his methods are a little ruthless, but Lombard is ruthless, too."

"Not like this," she said. "If he hit you, you'd see him coming."

His face cleared. He stared at her for a long moment. "How do you know?" he asked quietly.

She hesitated. "I've read some very interesting things about him," she said. She couldn't tell her brother that she'd spent several days alone with Kane Lombard, or that she'd been falling in love with him. In Clayton's current frame of mind, that would have been foolish. He was satisfied with her answer.

"No more Derrie," Clayton was mumbling dully. "I can't even believe it! She's been with me for years; from when I was first elected to the state legislature until I was elected to Congress, she was always there. And now she walks out over a triviality."

"It isn't a triviality," she said.

He glanced at her curiously. "Wake up, Nikki. You know what politics is like. Neither of us has ever been blind to what went on behind the curtains."

"Yes, but you've never been part of that kind of game before. You were an idealist."

"I can't change anything until I garner some political clout, and I can't do that until I'm reelected. Two-year terms for Congressmen are outrageous, we aren't even settled in office before we have to run for reelection. I want back in. I have plans, an agenda," he said, talking to himself. "How I win isn't that important. Stopping unemployment, which is growing by the day, is." His face hardened. "Derrie's worried about an owl while I'm trying to save jobs so that children won't go hungry. Hewett is a conservationist who will put trees above human beings. I won't, and if that isn't politically correct, tough!" He looked up. "I won't lose, Nikki. I can recoup enough support to get reelected. All I have to do is throw Lombard to the wolves. He's been dumping chemicals in a marsh. The media is having a field day at his expense," he added. "This is the first break I've had since the campaign began, and he brought it on himself. I got full credit for helping catch him and it's helped draw attention away from my stand on the environmental issues in the Pacific Northwest."

"Do you know what Mr. Lombard's been through in the past year?"

"Yes, I know, but it doesn't change things," he said shortly, rising. He held up his hand when she threatened to continue. "Enough, Nikki. He's an industrial polluter and I'm going to nail him to the wall."

"Is Miles behind you?" she asked.

"He's always supported me."

Nikki averted her eyes. Yes, he had. Miles even liked Nikki, but she could never forget the revulsion in his eyes the one time she'd tried desperately to arouse him by taking off her clothes in front of him. The damage he'd done to her image as a woman was never going to be fully erased. Kane might have helped, but he had his own emotional barriers.

"You've forgiven Miles," Clayton said slowly.

"Long ago," Nikki replied softly. "He couldn't help it."

Clayton winced. "If the reason you divorced got out, it would kill him," he told her. "He's a decent man, a very private man. He works hard for this country.

"You never even suspected, did you?" Clayton said

sadly. "Dad did, I think, but he wouldn't admit it even to himself. He was too bent on saving his own skin. Miles needed a wife, and Dad needed Miles."

"And the only one who suffered was me," Nikki said miserably.

"That's not quite true," Clayton told her. "Miles was devastated when he realized exactly how you felt. It took him a long time to get over it. He's more sensitive than most, and he doesn't like hurting anyone."

"I know that," she said. She looked at Clay. "But Haralson doesn't mind hurting people for gain."

He glared at her. "Haralson is my business."

"I won't let Haralson ruin you. Don't lose sight of why you ran for the office in the first place. Don't blow all that just because you want to stay in office."

"It's more than just keeping my job," he told her. "Now. When you get back on your feet, I thought we'd throw a few gala parties."

"I know, beginning with one in Washington, D.C., in September," she added, feeling brighter and happier as she considered the motif for the first party.

"The primary election will be over by then," he said.

"And we'll win," she assured him, smiling. "The party will be a celebration."

He hoped so, but didn't put it into words.

"I do love politics, Clay," she said wistfully.

"So do I," he seconded. "I'll try not to disillusion you too much with my campaign. Just remember, Nikki, we both have a lot to fear from Lombard. While he's occupied with defending himself against the EPA violations, his family will be busy trying to help him. Let's hope they won't have time to pay much attention to digging up scandals on us before the primary.''

Nikki wanted to agree with him, but she wasn't convinced he was right. Derrie had been the first casualty of this campaign. She wondered who would follow.

Miles Townshend sipped wine as he stood in front of his lofty window overlooking the traffic of nighttime Washington. He was barefoot, wearing a silver and gold robe that emphasized his blond good looks.

He felt triumphant over Haralson's victory against Lombard in Charleston. Now that Lombard would have his hands full trying to defend himself, he couldn't possibly have time to ferret out Miles's secret.

If the Lombards focused their attention on Clayton, their attack might include his sister, and then possibly Miles himself. Nikki was a thorn in his conscience to this day, and he feared what might surface if Lombard's family probed too deeply into her past. No one, however, knew the real reason for the breakup of their marriage. No one except Clayton and Nikki and Miles himself.

Miles leaned his head wearily against the cool glass. He'd always lived with the fear of public exposure. He was older than Clayton, raised in a generation with stifling attitudes toward anyone different from the norm. His parents had hidden what they called his ''character flaw'' from other relatives. They had made Miles ashamed of it. Because of his upbringing, he'd always had to hide what he was. No one would have understood. At least, that's what his parents had said.

But Nikki had understood. Even after she knew it all, she'd comforted him. Nikki, with her golden heart. He groaned out loud. It hurt him to remember the pain he'd caused her.

He knew that some people thought gay men chose, voluntarily, to be gay, but his sexual preference was something he couldn't help. There were no magic cures, no therapies that would make him heterosexual. He would be like this until he died, and the best he could hope for was to live discreetly and never permit his secret to be uncovered.

He dreaded the new political climate in which the media threatened to expose any and every personal secret. Fear had become a way of life lately, especially once the Lombards started sticking their noses everywhere.

It was a good thing Haralson didn't miss a chance. He'd provided Clayton with a soapbox from which to denounce Lombard's carelessness with his company's toxic waste. The man had a positive genius for making the most of publicity, and he always had an angle on how to make the other candidate sweat.

A friend had passed along some gossip regarding Haralson and his methods. He'd said his behavior had become erratic, his ethics questionable. Miles hoped his friend was wrong; Haralson had so far only been an asset to Clayton. And Haralson had always come through for him when he was campaigning. The gossip was probably just jealous chatter.

"Are you ever coming back to bed?" a quiet voice called from the silken depths of the king-size bed.

Miles put down his wine glass, relief draining away the fear. He slid the robe away from his body and walked, smiling, back to bed.

Fred Lombard puffed angrily on his big cigar as he paced around his son Kane's office.

"Damned stupidity," he muttered, glancing at his eldest son to make sure he was being listened to. "You know better than to run off on vacation and leave the business unattended. Think I've ever done that?"

Kane didn't answer. This speech was familiar. His father always asked the same question. The elder Lombard didn't make mistakes, always knew what to do, and was there on the spot with an I-told-you-so whenever he deemed it necessary.

"In my day, we'd have had that employee drawn and quartered," he continued hotly. "No questions asked, either, mind you. And the press would have been muzzled!"

"You're the press," his son pointed out.

The old man made a dismissive gesture with a big, wrinkled hand. His hands were almost out of proportion to his tall, spare frame. "I'm not that kind of press, I'm not easily led and fed lies. I print the truth!"

"No, you don't."

Fred Lombard glared down his thin nose at Kane. "I print it sometimes," he clarified, "when I think it needs printing. The rest of the time people expect to be entertained, and they pay through the nose for it. Don't you appreciate how to sell news?"

"Sure. Put two heads on the victim and draw in a flying saucer on a photograph, blow it up, and cover the front page with it," Kane returned.

Fred chuckled. "Sure, that's how you do it."

"You won't win a Pulitzer."

"I'm crying all the way to the Swiss bank where I keep my money," Fred returned. "No interest, but total confidentiality, and I like that. Don't expect to inherit everything," he added. "You have two brothers."

"I don't need to inherit anything," came the cynical reply. "I'm set for life already. I'll have free room and board and three meals a day at Leavenworth."

"Bosh." Fred waved the cigar at him. "They can't put you in prison for something an employee did in all innocence."

"Illegal dumping is a felony, didn't you hear the attorney?"

"Sure I did, but I'm telling you that the current administration is so slow about investigations that you'll be my age before any charges are brought."

"That could be true. But what if this administration loses in November?"

"Then we may find ourselves in a real tax crunch, my boy. And you'll have to walk on eggshells, because that young fellow not only has some bright ideas about the economy and the jobless, he's keen on keeping the earth unpolluted."

"More power to him," Kane replied. "I feel the same way. But even if I didn't do the dumping, I allowed it. It's my responsibility to make sure my employees hire disposal people who obey the law. I didn't."

"You weren't here," Fred returned. "I keep reminding you, you weren't here! If you want to take long vacations, sell the business!"

Kane sat down on the edge of his desk with a heavy sigh. He couldn't tell even his father where he'd been and why. Nikki, he groaned inwardly. Not a day went by that he didn't miss her.

"I've got the company attorneys working night and day on a defense, but my heart isn't in it. Did you see the photographs?" he asked, anger and sadness in his dark eyes. "My God, all that destruction. I hope they lock that idiot up in one of his own trucks and push him into a swamp."

"He'd pollute the environment," came the dry reply.

"I suppose so," Kane agreed reluctantly.

"Cheer up. I'm working on a way to save you."

Kane's head cocked. "If you dare put a picture of a flying saucer over a photograph of that marsh and print it . . ."

"Son, would I do that?"

"Hell, yes."

"Not this time," Fred promised. "I may be able to

get you some leeway from Seymour. I've got that fellow Sanders investigating a very odd little episode in Miles Townshend's past.''

Kane scowled. ''What sort of episode? And what has it got to do with Seymour?''

''It's very interesting. Did you know that seven years ago, Seymour's only sister married Miles Townshend and divorced him in a screaming rush?''

Kane felt his heart turn over. ''What?''

''The marriage lasted six months. After a quiet divorce, there was talk that Townshend had only married to stop some gossip about his continuing bachelor status.''

Kane's mind was spinning as he connected what he was being told. Nikki had been married. She'd told him that, but she'd once said that she was involved with a man who couldn't touch her. Townshend? Could she have been talking about Townshend?

Fred stopped pacing and stared at him. ''What are you brooding about?''

''What do we know about Townshend?''

''Not much. He's a secretive devil. I've got Sanders doing some discreet backtracking. We know that Townshend grew up in a little community near Aiken. Sanders has gone up there to talk to some people. If Townshend is hiding anything, we'll find it.''

''And if you do find something, what are you going to do?'' Kane asked suspiciously.

''We'll see,'' came the terse reply. ''You and I both know that Townshend supports Seymour against you. I suspect the plan is to keep your back to the wall so that you won't have time to do any digging and point any fingers in his direction. Seymour may have the same idea. If he does, he might slow down if we had something on his sister and her ex-husband.''

He didn't like the thought of involving Nikki in a scandal. ''That's underhanded,'' Kane said after a minute.

''Maybe so. But it's to your advantage,'' his father replied. ''Your lofty principles would land you in the hoosegow for sure otherwise.''

Kane could only think of Nikki and the time they'd been together, when he'd felt safe for the first time in his adult life. It seemed very far away right now, with his business in turmoil. He should have been honest with her from the beginning, and let her be honest with him. If he hadn't been so wary of commitment, anything could have happened. Now, each new day created more barriers. His eyes narrowed as he thought of her marriage to Townshend. He was getting a pretty sharp picture of the reason for the hasty divorce, and another of Nikki as he'd made love to her. What he was thinking was incredible. But it was most probably true. He wondered if he'd ever be able to ask her; or if she'd tell him, now.

The wheels of justice were slow, but relentless. Kane Lombard spent a lot of time with his attorneys and his production people and managers, trying to sort out the nightmarish complications of his own negligence. Both Will Jurkins and Ed Nelson came back to work. Nelson was feeble, but involved himself in the defense of his company. Jurkins provided the paperwork that showed CWC's lack of efficiency and showed a reason for firing them. However, Kane couldn't help noticing that Jurkins had dark circles under his eyes, and he asked if the man wasn't sleeping well. Jurkins had mentioned something about his child having a relapse, and he'd gone back to his office, looking haggard. Like the rest of the staff, Kane decided, Jurkins was feeling the pressure of public animosity. All of them had to pass through the picket lines daily, and only the security force kept them safe at all.

Meanwhile, Clayton was involved in fierce campaigning in the district as the primary election approached. He outdistanced his Republican competition in the polls because of the coup he'd pulled off when he had exposed the illegal dumping by Lombard International.

Nikki, recovered and back in form again, had waded into the ring with him. She gave speeches on his behalf to women's voter groups and local civic organizations. She was tireless and talented, using her communication skills to promote Clayton's position and gather more votes. Her brother had plenty of support here at home, but there were questions about his record in office, most of them having to do with his lack of attention lately to the woes of the manufacturing community. Jobs were being lost and his speeches offered no insight on any possible solution. Nikki suggested that he address the issue, but he was too concerned with working on a new denouncement of the EPA's continuing investigation of the Lombard company to listen to her.

Clayton was definitely ahead of his nearest Democratic opponent. But Sam Hewett, the Republican contender, was running almost unopposed, and the man had not only hired Derrie Keller, he'd just announced that he'd appointed her as his chief administrative aide. Many of her campaign strategies for the Republican were proving quite effective; clearly her skills extended beyond making coffee.

"I don't believe he's made this much progress." Clayton said disbelievingly as he lay in bed with Bett one rainy Saturday in Washington. "The primary's next week and it looks like Hewett is going to win the Republican nomination even without a runoff!"

"He's doing some pretty savvy stuff," Bett said. She rolled over onto her back, her small breasts brazenly revealed. She was painfully thin; her ribs showed through the skin. Clayton didn't look at her. She was exciting to make love to, but sometimes she felt boyish under his hands. He wished she were more endowed, more feminine in shape and contour. But, then, it was her intelligence that had attracted him from the start, and her body had very little to do with that.

"I'm going to win," he remarked.

"Of course you are. Isn't your sister planning some gala event two weeks from now, after the primary?"

"Yes," he said.

"I'll help if I can," Bett offered, taking him by surprise. "I can serve drinks or something."

He rolled over to face her, frowning. "You don't like Nikki."

"But, I do," she said. "She's very confident, isn't she? And she has an analytical mind. I admire the way she makes speeches and coordinates campaign functions for you." She hesitated for a moment before changing the subject. "Clay, I've had another offer from the British. They'd like me to lobby for them on this most recent agricultural issue. I said I'd think about it. They'd pay me a lot of money, and I could get out of the rut I'm in at the law firm."

"If you get a job as a lobbyist, we'll have to stop seeing each other," he said for the tenth time in as many days.

"But this is so important to me, Clay."

More important than I am, apparently, he thought irritably. "Bett . . ."

"Look at the time! I have to get a shower and get downtown," she said, rolling quickly out of bed. "I've got a meeting in thirty minutes!"

She dashed into the bathroom and shut the door. Clayton lay scowling at the closed door, feeling deserted and unhappy. Instead of concentrating on helping him in his campaign, Bett spent most of their time together talking about working as a lobbyist. She knew that he'd have to stop seeing her if that came about because he would be trapped in a conflict of interest.

First Derrie, and now Bett. Well, at least he still had his sister on his team.

Nikki had collaborated with one of Washington's leading hostesses to concoct the sort of party for September that people would be talking about years from now. Assuming that Clay won the primary, there were other parties planned for Charleston, fund-raisers and banquets and social evenings to garner more support. Nikki expected to be worn to a frazzle, but it would be worthwhile.

She was worn out from speech-making and social events. She'd had to put off her plans for a new series of sculptures of the founders of the South Carolina colony. She had no time to do anything except campaign. Maybe next year, she thought wistfully.

The latest polls indicated that Clay had the Democratic seat firmly in hand. But polls weren't actual votes.

On the day of the primary Nikki went with Clay to their local precinct to vote. Crowds were already standing in line at eight in the morning, and Nikki's heart lifted.

"This looks encouraging," she said.

Clayton didn't agree. The turnout frightened him. Usually when so many people went to vote, it was because they were angry and wanted to get someone out of office. He'd actually known some old-timers who only ever voted against, not for, candidates.

"Don't look so nervous," she chided.

A black lady next to them grinned. "That's right, it's not against the law to vote for the candidate of your choice."

Clay grinned. "Picked the best man, have you?" he teased.

"Oh, yes, sir," she said. "Going to have a new president this fall, so I figure we may as well get those other rascals out of there and put in some people who can get something done. I have no insurance. I can't make my house payment this month. I can't even afford to buy a new pair of shoes." She looked down at them, worn on both sides and scuffed. "The plant I worked for moved down into the Caribbean so it could get cheap labor and make more money. It don't bother the government that I wouldn't have a job," she added. "What a pity that we pay those people so much to represent us that they just forget how hard life is outside the Capitol."

She nodded politely and moved on as her line shortened. Clayton had gone pale. Nikki touched his arm in encouragement, but suddenly Clayton realized how preoccupied he'd been with keeping Kane Lombard under fire. He'd spent so much time feathering his own political nest and thinking of his own future that he'd forgotten the most important thing of all: that these people had elected him to represent their interests in Washington. How could he have been so blind?

"Derrie tried to tell me," he began.

Nikki looked at him and her eyes asked a question.

"I hope it's not too late," he said quietly.

"What do you mean?"

But the line moved, and so did they, and the question was drowned out by the low buzz of conversation.

"Those are ours," Nikki whispered, nodding toward two women who were shepherding people into the precinct.

"Ours?"

"Carpools, dear man," she said with a grin. "We've had telephone committees going for weeks and advertisements in all the local media for rides to the polls."

He was aghast when he began to realize just how many people were coming in. "I've never seen carpools organized on this scale to get people to the polls. How did you do it?"

Nikki glanced up at him, smiling. "I called in every favor I was ever owed. Of course, I can't guarantee that they're all going to vote for you," she added.

"Remind me to put you on the payroll!"

"And get us accused of nepotism? No, thank you!" she replied brightly, and brought the first smile to his face that she'd seen there all morning.

The polls closed at seven, but there were still lines of people waiting to get into the polling booths. Early returns gave Hewett a tremendous lead in the Republican primary, but on the Democratic side, Clayton was running neck and neck with a well-known Charleston attorney. It was much too tight a race for comfort. It meant that voters were unsatisfied.

"Will you stop pacing and worrying?" Nikki chided, sweeping into the hotel room in his headquarters in a blue and green silk pantsuit that suited her dark complexion.

Clayton, standing with his hands in his pants pockets, flanked by Haralson and Bett, glowered at her. "Do you see these figures?" he asked.

She handed him a plastic cup of coffee. "You're not going to lose."

Bett glanced at her. "You sound very sure."

Nikki smiled. "He's the best man, isn't he?"

"Of course," Bett agreed.

"Then he'll win." Nikki moved her eyes back to the television screen. "It's early yet, and these are small, typically Republican precincts they're reporting. Wait until we get the urban Democratic vote. That's where Clay's strength is."

Bett was surprised. "How do you know so much about all this?"

"I learned more in college than, how did you once put it, empty-headed hostessing," she said dryly.

It was a challenge from a face dominated by sparkling blue eyes. Bett smiled ruefully. "Sorry about that."

"Oh, we're all guilty of making snap judgments," Nikki said mischievously. "I won't mention what I asked Clay about you when I first met you, but I'll apologize for it, anyway."

"Thank you," Bett murmured sheepishly.

"Which makes us even," Nikki chuckled.

"Clay!" Haralson called suddenly. "Look!"

They all turned their attention to the television screen where new figures were being posted. The urban precincts were just beginning to be reported and Clay's two-percent lead had just turned into a twenty-percent lead.

"Hallelujah!" Clayton shouted.

"See?" Nikki asked, smiling. "I told you so."

"I knew that Lombard industrial pollution scandal would do the trick," Haralson said smugly.

Nikki stared at the man with cold eyes. "You sound almost as though you engineered it, Mr. Haralson," she said in a deceptively sweet tone.

He lifted both eyebrows. "Now, would I be stupid enough to admit it, even if I had? Besides, we won," he said, as if that explained away everything.

"There are more important things than winning," she told him flatly.

"Not many," he returned. "You aren't getting squeamish, are you, Miss Seymour?" he added, taunting her.

She smiled coolly and her eyes sparkled with repressed temper. "I'm an old hand at the political game, Mr. Haralson," she said levelly. "Be careful that you don't stand on my toes too long. You aren't the only manipulator around here."

He laughed shortly, as if he found that remark amusing, and gave her a careless, almost insulting appraisal before he turned away.

Nikki's hands clenched around the plastic cup. She didn't like the little man or his attitude. After this campaign was over, she promised herself, there was going to be a reckoning. Haralson wasn't going to get away with what he was doing to Clayton.

CHAPTER
ELEVEN

The celebrating went on all night. The leading opponent from Clayton's own party conceded early on, and Clayton and Bett and Nikki bathed in the adulation from his supporters.

Nikki noted that Sam Hewett had taken the Republican nomination with much less trouble than Clayton, and with a sizeable chunk of the vote. Nikki was certain that he was going to put up the most formidable competition Clay had ever had at the polls in November.

At midnight, Clayton went on television to make his acceptance speech for the Democratic nomination.

"I want you to know that I'm going to fight hard to win this time," he told the camera. "And I'm not going to sit on my record. I've had my eyes opened about some issues I haven't confronted. People are out of work because of jobs going to other countries. We have such people, right here in our city. It's time we stopped paying foreign countries to steal jobs from our workers. It's time we did something about the economy and learned to balance the budget. I've seen the light and I'm going to blind you with it until I get back into Washington, and then I'm going to tackle a new agenda. The environment is still an important issue to me, but we must get our people back to work. Thank you all for your support. Let's go on and win in November!''

The supporters cheered wildly. Clayton smiled, but there was a new fire in his eyes that everyone around him noticed. Bett saw it with trepidation, because in addition to the British offer, she had been approached about representing a lobby that supported foreign expansion of American businesses in the Caribbean. She hadn't mentioned that one to Clayton. Her smile was a little strained as she contemplated the future.

Nikki was oblivious to the other woman's thoughts. Her eyes were on her brother, and she was bursting with pride.

The only thing that dimmed her happiness right now were thoughts of Kane Lombard.

She knew that he wasn't responsible for that illegal dumping of industrial waste. That fiasco had to have happened while he was lying injured in her beach house; or perhaps while they were spending time together or when he was nursing her. She wondered if he'd kept that quiet because he was trying to protect her reputation or if he was keeping it as an ace in the hole. She wondered if he ever thought about their night together. She knew how frequently she thought about it.

She'd seen Kane on television several times, and she'd felt sickened by the trials he was facing because of her brother's supporters. She wondered if it had made Kane hate Clay even more. She worried about how he might counterattack, and she'd almost telephoned Kane once to discuss it with him. But he wouldn't have spoken to her, most likely. She glanced around at the other people present and saw beneath the polite smiles. So many secrets lay behind all this sparkling hoopla of politics. Everyone had a skeleton in the closet. Some rattled louder than others.

Soon after Clayton went back to Washington, Nikki moved temporarily into the small cottage at the Royce Blair estate in Maryland which Madge Blair had made available to her. Madge was contributing the setting for a gala evening to celebrate Clayton's party nomination and also to garner support for his campaign. Nikki's genius for organization was being put to good use as she hired caterers, made arrangements for entertainment, and played overseer for the immaculate theme decorations that were being installed in the mansion's great ballroom. Several of Nikki's sculptures were displayed in the Blair home, and Nikki beamed with pride as she noted Madge and Claude's honest pleasure in her work.

"You never cease to amaze me, Nikki," Madge confessed while she helped hang delicate silver filigree musical notes against a background of golden staffs on white satin. "A theme party built around opera, with all the guests to come dressed as their favorite singer or operatic character. I expect we'll have twenty Pavarottis," she confessed, laughing. "Don't you adore him? Did you get to hear him in Puccini's *Turandot*?"

"No, I saw it when Placido Domingo had the title role," Nikki said. "It's beautiful, isn't it? I could listen to someone singing 'Nessun Dorma' all my life and never tire of it. Where's Claude?" she asked, looking around the room.

"In hiding," Madge said, laughing. "He does so detest parties, my poor darling. He's shut himself in the library with Mudd and he's furiously reading Greek tragedies. It inspires him, he says."

"Madge, he writes sexy murder mysteries," she commented. "He's world-famous. Everything he writes is made into a major motion picture. There's one debuting next month."

"I know, dear, I'm married to him," Madge returned, tongue-in-cheek.

Nikki laughed. "Is he going to come to the party, at least? He does live here."

"He might. But rest assured that he'll roll himself in flour and come as something disgusting like the ghost in that Mozart opera I hate." She tacked a note into place. "Who are you coming as? I know; Madama Butterfly! With that jet black hair, you'd be a natural.''

"Actually, I'm going to wear a gauzy gown and come as Camille. I feel tragic.''

"Oh, Nikki, not you. You always sparkle so.''

"I've had my share of sadness.''

Madge glanced at her. "Indeed you have. But your face doesn't show it. You look almost untouched.''

Nikki could have howled. She was almost untouched, but Madge didn't know why; she only knew that Nikki had a failed marriage behind her.

"Hand me that stapler, could you?'' Nikki asked.

"Here, dear. The invitations have all gone out, and we're very nearly through here. Only a few more hours. Clayton and Bett will be ontime won't they?'' she added worriedly.

"They promised.''

"Nikki, Claude insisted that we add a couple of names to the list, so I sent out a few extra invitations. I hope you don't mind?''

"How silly. It's your house and you're our friends. You're even loaning us your home for this oh-so-discreet fund-raiser. How could I possibly mind?''

A loud yowl broke the silence and Madge groaned.

"Just listen to those cats! Mudd is Siamese and Claude has the two Persians as well; they drive me mad! How he can write with those furry assassins all over his desk is beyond me!''

Nikki felt dizzy all of a sudden and gripped the stepladder hard, aware of Madge's curious stare as her wide eyes opened.

"Nikki? Are you all right?" she asked with concern.

"Of course. I'm fine. I just got a little dizzy. I haven't eaten anything."

"Then you must have a sandwich. Come with me. I'll have Lucie make you one of her famous Philly steak sandwiches and cottage fries."

"Thanks just the same, but I really don't want to die of cholesterol poisoning," Nikki chuckled. "Make that a small salad and some breadsticks instead, if you could."

"You sparrow, you." Madge smoothed her hands over her ample hips with a grimace. "If I liked lettuce leaves, I could look like you in places, at least."

"You're very nice as you are, as I'm sure Claude tells you constantly." She linked her arm with Madge's. "Now, let's go over these catered items just once more."

The day's activity was frantic, but Nikki excelled. The brief faintness vanished and she was sparkling like a jewel by evening. She looked around the room at the arrangements, satisfied, and went toward the staircase. It was nearing time for people to start arriving. If only it would go smoothly. She always worried about the food and musicians arriving on time.

"I can see the wheels turning in your head," Claude

observed, coming into the hall with a cat under one arm. It was Mudd, a big, chocolate-point Siamese with blue eyes that appraised Nikki and found her uninteresting. It closed its big eyes and curled closer into Claude's jacket.

"Mudd is hopeless," he remarked, nodding toward the sleeping cat. "He only wakes up to eat. He's so lazy that he even lets the others bathe him. His psychologist says it's because he's depressed. He isn't let outside you know, and it's frustrating him."

Nikki didn't dare grin. Claude took Mudd's therapy sessions very seriously indeed.

"How is he progressing?" she asked cautiously.

"Well, I don't notice much change, but at least he's stopped chewing on my computer keyboard. Damndest thing, all those tooth marks. Jealousy, you know. He's jealous of the computer when I'm writing."

"Are you coming to the party?" Nikki asked her host.

"I might. I think I'll come as Ravel, with Mudd under my arm," he added. "Ravel kept cats, you know. Dozens of cats. He even spoke to them."

"I used to speak to my cat," Nikki pointed out.

"Not in its own language," he returned with a wicked grin.

"Puff understood me well enough. He could hear the sound of a can being opened from the balcony upstairs," Nikki recalled wistfully. Puff had died of old age a few months back, and she was still sad about it.

"You need a new cat," he said gently.

She shrugged. "I'm too busy for cats," she lied. It was unthinkable to replace Puff so soon.

"What are you coming as?" he asked curiously.

"Camille," she said.

"A tragic heroine? Any particular reason?"

She smiled. "Perhaps I feel tragic."

"Clayton won the nomination," he reminded her.

"That isn't what I feel tragic about."

"Then it must be lost love."

She laughed. "How do you know so much about people?"

"My dear girl, I'm a writer. Who knows more about people than we do?"

"Good point."

"Didn't Camille have a cat?" he asked, frowning. "You could carry one of the Persians."

"I think having a woman with tuberculosis carry a cat would be a bit . . . how shall I put it . . . unexpected?"

"Oh. Oh, yes. I see." He chuckled. "Bad suggestion."

"He has three cats," Madge reminded Nikki. "They get his box of fanfold computer printer paper and eat it if he leaves them alone. Or they chew up manuscripts. Mudd can even open the cabinet under the desk."

"You need a filing cabinet."

He frowned. "That's cruel."

"What is?"

"Suggesting that I lock Mudd up in a filing cabinet!"

Nikki gave him an exasperated look and dashed upstairs to the sound of mischievous laughter.

The gauzy white costume suited Nikki. She felt as if she were a floating cloud among all the brightly colored costumes of the guests. Bett and Clayton had driven over from Washington, D.C., dressed as Carmen and her soldier. Clayton looked uncomfortable in the high-collared uniform, but Bett was convincing as a peasant girl with her sparkling eyes. They waved to Nikki, and Clayton gave her a thumbs-up sign as he found himself surrounded by monied supporters.

Claude and Madge were exceptionally colorful as Maurice Ravel and Madama Butterfly.

"It's the odd couple," Nikki quipped when they joined her.

"Look who's insulting whom, the coughing courtesan," Claude returned, clutching Mudd under an arm. Mudd was wide awake and very obviously irritated at the company he was having to keep. He gave his human friend a pie-eyed glare and suddenly sank his teeth into Claude's arm.

"Ouch!" Claude cried.

"Repressed hostility can stunt mental growth," Nikki said, nodding. "Better allow him freedom of expression. We wouldn't want to inhibit him."

"I'll inhibit him into a boeuf bourbonnaise if he does that again," Claude said, glaring at the cat.

"Don't be absurd, dear, you can't cook a cat with *red* wine, it's so bourgeois," Madge told him.

Nikki laughed. These two were the closest friends she'd ever had, and the most loyal. They didn't know all of her background, but it wouldn't have mattered if they had. They were the least judgmental people she'd ever known.

"What a crowd," Clayton murmured, joining them. He scowled at his sister with her stark white complexion and painted cheeks. "What are you supposed to be, Vampira?"

"I'm dying of tuberculosis, can't you tell?" She glared at him and coughed loudly. "I'm Camille."

"I hate opera," Clayton remarked to no one in particular.

Nikki didn't say a word, but she raised an eloquent eyebrow for her brother's benefit. He gave her a hard glare.

"Where is Miles?" Madge asked.

"He had other plans and sent his regrets," Clayton said with a smile. "He's not much of a mixer. Parties make him nervous."

"It's because all the women throw themselves at his feet," Madge said with a wicked smile. "He's so handsome, isn't he? Oh, my, even my knees go weak when I look at him."

Nikki's had once, too. But now she thought of Miles with sadness and pain. She didn't reply.

"Look, more guests are arriving," Claude said enthusiastically. "I must mingle, my dears."

The party lasted into the wee hours, and was pronounced a grand success. By its end, Clayton had more pledges than he needed, and Nikki was the woman of the hour.

The only thing that disturbed her was that twinge of weakness she'd felt. Nikki was never faint. She climbed into her borrowed bed that night more disturbed than ever. It had been almost two months now since she and Kane had been together. She didn't like the suspicion that was beginning to occupy her.

CHAPTER TWELVE

Nikki was more fatigued than usual following the gala at the Blair estate. Combined with the faint nausea and dizziness, plus the length of time since she'd been intimate with Kane, the fatigue pointed straight at pregnancy.

She went to her family doctor and was hardly surprised to find that she was carrying Kane's child. She didn't know how she was going to tell Clayton. The Capulets and the Montagues had nothing on the Lombards and the Seymours just lately. But oddly, her first thought was of how delighted Kane would have been about the child before he knew her identity.

For several days after she found out about her pregnancy, she walked on a cloud. Even with the drawbacks and the potential scandal, she was happy about it. Somehow, the obstacles didn't matter. She dreamed of Kane and how he might react to the news, if she only dared tell him.

But it was a startled Nikki who came face-to-face with him at a charity ball for cystic fibrosis in Charleston just a week after her visit to the doctor.

Nikki was just refusing a dance in favor of a soft drink when she turned, laughing, and walked right into Kane.

He caught her instinctively, and they stood there just staring at each other until the woman with Kane coughed politely.

Nikki's knees all but gave way, and she moved back from him. But his whole attention was focused on Nikki, and there was accusation and anger and pain in his dark eyes.

She understood the anger. She was Clayton's sister, and the media blitz had hurt him. Perhaps he even thought she'd encouraged her brother, because Kane had been unkind to her. But the sight of him fed her heart.

"I'll get something for us to drink, shall I?" Kane's brunette companion asked with a mischievous smile. She nodded at Nikki and made herself scarce. Kane hadn't even looked her way.

"This is expensive company for a beachcomber, isn't it?" Kane remarked. "The tickets were a hundred each."

"Clayton and I aren't quite that poor," she replied. "And it helps him politically to be seen at charity do's." The silence stretched between them, and she looked at him with eyes that had gone hungry for the sight of his broad, tanned face. "You look so tired, Kane," she said softly. "It's been terrible, hasn't it?"

His jaw clenched for an instant. Then he lifted one thick eyebrow and smiled cynically. "Gathering tidbits to feed your brother?"

She touched her waist absently and wished, so much, that she could tell him about the baby. The dress was a little snug through the stomach, but she wasn't showing yet.

She knew that Kane must feel betrayed. Certainly he looked it. "No. I was asking about the health of my friend," she returned. "You were that, once."

He felt the ground going out from under him as he looked at her. He'd missed her. In that elegant blue-sequinned gown, she was all his dreams rolled into one. "Are you completely well this time?" he asked.

The concern he couldn't hide thrilled her. "I think so. I've been taking it easy."

"That isn't what I've heard," he replied. His eyes scanned the room until he saw Clayton dancing with Bett, and then they narrowed angrily. "Your brother plays dirty pool. He's going to discover that the mud sticks when it's thrown. Remind him what my father does for a living," he added, glancing back down at her so quickly that she started. "And tell him that I said not to get overconfident. I'm on the firing line because one of my employees made an error in judgment, but your brother could be there for another reason entirely, along with his ex-brother-in-law."

He was fishing, but Nikki didn't realize in time, and her face gave her away.

"So there is fire behind the smoke," he said with a faint glimmer in his eyes. "Did you hope I'd forgotten what you said about your ex-husband, Nikki?" he added so softly that only she could hear him.

She felt the blood draining out of her face. "Whatever Clayton's done—and I'm not defending him blindly—you have no right to hurt Miles," she said huskily.

Her defense of her ex-husband irritated him. "Why not? He launched Haralson at me. He's got a secret, hasn't he, Miss Seymour? And he thinks keeping my neck under his foot will keep us from digging for it while he uses every gutter tactic in the book to put Clayton Seymour back in office!"

"Miles isn't underhanded," she began.

"No? I'm getting pressure from a new angle," he said suddenly. "It seems that I'm about to be investigated for income tax evasion."

She just stared at him. It was inconceivable that Clayton would do that. But Haralson might.

"Neither Miles nor Clay would do that," she said. "They're honorable men."

"Really?" he asked coldly. "Miles will be out of office in no time if he's behind that IRS probe."

She moved closer to him, looking up with a plea in her eyes. "Don't hurt him," she said softly. "He isn't what you think."

"What is he like?" he demanded. "You ought to

know, you married him, didn't you?" He caught her arm tightly and his dark eyes glittered down into hers.

She winced and he felt a twinge of guilt. His hand relaxed its steely grip and became involuntarily caressing. He looked into her eyes and felt himself caving in all over again. He missed her so badly that his heart ached.

"Did you love him?" he asked harshly.

She bit her lower lip until she tasted blood. Her eyes were huge, tragic.

"Well, did you?!" he demanded.

"At the time, yes!"

"You still love him, don't you? You love him enough to help him further any political scheme. There hasn't been another man in your life since the divorce until I came along and knocked down your defenses. Oh, yes," he said smugly, "we checked."

"We?" she asked uneasily.

"My father owns a tabloid," he reminded her. He smiled slowly. "There's nothing he can't find out. In fact," he added, "he's on the trail of something very big. If he finds it, your brother may be very sorry indeed that he took advantage of my unfortunate circumstances to feather his own political nest."

She felt her heart stop. Had Miles covered his tracks well enough over the years to throw off an investigative reporter for a tabloid? It didn't bear thinking about! "He wasn't taking advantage," she said defensively. "Clayton was doing what he thought best to protect his constituents."

"I'm one of his constituents," he reminded her. "He didn't show me any of that concern."

"You're supporting his major opponent, a Republican," she pointed out.

"And I'll support him even more, now," he returned. His face went even harder. "I'm going to see your brother thrown out of office in November. I promise you I am, no matter what it takes."

She felt chill bumps run down her arms. "Revenge, Kane?" she asked.

"Call it what you like." He felt regret like a wound. "Why didn't you tell me who you were?" he asked raggedly.

"It wouldn't have mattered," she replied. Her eyes were sad, haunted. "It was impossible from the beginning."

She sounded torn. Sympathy welled inside him. He reached out and touched her cheek, as lightly as a breath. She didn't pull back. Her soft, misty eyes sought his and gloried in their admiration of her beauty.

"Did you know what he planned to do?" he asked, the bitter anger gone from his voice.

Her mouth pulled into a sad smile. "What do you think?"

"You're too honest for your own good in some ways, and a little liar in others. It hurt me to send you away, Nikki. It hurt like hell."

The pain she felt was naked on her face. "It hurt me more," she whispered unsteadily. Her eyes went to Kane's companion, who was talking to another woman at the refreshment table. "I don't have a lover hidden away to console me."

His jaw tightened and he dropped his hand. "If you mean my companion, she's my sister-in-law. My youngest brother's wife. Her name is Charlotte."

"Oh." She hated the relief she felt. "What does your youngest brother do?"

He smiled. "He's a dentist."

"That's nice." She searched his eyes, feeling light-hearted because Kane hadn't been with another woman.

"Nice," he echoed. The smile faded and he looked at her with something like anguish. "Do you think I could touch another woman, now?" he asked harshly. "In fact, could you let another man touch you?"

Her teeth bit briefly into her lower lip as her face echoed the torment of his. "No," she said huskily. "Oh, no, I couldn't bear to!"

He looked hunted as his dark eyes roved the room and found no privacy within reach. "We can't talk here," he groaned.

"We can't talk anywhere," she said miserably, her blue eyes tragic as they met his. "My brother hates you."

"The feeling is mutual, I assure you." He caught her hand where it fell at her side and clasped it tightly in his, out of sight. It felt warm and comforting. "Are you . . . all right?" he asked quickly, searching her eyes.

She went very still. She knew what he was asking. She wanted to tell him. She should tell him. Her eyes darkened with pain and joy, mingled, as she realized how dangerous it would be right now to make such an admission.

"Yes. I'm . . . I'm fine," she lied.

"Did you tell your brother that you knew me?" he asked.

Her face contorted. "No," she said huskily. "Why didn't you tell the reporters?" she asked. "It would have hurt Clayton in the polls to have it known that his sister was involved with you, after all that publicity about your environmental problems."

"It would have hurt you more. I don't have to stoop that low to win battles." His free hand traced her cheek down to her small, rounded chin, and he smiled as he touched the faint hollow at the base of her long, graceful neck. "I won't sacrifice you. Not even to save myself."

The shock of what he was saying went all the way down to her toes. She stared at him with aching need, with a terrible sense of loss.

"Clayton won't stop. Neither will his campaign manager," she said miserably. "They'll carry the pollution charges all the way to the court of last resort if they have to."

"It was a nasty piece of work, wasn't it, Nikki?" he asked quietly. "I hated the photographs, the damage it did. It wasn't my fault, but I can't prove that."

"If you told about your accident, on the beach . . ."

He shook his head, smiling. "Even that wouldn't exonerate me. I told you. I won't sacrifice you."

"Why not? Everyone else has, at one time or another," she said bitterly. First her father, then Miles.

"Your brother is glaring at us."

"My brother is glaring at you," she corrected. "He likes me."

He smiled. "So do I."

"Kane, it's all so hopeless," she said suddenly.

The band was playing, and out of the corner of his eye, he could see Clayton glaring at them.

He tugged at Nikki's hand. "We're going to be burned at the stake before the evening's over," he said. "We might as well enjoy it. Come here."

He drew her into his arms, into his body, and wrapped her up tight as he began to move to the lazy two-step. Nikki shivered and tried to stop.

"I can't bear losing you again!" she ground out, clutching his lapel.

His big arm contracted, bringing her breasts right into his shirt front. "Relax," he said huskily, his voice deep and sultry in the space between them. "It's all right to let me see that you want me. I want you, too."

Her legs trembled as they brushed his. She couldn't remember feeling anything so explosive since their long, sweet night together. She shivered as she let it happen, and her body melted with little jerks into the warm strength and power of Kane's.

"Chemistry," he said deeply, feeling her tremble. "We mix like oxygen and hydrogen, bubbling where we touch. Blood rushing into empty spaces, churning, making heat and magic. Feel it, Nikki?" he asked, and his arm dropped just a fraction, rubbing her against the suddenly changed contours of him.

"Want to go out and sit in the car with me?" he asked in a strained voice.

She laughed softly. Her fingers curled into his chest under the dark evening jacket, against his spotless white silk shirt. She could feel the thick hair under it, the warmth. "No."

"No," he repeated. "It's unrealistic, isn't it? But we both remember, don't we?" He moved, deliberately letting her feel the power of his body as his cheek lay against hers and his breath feathered the hair at her ear. The music, the people, the world vanished in the heat of what they were sharing. Her eyes closed. She felt him in every cell of her aching body.

"Come closer," he said, his voice harsh.

She pressed into him, shivering.

"Move, Nikki," he challenged. His hand slid to her lower back, pulling, pressing.

"Kane," she protested once, the fragile sound lost in a gasp as she felt herself going helplessly on tiptoe to search for a more intimate contact.

His other hand clenched in the thick hair at her nape and he made a muted, hoarse sound at her ear.

"Oh, God," he groaned, shivering.

She couldn't stop. She knew they were being watched, because she couldn't stop what was happening. The sheer heat they were generating was becoming a throbbing pleasure that outweighed every single thought of modesty.

The sudden change of tempo in the music was a shock like ice on fire.

"I can't dance any more." Nikki's voice sounded choked, thick, as she looked up at Kane.

His face was faintly flushed, high on his cheekbones. His dark eyes were fierce as they searched her face. "We'll have to," he said huskily. "Would you like to look down and see why?"

She felt her cheeks color. "No need, thanks," she said huskily, and forced a smile. "I won't ever dance with you again, you know."

"I would very much like to take you into a closet or a bathroom or even a recess in the wall and make love to you until you fainted," he said roughly. "We belong together, Nikki."

"My brother, your father, Miles, the other candidate," she moaned. "It's too complicated."

He felt his body begin to unclench as he concentrated on the music to the exclusion of everything else. "What do you want to do, then?"

"I can't hurt my brother, Kane."

"But you can hurt me?"

"Do you think it isn't hurting me?" she whispered. And she couldn't even tell him the rest, that she was carrying his child under her heart. That hurt most of all.

She dropped her eyes to the swift, hard rise and fall of his chest. "You just want me. It will pass."

"Like hell it will," he said. "I was wrong to let you go in the first place. I got cold feet, but that's not the case any longer. I'm on fire for you, Nikki."

She stopped dancing. The memories were painful. "Let's sit down."

"Thank your lucky stars that what you feel isn't noticeable," he said with dry humor.

She cleared her throat, refusing to look at him as he escorted her off the floor and toward the refreshment table.

"It isn't over," he told her firmly, holding her eyes. "I'll find a way. I swear I will. I'm not going to let you go without a fight this time."

"You don't understand," she said weakly.

"No. You don't." He brought her hand to his mouth and kissed it hungrily. "What I want, I get. And I want you."

Clayton watched Kane walk back to the woman who'd come with him. He was fuming when he joined Nikki.

"Do you know who you were dancing with?" he asked furiously. "That was Kane Lombard!"

"I know who he is, Clay," she said.

"Then why did you dance with him?" Clayton demanded. "And like that, for God's sake, like lovers!"

She managed not to give herself away—barely. "You're imagining things. We were talking."

"That's a new word for it." He stared at her for a long moment, torn between anger and curiosity and concern. She looked drained. "Nikki . . . you know him, don't you?"

"We've met before," was all she volunteered.

He started to pursue it, but she looked exhausted.

Whatever she'd done, she was his sister and he loved her. He moved restlessly. "We'll talk about this later," he said.

She nodded, but didn't say a word.

CHAPTER
THIRTEEN

A
s Derrie slid her key into her apartment door, she felt a tap on her shoulder. She whipped around, dropping the key in the process, and found herself face to face with Cortez.

"You might try walking like normal people, so that you make noise," she pointed out.

"What? And blow my reputation?" He sounded whimsical. She chuckled.

"Just as well you didn't scream," he mused.

"Why?"

"Because I don't want to have to show my credentials to a police officer. I'm supposed to be on vacation, remember?" He bent and picked up the key she'd dropped. He handed it to her. "I need to talk to you."

She led him into her small apartment. There was a framed photo of Clayton, in color, smiling at her from the end table. She turned it face down. "Traitor," she muttered at it, and went to make coffee. She felt proud of herself for doing that until she realized that she would only put it back up later. She was such a wimp.

"Still mad at your boss, I gather?" he asked, leaning against the door frame with his hands in his pockets to watch her.

"Yes," she said, glancing back at him. "Except that he's my ex-boss now."

"I know. Haralson phoned me earlier to tell me that you'd deserted. He doesn't know why. But I think I do. That's why I'm here." His dark eyes narrowed. "Good thing he doesn't know that we're acquainted."

"I suppose so."

He moved to the table and sat down, letting her hand him a cup of black coffee. He waved away her offer of cream and sugar and waited for her to sit down.

"Why did you quit your job?" he asked.

She knew that it was more than idle curiosity. Cortez still worked for the government, and he knew more about Haralson than she did. She told him the events that had led up to her resignation, including the placement of a line of picketers at Kane Lombard's plant.

His dark eyes narrowed. "Did you say anything to Haralson about why you were leaving?"

"I did not," she assured him. "Nor did I tell Clayton or Nikki Seymour anything about Haralson, but I wanted to." Her eyes pinned him. "Is he doing something illegal to help Clayton get votes?"

"Derrie, I couldn't tell you anything even if I knew it," he added.

"I'm sorry. It's just that I feel like the rat that deserted the sinking ship," she said. She glowered at her coffee. "If Haralson does something outside the law, Clayton could get blamed for it. And that's not all." She hesitated, wondering how far she could trust him.

"Come on," he said. "You and I have no real secrets."

"There's some kind of skeleton in Nikki's closet," she said quietly. "Something that Haralson might know about, and use."

"I see." He didn't say anything else.

"Try to save Clayton, if you can," she said quietly.

"I'll do my best." He leaned back and stared at her. "I had lunch at the Calico Café."

That made her brighten. "Did you see Phoebe?"

"Yes, I saw Phoebe." He smiled. "She looks a lot like you."

"I think I told you when we first met that she's my sister's step-daughter. Her father was killed in the Middle East a few years ago. Remember the Marine barracks that was bombed during the Reagan administration?"

"Yes. I'm sorry."

"So were we. Phoebe comes to see me fairly often."

"She's very young," he said.

"She'll mature."

"She helped me find the toxic waste dump."

"And you reported it."

"Yes." His eyes were cold as he remembered the convenient timing of the discovery and the bright orange stencils. He smiled at Derrie to dispel his preoccupation. "I work for the government. I can't cover up a crime." He didn't add that he knew Lombard wasn't guilty.

She hesitated, then picked up the thread of their discussion. "Nikki doesn't like Haralson. But Clayton won't believe he's up to anything. At least, he won't admit it."

"What do you know about Townshend's past?"

She hesitated.

"Derrie," he said. "I understand loyalty. You're going to have to trust me."

"That's hard."

"I know."

His eyes were without guile, without secrets. They were very large and black, like coal. He didn't look away or fidget.

"There is something to do with his marriage to Nikki," she said finally. "I never knew what, because nobody ever talked about it." She hesitated. "Don't let him hurt Nikki."

"I'll do my best." His high-cheekboned face hardened. She got a glimpse of what it would be to have him for an enemy. The look in his eyes made her nervous, even though it was meant for someone else.

He finished his coffee and got up.

She did, too. "You aren't going to get in trouble for getting involved in this, are you?" she asked.

He chuckled. "I told you, I'm on an extended vacation."

"Pull the other one. You don't take vacations."

He studied her quietly. "Yes, but that's just between you and me. I'll do what I can for Nikki," he added quietly. He opened the door and turned, his dark eyes meeting hers. "I won't mention that I've been here."

"Cortez, what did you and Phoebe find at that waste site?"

"Toxic waste, of course. Goodnight."

Exasperating, she thought, that's what he was.

She locked the door behind him. Then she picked up the telephone and dialed Phoebe.

"Hi, Aunt Derrie! What's up?" Phoebe asked.

"Cortez was just here," she said bluntly. "Listen, what did you two do out at that waste site?"

Phoebe brushed back her long hair and felt a faint twinge of jealousy that surprised her. Why had Cortez gone to see her aunt? "Well, he pushed me down in the long grass and ripped off my blouse . . ." Phoebe began wickedly.

"Phoebe! This is serious," she added. "And strictly business, if that's what's unsettled you. Cortez is just a friend, although you mustn't tell anyone that I know him. Promise me."

"Of course, if it's important."

"He's the man I mentioned to you before," Derrie continued. "The one you didn't want to meet . . ."

"Oh! Really? Well!" She hesitated. "I was just briefly jealous when you mentioned he'd been to see you. Sorry. Isn't it silly to feel possessive about a man you've only just met? He's probably too old for me, and our backgrounds are so different, but he's just devastating."

Derrie chuckled. "I suppose he is. Now back to the waste dump. Think hard, dear, what did you see?"

"A lot of oil drums," Phoebe recalled. "With emblems on them."

"What kind of emblems?"

Phoebe hesitated, trying to force her mind back. "Well, they were Lombard logos," she said. "Painted bright orange."

"Thanks."

"Uh . . . Cortez didn't mention me, did he?" Phoebe added offhandedly.

Derrie grinned to herself. "In fact, he did," she returned. "He thinks you're very attractive."

"Oh." Phoebe's heart lifted. She smiled to herself. "Good night, Aunt Derrie."

There was a smile in the voice that replied, "Good night, my dear."

CHAPTER
FOURTEEN

Nikki was deeply worried about the way Clayton was acting. He hadn't been the same since the charity ball when he'd seen her dancing with Kane, and he was increasingly preoccupied.

The campaign was escalating. There were new headlines in the paper about the legal battle Kane Lombard was facing with the environmental people. He was probably not going to face criminal penalties, according to the ongoing stories in the newspaper, but his company was in violation of several statutes of the Hazardous Waste Management Act, not to mention the pollution control act overseen by the state people at the Department of Health and Environmental Control.

Derrie had telephoned Nikki earlier, before Clayton got home, with a discreet bit of information. She'd sworn Nikki to secrecy about the source of it first, then she'd gone on to relate what she'd heard about the markings on the oil drums containing Lombard waste. Why would anyone use bright orange stencils to label waste drums? The more Nikki thought about it, the more concerned she became. Something was shady about the whole business of that waste dumping.

Clayton noticed her frown over supper. "What's wrong?" he asked.

"Oh, nothing. I was just thinking about Derrie. She called to ask how I was," she added, not mentioning what Derrie had told her.

He looked up from his plate. "Is she all right? Liking the new job? Missing me, maybe?" he added teasingly.

"I'm sure she misses you," she agreed.

"I miss her, too." He stirred a couple of green beans around his plate. "I don't suppose you've noticed that Bett and I have gone our separate ways."

Her eyebrows lifted. She'd been too busy campaigning for him and worrying about her pregnancy to notice much. "You have?"

He nodded. "She's going to work for a Caribbean lobby, and probably a British one as well. We were good together while it lasted, but she decided that I was more expendable than this job opportunity. I can't blame her," he added quietly. "Bett overcame some pretty rough childhood obstacles to get where she is. She couldn't pass up a chance like this. And it wasn't as if we ever discussed marriage."

"I'm sorry."

He shrugged. He smiled at his sister. "Do you suppose Derrie might like to console me?"

"You know what she'd say to that kind of insult."

"Maybe if I phrased it right, she wouldn't throw me out. I never really saw Derrie until she left," he added seriously. "Do you know what I mean?"

"You didn't miss her until she was gone," she translated.

"It was more than missing her." He smiled. "I can't ask her to come back to work for me. But after the campaign, she might be persuaded to take a private interest in a poor, lonely congressman."

"Hmmm," she said noncommittally, and didn't mention that she knew Derrie yearned for news of Clayton.

He ate a green bean and his eyes went back to Nikki. She'd worked too hard lately, and it was telling on her. "You need another vacation," he remarked.

She toyed with her food. She wasn't eating much lately. "Not until after you're reelected," she teased.

"You've been subdued since you saw Lombard." He studied his fork. "We haven't really talked about him or the pretty woman that he had in tow at the charity ball the other night." He watched her surreptitiously, trying to draw her out. She'd previously refused to talk about Lombard whenever he'd broached the subject.

"She was his sister-in-law," she replied absently.

He put down his fork. "Nikki, you have to tell me what's going on. You said you'd met Lombard. When?"

She put down her own fork. "If you must know, he was injured and washed up on the beach the last time I went to Seabrook, after Spoleto. Chad and I looked after him."

"Chad Holman?"

"That's right."

He frowned. "Chad stayed at the beach house with both of you?"

Her eyes met his levelly. "No."

"My God, you didn't stay there alone with him?!"

"He had a concussion and couldn't remember who he was," she said stiffly. "I had no choice."

He whistled. "Oh, boy. Nikki, you've got more than your share of political savvy. Think about what the press would make of that."

"Nobody's going to find out. Which means that you'd just better not tell Haralson, do you hear me?" she threatened. "This is between you and me, Clayton."

He grimaced, but he agreed. "What about Lombard? Will he keep it quiet?" he asked with mocking laughter.

"Yes, he will," she said surprisingly.

"What makes you think so?"

"It wouldn't do him much good."

"I wouldn't be so sure. This isn't some great cosmopolitan city, it's Charleston, where reputations and family honor still mean something. That little bit of gossip could be very unpleasant for us, just before the election."

"I told you, it won't get out," she said quietly.

"No? What if Lombard is faced with a jail sentence for that dumping?"

She shook her head. "They'll fine him. That's all."

"Illegal dumping of toxic waste is a felony. CEOs and presidents of companies have gone to jail for it. Lombard could, too. Faced with years in prison, why wouldn't he throw you to the wolves?"

"I told you, it wouldn't help him," she pointed out.

"It would if he could claim that his accident prevented him from finding out the truth about what was going on back in Charleston. He might even claim you kept him in the dark deliberately."

"That employee of Lombard International's who hired Burke's is Burke's brother-in-law. He swore that Burke had a good record and that the media had just pounced on a couple of unfortunate incidents in the past. They interviewed him on television, don't you remember?"

"Nevertheless, Lombard can be charged for that," Clayton said with an attorney's knowledge of penalties. He'd studied environmental law. "The fact that he didn't check out Burke's is enough to make him liable under the environmental statutes. He's guilty of negligence, if nothing more criminal. The environmental people are very militant these days, and they should be. Pollution is easy to cause, hard to correct. Prevention is the only way we can ensure future supplies of clean water and air."

"But it's okay if we wipe out a species of owl to temporarily save loggers' jobs," she said deliberately.

"Don't change the subject." He got up from the table and started pacing.

"I have to win this election, Nikki."

"Why?" she asked bluntly. "Why do you *have* to win?"

He hesitated. Campaigns had always been important to him, of course, but only in the past two or three months had this one become the most important thing in his life.

"Because I want to go back to Washington, I suppose," he began. "I have programs I haven't been able to implement, unfinished projects to work on . . ."

"You weren't like this until John Haralson came down and started working for you."

"Haralson is a means to an end. Miles recommended him and Haralson has been more than helpful."

"Miles means well, but he walks around in a fog," she said. "He doesn't want to know how things are done, just that they get done. He's very naive in some ways, and altogether too trusting."

"You aren't still . . . ?"

She laughed gently. "Still grieving for him? Oh, no. I have scars, but I gave up hope long ago."

She shook her head sadly. "I'm tired of arguing with you about this, Clayton." And she was. Right now she was also nauseous. It was a good thing that her condition wouldn't show for a while. It gave her a little time to work and plan.

He dug in his pocket for his keys. He hesitated. "I might go and see Derrie."

"That would be interesting, considering that she's working for your major opponent in the campaign."

He laughed unamusedly. "Yes. I guess it would." He started out. Then he paused and looked back at Nikki. She looked fragile these days. "When you got sick, was it really Chad who looked after you?" She hesitated. "You'd better tell me. I see him occasionally."

"No," she confessed quietly. "It was Kane. He took me to another doctor and then took good care of me." She avoided his eyes. She might as well tell him all of it. "I love him, Clay."

He stared at her blankly. She hadn't said anything at the time, but she must have bitterly resented the way Clayton had treated Kane Lombard in the press. She didn't approve of polluters any more than he did, but she didn't seem to feel that Lombard was guilty. Clayton had been sure that he was. Now, with Nikki defending the man so loyally, he began to doubt.

Clayton felt guilty, and that made him mad. He didn't want her to be in love with his enemy's biggest campaign contributor. That reporter from the Lombard tabloid was still in Charleston and snooping around, and Haralson was getting pretty nervous. So many undercurrents were at work here, he thought. Too many.

"I need to win the election. I can't have the Lombards digging into our pasts."

"Clay, if they published everything they know, they

still wouldn't have a story,'' she said quietly. "Miles is a victim. It would hurt him if things came out, but perhaps not as much as you think.''

"What would Miles do? You know how privately insecure he is. He could consider suicide.''

She frowned. "I don't think he would. He's made of sturdier stuff than that. Listen, Haralson is keeping you on a very short rope,'' she said bluntly. "He's the one who's obsessed with getting Kane Lombard. Why don't you find out why?''

He frowned. "I know why. He's trying to help me.''

"Clay . . .''

"I'll be in later,'' he said, smiling easily. "Don't worry. It will be all right. So long as you don't have any more public tête-à-têtes with Lombard,'' he said firmly.

"All right.'' She sounded reluctant.

He started out the door and hesitated, glancing back at her. "Nikki, how does he feel about you?''

She lifted her eyes and smiled wistfully. "He'd let them put him in jail before he'd involve me in any scandal,'' she said frankly. "Neither of us can help how we feel, Clay. If it weren't for the campaign, I'd have gone to him long before now.''

Nikki had done so much for him, and he was asking her to give up what might be her one chance of happiness. He felt like a dog.

"I see,'' he murmured. "Well . . . I won't be late.''

Nikki was tempted to go and see Kane after she

watched the evening news. The environmental people had found another toxic waste dump on a deserted piece of farmland. Burke's wasn't implicated in this one, and there were no logos on the old oil drums full of toxic waste they found there.

The cleanup crew was putting the drums in over-packs—metal envelopes the purpose of which was to prevent further leaking. Hundreds of gallons of the un-identified toxic substances had already leaked out, how-ever, and leached into the soil. The extent of the damage would be found over time, but first the waste had to be analyzed and identified, and then cleanup operations would begin. The on-site EPA coordinator was hopping mad, promising retribution for this latest "midnight dump" and prosecution to the fullest extent of the law.

Along with the new report came a rehash of the site that Burke's disposal operation and Lombard Interna-tional were accused of having created. Charges were pending, and there had already been a red flag beside the company on the EPA list because of an earlier sew-age leak. The news report made that one sound deliber-ate now, which was, Nikki thought, sure to make Kane's defense even harder. Her eyes narrowed. How unfortu-nate that the company should change waste handlers on the heels of the leak, and that Burke's should be so easily traced to the site; how fortunate for the environ-mental people that the dumping site had been so quickly and easily located, and that the logos from Lombard International had been so very readable, indeed.

She got up from her chair and moved to the telephone with no doubt in her mind that it had been a frame. Why hadn't anybody else thought of it? Why hadn't Kane?

She knew the number of his beach house on Seabrook Island. He probably wouldn't be there, but even if he weren't his housekeeper might know how to reach him. She dialed the number. The phone rang once, twice, three times, four. She started to hang up when there was a click.

"Lombard."

It was Kane himself. The shock of his deep voice, unexpected, almost caused her to drop the receiver. She fumbled it back to her ear.

"Who is it?" came a curt demand.

"It's . . . Nikki."

"Well, hello. I've had my hands full, but I did try to call you. Three different times, in fact, but I gather that you're busy with the campaign trail. I didn't want to get you in trouble with your brother by leaving messages on the answering machine."

She felt warm all over hearing that. She'd thought he hadn't bothered to call. "That was nice."

There was a pause. "Are you all right?" he asked, and his voice was deep as velvet, soft.

Tears stung her eyes. She blinked them away. The concern was immediate, awesome.

She smiled. "I'm fine," she said. "How are you?"

"Notorious," he returned dryly. "I trust your brother is enjoying the public airing of my alleged sins in connection with this latest dumping scandal?"

"He isn't here."

There was another pause. "Dangerous, isn't it—calling the enemy just to talk?"

"Could I see you?" she asked.

"Sure. They're showing a file photo of my back on TV right now. Turn on channel . . ."

"Kane, don't joke. I've . . . found out something. Thought out something," she corrected. "I have to talk to you."

"Do you trust me, Nikki?"

"Of course," she said at once. "I don't have anything to say that could compromise you any more than you've already been compromised. But I think you should listen to me."

"Go ahead," he invited.

She started to speak and then thought better of it. If what she expected were true, the telephone could be bugged.

"Suppose I meet you somewhere?" she asked.

"Risky. Deliciously risky," he added softly.

"It's more risky to talk on the telephone. Someone might be listening."

"That isn't likely," Kane said, amused. "You've been watching too many spy thrillers."

"Indulge me," she teased.

"Okay. Where do you want to meet me?"

"Where I found you when you were hurt."

"When?"

She was getting the hang of this. It was almost fun. "I'm leaving now."

"I'll be waiting."

Nikki put on a pair of dark jeans and a white sweatshirt with a jeweled rose on the front. Her heart beat wildly as she ran out the front door and got into her car. The information she had might help Kane, but she had to admit to herself that the real reason she was going didn't have a lot to do with politics or toxic waste. She was going to see Kane because she loved him.

She found him sitting on a sand dune next to a clump of grasses, smoking a cigarette. It was his second.

"I didn't know that you smoked," Nikki said.

He turned and waited for her to join him. They were secluded here in the darkness near the water's edge and couldn't be seen from the neighbors' houses.

"I stopped smoking," he said. "Until a few weeks ago. I'm living on my nerves. Missing you hasn't helped," he added wryly.

She sat down beside him and wrapped her arms around herself. She could see him very well in the moonlit darkness. She felt the warmth and size of him and felt secure despite the hostility between them.

"Something is going on," she told him. "I seem to be in the middle of it, and so are you."

"Explain that," he replied.

Her eyes were soft on what she could see of his face. She wanted so badly to slide across his lap and let him hold her. It had been a long time since he'd held her so intimately at the charity ball; even longer since she'd lain in his arms and been loved by him.

"Someone is framing you."

"What?"

"Haven't you figured it out?" she asked. "The sewage leak may have been accidental. But the dumping came right on its heels, as if somebody knew you'd be on the EPA's hit list for a prior offense. The dumping site was found with ridiculous ease. The logo of your company was stenciled on those containers in bright orange fresh paint. Add it up."

His cigarette was hanging in mid-air. He'd been so upset by the charges and the publicity and the unrelenting persecution and missing Nikki that his ability to reason had been impaired. She was right. He hadn't appraised his situation at all. He'd been too busy defending it.

He shifted closer to her, and bent to talk more softly. "If your brother was behind it, would you tell me?"

"I love my brother," she said quietly. "I can tell you for a fact that he wouldn't sanction anything illegal—if he knew about it. He doesn't realize that he's become entangled in this mess, too, but I do. Someone is trying to destroy your company and your credibility. I get chills just thinking about what could happen. It's cold-blooded and shrewd, and there has to be a very intelligent purpose behind it. I just can't think what. But it has to be more than an underhanded way to help Clayton win the election, don't you see?"

He didn't. His eyes narrowed as he finished the cigarette and stabbed it out in the sand. "What good would it do to put me in front of the media as a target?"

"I don't know. But there must be some reason. Kane, I know you weren't responsible for what happened," she said stubbornly.

He searched what he could see of her features. His head turned then and he stared out over the bay, toward the ocean, his eyes unseeing in the moonlight that sparkled on the waves.

"Why don't you think I did it?" he asked.

She smiled. "You love the ocean, don't you?" she asked. "You're a naturalist through and through. People like that don't try to destroy the environment."

His head turned toward her. "You're perceptive."

"I suppose so, at times. What will you do?"

"I'm not sure yet."

"Kane, you won't go to jail, will you?" she asked worriedly.

"There's very little chance of that. Why?" he murmured dryly. "Are you afraid I might drag your name into it for an alibi?"

"I know you wouldn't," she said quietly. "But I would, if it meant a jail sentence for you otherwise."

His heart jumped. "And throw your brother's political career into the garbage?"

She didn't blink. "Yes."

He felt himself moving, without conscious volition. He reached for her, pulled her across him, riveted her to his powerful body. Then he kissed her, with the wind blowing in from the bay rippling her hair as the kiss rippled her mind.

He backed her into the sand and edged himself between her jean-clad legs, shifting her abruptly so that the core of her was suddenly pressed to his raging arousal.

She gasped, but he didn't slow down. If anything, he became more ardent. She felt his hands on her thighs, under her taut bottom, lifting and pulling her into his hips so that only the fabric kept his body from penetrating hers right there.

"That coarse sand would hurt your bare back," he said tightly, his breath moving against her lips as he spoke. "That's the only reason I haven't unzipped your jeans."

Her senses were dimmed, but returning. She shivered. The contact was so intimate that she was glad he couldn't see her face.

He moved sensually against her hips and she heard his breathing deepen. "Feel it?" he whispered.

She caught her breath and buried her face in his throat.

He felt that nosedive with a sudden curiosity that temporarily overcame his desire. His body stilled. "Nikki . . . what's wrong?"

She made a gesture with her head, and her burning face pressed closer.

"You'd better tell me, Nikki," he said slowly.

"Tell you what?"

"Don't prevaricate."

She drew her closed eyelids against the furious pulse

in his throat. "You know already," she whispered. "Don't you?"

"I've shocked you. Nikki, that night we spent together; the reason you were uncomfortable was because you were a virgin, wasn't it? You didn't actually know what sex was."

She laughed breathily. "Oh, I'd say I have a pretty good idea of what it is, now!"

He lifted his head and moved her so that he could see her flushed face in the moonlight. His own was curiously elated.

He smoothed back her disheveled hair with trembling hands. Then he began to unbutton his shirt, slowly, letting her see his chest come into view. There were beads of sweat clinging to the thick hairs that covered him to the collarbone, and his bronzed muscles were damp.

"You're sweating," she said, surprised, because it was cool on the beach.

"Of course I am. I want you," he replied simply.

He pulled her cheek to his bare chest and smoothed her hair, kissing her forehead while his big hands slid around her, under the sweatshirt, against her bare back. They unclipped her bra. He bent and brushed his open lips lightly against her mouth.

"It's been so long," she whispered unsteadily, pulling his hands over her breasts. She lay back and her eyes were hungry. "So long, Kane!"

"Forever," he agreed huskily.

His hands bunched the fabric of the sweatshirt and slid it up, with her bra, baring her breasts in the moonlight.

She shivered. It was erotic; the breeze on her bare breasts and his sultry gaze appreciating them.

"Arch your back, little one," he whispered. "Offer them to me."

She did, arching slowly, her breath coming rapidly through parted lips. She shivered in the breeze, and then his warm, moist mouth was covering her, his tongue moving softly over the hard nipples, making her body undulate while she moaned with helpless pleasure.

"Nikki," he whispered hoarsely. His hands fought snaps and a zipper while his mouth made a banquet of her. "God . . . Nikki!"

He pushed part of his jeans under her, to protect her back. Then he was touching her. She gave in at once, with remembered pleasure. Her legs parted for him and he worked witchcraft on her aching, helpless body. She clutched his mouth to her breast and shivered again and again as he brought jolts of white-hot pleasure that robbed her of breath and strength.

She couldn't bear it. The tension was making her frantic. She lifted to him, her hands clawing at his shoulders as she tried to make it happen, tried to make the tension snap, tried to help him . . . help him . . .

She cried out, desperate. His mouth quickly covered hers to silence the sharp little cries, and he laughed against it with arrogant, wicked delight.

Dimly, she heard the sound of another zipper moving.

The pressure of his mouth grew suddenly insistent. She was more than ready, but the hard thrust shocked her. He lifted her, and she felt him all the way inside her body.

She made a sound, a gasp, a hungry moan, and he felt her shudder endlessly with pleasure. He helped her, completed her. But when she relaxed and shivered, he was still aching for his own relief.

"Help me," he whispered into her lips. His body was faintly tremulous, like his voice. He was stimulated beyond stopping, beyond reason. He wanted the mindless pleasure she'd given him before. He wanted to feel it like silver knives through his powerful body.

"Yes," she whispered back, her voice loving as she lifted up to him. "My darling!"

He groaned. His big hands cradled her hips. He kissed her ardently and lifted, thrust, with tender, smooth motions. He was desperate for her, but the tenderness he felt made him careful, made him considerate. And the soft, subtle movements intensified the monstrous pleasure inside him.

"I've never done it like this," he whispered huskily. "I've never felt it like this. I can't be tender enough, I can't touch you . . . inside . . . deeply enough," he choked. His hands contracted bruisingly and he groaned in hoarse anguish as he pushed as deep as he could and felt himself going off the edge of the world. "Nikki, make . . . it . . . happen . . . to . . . me!" he choked.

He felt the white-hot throb all around him and he kissed her mouth, his body clenching fiercely as he felt a blaze hotter than the sun burst inside him.

She followed him, blind with the incredible ecstasy he gave her. She shivered as she began to fall to earth again, and her arms cradled him, her tired eyes closed, smiling, glorying in her part in his downfall. She thought of the child they'd already created together. The joy she felt was almost unbearable. He was hers. He belonged to her.

When the shuddering stopped at last, he fought for breath, enveloping her against his broad, hair-roughened chest while he came back to the world.

She kissed his bare shoulder with soft, tender lips and curled herself into his warm body. Her hand rested over his flat stomach possessively. "If you ever do that to another woman," she said breathlessly, "I'll pitch you into the nearest swamp."

He chuckled, winded. "I wouldn't have the energy."

He turned and began to kiss her, with breathless tenderness.

"You didn't use anything," she pointed out demurely.

"Yes. I know." He pulled her cheek to his chest and pressed it there, over the dull, heavy throb of his heart. "I know we're in a hell of a situation, and that it's a little late to ask you how you feel about it. But I lost my little boy, and I miss him like hell." He hesitated uncharacteristically. His big hand pressed softly against her hair, holding her closer. "Nikki," he whispered, and his voice was unsteady, "would you give me a baby?"

CHAPTER
FIFTEEN

Nikki could have danced on the beach naked. She could hardly believe he'd actually asked her that.

"You love kids," he continued persuasively. "So do I. There are hundreds of other things we have in common. The baby would be the foremost thing."

"It's happening so fast," she began dizzily.

"Not fast enough, to suit me," he corrected. He looked down at her and his big hand pressed down gently on her belly. "I didn't do a lot to prevent it the first time. I knew then, but I had a momentary lapse and backstepped. By the time I came to my senses, I knew who your brother was and I blew up. You can't know how I've regretted it."

"I should have been honest with you," she said.

"We both should have been honest. But I'm digressing. I'm sure I read somewhere that virgins always get pregnant right away,'' he teased.

She hit his chest. ''I am not going to have a child out of wedlock in Charleston!''

''We'll get married,'' he said. ''The sooner the better, in fact.''

She gasped. ''My brother would kill you before he'd let me marry you!''

''Not when we tell him you're pregnant,'' he said smugly, and heard her catch her breath. ''Well, even if it's not true now, it will be soon enough. I hope you like short engagements, because we can be married in three days. And we will be,'' he added when she looked inclined to argue. ''I don't know what's going on around here and I don't give a damn, but you're going to live with me while we're finding out.''

''I have to go home!''

''Why?''

The feel of his body against hers made her warm and cozy. She lay down and sighed as he absorbed her weight. ''Because I can't be underhanded. I'm not ashamed of the way I feel about you.''

He was still. His hand smoothed at the nape of her neck. ''And how is that?''

''Deeply affectionate. Passionately desirious. I'd think up more adjectives, but I'm sleepy.''

''Making love is tiring,'' he whispered, and his voice smiled. ''You won't come home with me?''

''I want to. Oh, I want to! But let's do it properly,''

she pleaded. "If you're sure you want to marry me, that is."

He lifted an eyebrow. "I'm sure, all right," he said solemnly. "The baby would be a nice consequence, but it's my backbone I'm thinking of mostly."

"Your what?"

"My backbone," he murmured with deep satisfaction. "I like having it melt and blaze up like fireworks. Couldn't you tell how much pleasure you gave me, or is it still too new to you?" She looked puzzled and he laughed, whispering in her ear.

"Oh," she gasped.

"You won't be so easily shocked a few weeks from now," he whispered. "In fact, there's every possibility that you'll be shocking me."

"I wouldn't bet on it." Her fingers curled into his chest. She stared across it at the movements of the ocean. It was all so sudden. She felt as if she had emotional whiplash.

His fingers traced over her face, down to her mouth. "I've grieved for you, Nikki, night and day. It knocked me for a loop when I found out who you were, but that didn't stop the longing. Seeing you at the charity ball was the most painful thing that's happened to me in recent months."

"You really tried to call me?" she asked.

"Yes. After the charity ball. I know your brother would like to see me in prison. I have no love for him, either. I didn't want to put you in the middle, put you in the position of having to choose between us. But I can't give you up, Nikki. I won't.''

"And this has complicated things, hasn't it?'' she murmured.

"This was delicious,'' he murmured deeply. "Have you any idea what it feels like for me when I have you, to feel you having me, wanting me?''

"Oh, yes,'' she said, her eyes bright. She lifted her mouth to his and kissed him softly. Her body sought the length of his and pressed there gently, feeling him wanting her. "You're very big,'' she whispered daringly, and heard him groan as he answered the kiss. It was a long time before he lifted his head.

"You have to go home,'' he groaned.

"You don't want me to go home,'' she said. She nuzzled close and shut her eyes, thinking about their baby. Her fingers traced the hair on his chest and tangled there. "Do you really want a baby with me, Kane?'' she asked softly.

"More than anything,'' he confessed. His hand tightened on her head.

He rolled over and she opened her arms, cradling him against her. Perhaps grief was making him vulnerable, but she loved him. And given time, he might admit to loving her, particularly if there were a child. It was evident that he wanted her obsessively, and he was certainly fond of her.

"I'm so glad you said that.'' She reached up and kissed him with slow tenderness. "You see, Kane . . .

we can tell Clayton I'm pregnant and it won't be a lie. I really am pregnant,'' she whispered.

He searched her eyes. His hand pressed back the strands of dark hair that clung to her cheeks.

He made a rough sound in his throat. ''What?''

''I'm carrying your child,'' she whispered, smiling at his expression.

''You mean . . . really . . . that first time, that first night . . . ?''

She laughed. ''Yes.''

His face brightened. He chuckled with deep pleasure and his hand flattened over her stomach, pressing there possessively.

''It's useless to ask how you feel about it,'' she mused dryly.

''I'll buy a baseball bat and a glove tomorrow. Whatever we get, boy or girl, is going to love baseball as much as I do. Genes, you see.''

She laughed and pulled him close, kissing him with pure adoration. ''I love you so,'' she whispered shakily.

He wrapped her up against him, closing his eyes. ''My Nikki, my very own,'' he whispered back. ''I adore you!''

After a minute, he felt her shiver and realized that her skin was cool.

''We can't let you catch another chill, my darling,'' he said quietly. ''This was irresponsible. But it had been too long.''

''For me, too,'' she agreed. ''I don't have any regrets, and I won't believe that you do, even if you swear it.''

He laughed. ''I regret nothing.''

He helped her dress and then put his own clothes back on.

He got to his feet reluctantly and helped her up. As he held her in front of him, his eyes were watchful and tender. ''You look different. Radiant.''

She searched his eyes. ''You meant it? About wanting to get married, not minding about the baby?''

''I meant every word,'' he said softly. His eyes were meltingly tender, and he seemed suddenly awed as he looked at her. ''I may die of happiness any minute.''

''Please don't.'' She smiled, her eyes misty with feeling, with delight. ''Will you call me tomorrow?''

''What a silly question. Come home with me. We'll lie naked in each other's arms until morning, even if that's all we can do.''

''I want to. But I have to go home.'' She nuzzled her face against his chest. He was hers. She looked up and possession was written on her face. ''You belong to me now.''

''I know.''

He caught her hand and lifted it, palm up, to his lips. ''Dream of what we did. And be careful. Be very careful. You're my life now, Nikki.''

She reached up to kiss him, gently. ''I'll be all right.''

''I'll be in touch very soon, after I've made all the arrangements. Wait before you tell your brother. I'd rather he heard it from both of us.''

She nodded. "So would I. Good night."

He walked back toward the beach, where he'd left the small motor launch that he'd piloted over to see Nikki. She watched him go, her body tingling, her heart full. Life was very good, she thought. She couldn't regret what had happened. She was a woman now, and soon she'd be a wife; Kane Lombard's wife. Her feet hardly touched the ground all the way back up to the beach house.

The telephone call early the next morning was so unexpected that at first she simply held on to the receiver and stared blindly at the wall.

"What did you say?" she asked shortly.

"I said, I've got some very racy photos of you and Lombard last night on the beach. Hot stuff, lady. Suppose I turn them over to the tabloids?"

"Kane Lombard's father owns a tabloid," she said angrily.

"Not the only one. He doesn't mind slandering other people. But how is he going to like having his own son on the front page of somebody else's tabloid? How is your brother going to like having you on the cover of one? Sister of congressional candidate makes out with her brother's political enemy on the beach," he rattled off. "What a headline!"

She slid down the wall to the floor. That kind of photograph would finish Clayton in Charleston. She couldn't think straight for the fear. "What do you want?'' she asked. If the telephone was bugged by any of Clayton's enemies, she was finished. Her whole life flashed before her eyes.

"I want you to stay away from Lombard," he said. "And I want you to keep your mouth shut about why."

"But . . . !"

"If you go near Lombard, those pix go straight to the papers, with four-column cutlines. And we'll be watching."

The line went dead. If only she'd had the presence of mind to tape it! She hadn't dreamed that anyone had followed her to the island. Now, when it was too late, she realized how careless she'd been.

She buried her face in her hands. This couldn't be happening! Kane wanted to marry her. What would he think when she wouldn't talk to him, or see him? What if he caused a scene and these people were hiding outside with cameras to capture it all on film? Her heart stopped. It would be on all the news shows. Irate lover attacks congressional candidate's sister. Publicity. Bad publicity. Clayton would be knocked out at the polls with such sordid goings-on. And she was pregnant.

She didn't know what to do.

Derrie answered the knock on her door dressed in a beige, gold and white caftan with her hair trailing down her back. She was ready for an early night, and not expecting company. She opened the door quickly.

Clayton Seymour stood there. Her heart skipped wildly.

The sight of her made Clayton stop in his tracks and just stare. He'd rarely ever seen Derrie like this. For some reason, he found it much more affecting than he should have. He smiled lazily. "Well, hello. Have you missed me?"

"Not particularly," she said. Her legs were trembling, but she managed to keep him from seeing.

He sighed. "Ah, well. Can I come in?"

She stood aside and let him in, closing the door behind him. She turned. "What do you want, Clay?"

He shrugged. He jammed his hands deep in his pockets. "I thought we might take in a movie."

She shook her head. "I don't think that would be wise considering the circumstances."

"You've done some wonderful things for Hewett," he tried again. "I like your promotional ideas. They're solid without being sensational."

She glared at him. "How's Bett?" she asked.

He grimaced. This wasn't going to sound good. "She went back to D.C. to work for some lobbying groups. It would be a conflict of interest if I continued to see her. We've broken up."

"Oh. So that's it." She sounded resigned.

"Bett is a hell of a woman, and I'll always be fond of her. But it was no great love affair, and putting an end to it was her idea."

Belatedly, he realized that everything he said made it worse, and he groaned.

She didn't say a word. He could see in her face that she was wary of his reasons for being here. And beyond that, he could see the helpless attraction she felt for him.

Derrie had loved him. Why hadn't he realized it before?

"I've been unfair to you," he said. His blue eyes searched hers. "I took you for granted, refused to listen to you, and finally fired you. And do you know what, Derrie?" He laughed bitterly. "The girl I hired to replace you has to ask me about every decision she makes. She has no self-confidence at all."

"Why didn't you let Bett run the office for you instead of becoming a lobbyist?" she asked. "She'd have been a natural."

"Bett didn't want to work for me. She was ambitious and she decided that I wouldn't fit into her life anymore." He studied her. "Don't you miss me?"

"I miss working for you, but I'm very challenged with Sam. He's a good boss." She forced a smile. "And we're going to beat your socks off at the polls in November."

His eyebrows levered up. "You've got it to do," he replied with a twinkle in his eyes. "I'm no lost cause."

Keep Haralson on and I can guarantee that you will be, she thought, but she didn't say it.

He studied her with a lifted eyebrow. "Derrie, did you ever wonder how it would feel to sleep with me?"

She shrugged. "Once or twice," she confessed.

His eyes narrowed and he smiled. "You're embarrassed. Haven't you ever done it?"

She hated that superior attitude. "If you're thinking that I'm as pure as the driven snow, and that I've spent my life waiting for you to fulfill all my virginal dreams, you've got the wrong woman," she said quietly.

He was surprised, and it showed.

"Were you in love?" he asked.

"At the time, I was trying to forget that I was in love," she said enigmatically. "He was kind, when I needed kindness, and I have no regrets whatsoever."

"And there were no consequences?" he asked.

"Of course not," she said.

His eyes slid down the caftan, lingering where her breasts thrust against it. Her silky hair flowed like waves of gold around her shoulders. She wasn't a beautiful girl, but she was attractive. She was sexy, he decided finally. And why he should have expected her to sit home alone when he'd been sampling bedrooms was absurd. He smiled at his own vain misconceptions about Derrie. It amazed him that he'd never thought about her private life before.

"Look, Derrie, I need to talk business. You've never liked Haralson," he said suddenly. "You wouldn't tell me why. But now I need to know."

She moved away from him toward the living room. "It's nothing that you won't find out eventually," she said, honoring her promise to Cortez to say nothing.

He followed her in and sat down on the couch across

from her easy chair. His face was troubled. "What you aren't telling me could cost me the election."

She turned. "Would that bother me, when I work for your closest competitor?" she asked mischievously.

He pursed his lips, smiling faintly. "You could come back."

"I might think about it. But not until after the election," she said smugly. "I won't fraternize with the enemy."

He lifted an eyebrow. "All right. After the election."

She laughed with delight. "We'll see."

He smiled wickedly. "Finally something to look forward to. You're sure you won't talk to me about Haralson?" he added.

She grimaced. "I wish I could." Her eyes searched his. Her loyalties were really divided now. She couldn't help him without hurting Sam, but she didn't want him to suffer, either. "Don't trust him very far. Will that do?"

"It will help." He turned toward the door, paused and turned back, surveying her. "I guess I've let Haralson run things as he wanted for long enough. I'm going to start paying more attention to him and see if he's really as bad as you and Nikki seem to think."

"I can't possibly agree with you, because I work for the opposition," she pointed out, although inwardly she was delighted to see him coming to his senses.

"So I noticed."

She pursed her lips. "Remember who helped me right into his political lap."

"How could I forget?" he groaned, smiling. He studied her for a long moment. "You know," he paused, "I've just realized why the office is so empty without you."

"Why?"

"I'll tell you," he promised, going out the door. He stuck his head back in. "*After* the election!"

CHAPTER
SIXTEEN

Nikki avoided calling Kane all morning. She wasn't a coward. If Clayton hadn't been fighting for his political life, she'd have invited her faceless tormenter to publish those photographs and she'd have taken the consequences. But she didn't have the right to cost Clayton everything he'd worked for.

The question foremost in her mind was who was behind it. She didn't trust Haralson. She couldn't figure out why he'd want to cost Clayton the election. Even if she didn't approve of his tactics, he had only tried to further Clayton's—and his own—career. It could be someone from the Hewett camp, but Derrie would have told her anything she knew.

She avoided answering the telephone every time it rang. But that afternoon it started and refused to stop. She put on the answering machine. That was worse.

"Answer me, Nikki," Kane growled when the tape started. "I know you're there. What the hell is wrong with you? Have you had second thoughts? Changed your mind?"

She bit her lip. In order to save Clayton, she was going to have to lie. There was no other way.

She picked up the receiver and fought down nausea. "Kane, I have had second thoughts," she said in a dull, defeated tone. "I'm sorry. I really can't do this to Clayton."

"Your brother has his own life to live," he pointed out. "Nikki, we're going to have a baby!"

"Well, we . . . I might not be, after all," she stammered, clutching the receiver. "Tests can be misread . . ."

There was a shocked pause. The receiver clicked down in her ear. So much, she thought, for victories.

Clayton noticed Nikki's pallor, but he didn't understand what had caused it. She was secretive, tense.

"Are you all right?" he asked.

"Sure. You never told me if you saw Derrie. How was she?" she returned.

He chuckled. "Spitting fire. But I think she may come back after the election." He paused thoughtfully. "Odd that I never really noticed how alike we are, how well we get along."

Nikki brightened at the look on his face. "Yes, I always thought so," she confessed.

"She's full of surprises, our Derrie." His smile faded and he began to look worried. "I wish I had time to explore them all. But there's a campaign waiting to be won and a few problems to solve," he said, facing his sister.

His eyes narrowed. "I've had time to do some serious thinking about Haralson. You and Derrie seem so against him and although he was instrumental in exposing Kane Lombard's toxic waste dump, his methods may not have been the most ethically sound. I shouldn't have ignored that and I'm willing to admit I made a mistake. I've decided to send him back to Washington."

She looked relieved. "I'm glad. You're doing the right thing."

"I suppose so. But he was a hell of a campaign manager. I don't know who's going to replace him."

"Me."

His eyebrows lifted. He chuckled. "You'd be a natural! But I need you to make nice speeches to women's club and organize carpools," he said, tongue-in-cheek. "Nikki, your natural talents would be wasted ordering a bunch of campaign workers around. You've already had to give up your sculpting for the campaign. This would be too much. I'll manage. I already have a couple of people in mind."

She pursed her lips and stared at him. "Just wait. One day I'll run for office myself. Maybe for yours."

"I tremble at the thought of facing you in the political arena," he murmured affectionately.

Nikki watched him move toward the door. "Where are you going?"

"To give Haralson his walking papers, of course," he returned.

After he left, Nikki thought about how she had hurt Kane. That made her angry. If only she could find some way to protect Clayton and still be free to marry Kane!

Mrs. Yardley knocked on Kane's office door and peeked around it. "It's Mr. Jurkins," she said. "He'd like a word with you, if it's convenient."

"It's convenient," he said shortly. "Send him in."

Jurkins was wearing a two-year-old suit with scuffed shoes. Kane stared at him for a long moment. If he'd suspected Jurkins of taking kickbacks to change solid waste companies, it was hardly evident.

"Yes, Jurkins? What can I do for you?" he asked with faint impatience.

"I keep hearing gossip," the other man said slowly. He was twisting a paperclip in his nervous fingers. "I just would like to know if they plan to try to put you in jail over the waste dumping, sir."

"Bob Wilson says that it's unlikely," Kane replied. He perched himself on the edge of his desk. "Probably we'll be fined. But that sewage leak didn't do us any favors with the state and federal environmental people."

"Yes, I know, and that's my fault. That leak was a legitimate accident, Mr. Lombard," Jurkins said earnestly. "I wouldn't do anything illegal. I mean I wouldn't have. I have a little girl, six years old," he stammered. "She has leukemia. I can take her to St. Jude's for treatment, you see, and they don't charge me for that. But there's the medicine and she has to see doctors locally and the insurance I had at my old job ran out. She isn't covered under the insurance here. It's that pre-existing conditions clause," he added apologetically.

"But that isn't why I came."

Kane lifted a questioning eyebrow. Jurkins was almost shaking. "Sit down, Jurkins," he said, gesturing to a chair.

Jurkins looked oddly thin and frail in the big leather armchair. He was still twisting the paperclip. "I hope you won't get in too much trouble. My brother-in-law isn't an outlaw. Truly he isn't."

"So you keep saying. At least they aren't going to shut us down," Kane returned. He was waiting. Waiting.

Jurkins hesitated. He looked up and opened his mouth. He wanted to speak. But he couldn't make the words come out. He got to his feet again, jerkily, red-faced.

"I'll, uh, get back to work now, sir," he said. His voice was unsteady. So was the smile. "I hope it works out."

"So do I."

Kane sat on the edge of the desk when the man had gone and his mind kept going over the odd conversation. Something was definitely wrong there. Jurkins was in-

301

volved in this somehow and he was afraid to tell what he knew. He pushed the intercom button. "Get me Bob Wilson," he said.

"Yes, sir," came the quick reply.

Haralson stared at Clayton Seymour as if he couldn't believe his own ears.

"You want me to leave?" he asked the other man. "Are you serious?"

"I'm afraid so. I'm going to replace you."

Haralson, always so cordial and kind, suddenly turned nasty. He sat up in the chair, holding his cigar between his cold fingers, and reached into his desk drawer. "No, you aren't. Want to know why?"

"Do tell me," Clayton invited with smiling, cool confidence.

He was unprepared. Totally unprepared. Haralson drew a photograph, an eight-by-ten glossy, out of the drawer and tossed it across the desk to Clayton.

"If you want to see that on the front page of every tabloid in the country, fire me."

Clayton gasped. It wasn't blatant, for a photograph of that sort, but it made innuendoes that were unmistakable. That was Kane Lombard—and Nikki!

"I've got several other pictures on that same order. I'm sure you'll see things my way," Haralson said pleasantly. "I'm going to get you back in office, of course, that's a by-product. But my main purpose is to bury Lombard. I don't suppose you know that he cost my father his Senate seat?''

Clayton was stunned.

''That's right,'' Haralson continued. ''Lombard found out that my father was having an affair with another senator's wife and he told his family and they told the whole damned world! I was in my last year of school when it happened, but I never forgot. I never could forget! We lived in a small town in Texas, and that sleazy tabloid ran the story week after week after week! My mother killed herself over it, and I swore I'd make Lombard and his family pay! It's all been a means to an end. I worked hard for Miles Townshend so that I'd have a foot in the door in Washington. When Lombard opened his plant I maneuvered myself into the perfect position of working for a candidate who was situated right in Charleston, who could ruin Lombard, with a little help from me.''

''You've had this in mind all along,'' Clayton said, aghast. ''It must have taken . . .''

''Months,'' Haralson agreed coolly. ''Yes. It's taken months of planning. I haven't forgotten a single detail, and it's all been toward one end, to bring down Lombard. He'll go to jail. I promise you he will, because you're going to keep the pressure on him in the media until the public demands it.''

''You think I'll play along just because of one photograph?'' he said, disguising his fear. ''My sister loves Lombard, and it's mutual.''

Haralson had an ace left. He played it. "That's not all I have, that little photograph," he said. "The man who took those photos is a private detective. I've had him follow Sanders, the *Weekly Voice* reporter, down to Aiken, to the Secretary of the Interior's home town. He found out that Miles Townshend never touched a girl all the way through school, college included. And when a rumor about his sexual preference started traveling, when he was first elected to the Senate, he rushed into marriage with your sister to scotch the gossip. I know why."

"What do you know, exactly?" Clayton asked with a feeling of utter dread.

"The best kept secret in Washington: that Townshend is gay."

Clayton couldn't reply. He didn't dare say a word. He looked down at the photo instead, torn between fear of exposure for Nikki and Miles and the urge to strangle Haralson where he stood.

"Take that with you," Haralson invited. "I still have the negatives. Your sister will have no opportunity to make that monster, Lombard, happy. He may love her, but he'll never have her. I had my detective call and warn her that those photographs would go on public display if she went near Lombard. He's going to pay and keep on paying until he's as dead as my mother is!"

Clayton wandered back to his office. He'd been an utter fool. How could he have missed the signs? Haralson had taken him for a hell of a ride, and now he had Nikki and even Miles on the run. Clayton didn't know what to do. He stared at the photograph with distaste. Looking at it, there was no doubt that Nikki loved the man. So she knew that these had been taken. That would explain why she had looked so strained and upset this morning.

The election was barely a month away. Haralson had to have something else up his sleeve. He was going to publish those photos anyway. He'd probably wait until the last possible minute and then let fly. The scandal would destroy Nikki socially. It would ruin Clayton's chances for reelection.

He only knew of one way to stop Haralson. He got in his car and drove out to Seabrook, to the Lombard beach house.

If Kane Lombard was shocked to find Clayton Seymour standing on his doorstep, he hid it quickly. He had a glass of scotch and ice in one big hand. His eyebrow jerked as he stood aside to let the shorter man enter.

The beach house was luxurious, Clayton thought, and right on the marina. It must have cost a fortune.

"Is this a social call?" Kane drawled.

"Thank your lucky stars that I'm not homicidal," Clayton returned. He glanced around. "Are you alone?"

Kane nodded. "What is it?"

"I think you'd better have a look at this." He took the photograph from the inside of his suit jacket and tossed it on the coffee table.

Kane's eyes darkened, narrowed. He cursed roundly and violently.

"Who?" he demanded, his eyes promising retribution.

"My reelection campaign manager, John Haralson," Clayton said heavily. "I went in to fire him this morning and he handed me that." He glared at Kane. "I could kill you for doing this to Nikki."

"I made love to Nikki," he returned solemnly. "Please notice the wording. I didn't seduce her, have sex with her, or any number of less discreet euphemisms. I made love to her."

Clayton relaxed a little. Not much. He was still furious. "Did it have to be on the beach?"

"I couldn't make it to the house," came the rueful reply. The smile faded quickly though. "Has Nikki seen this?" he asked suddenly.

"I don't know, but she's been told that photographs had been taken," he said. "She was warned not to go near you or they'd be published."

Kane smiled with relief. "So that was all it was. Thank God." Kane relaxed.

"Haven't you talked to her?"

"I've tried to do nothing else," the other man said heavily. "She said it was all a mistake, and I believed she meant it." His head lifted. "But now I'm going to marry her. If you don't like it, that's tough," he added without blinking, his face hard and relentless.

"At least you're honorable enough to stand by her," Clayton said stiffly.

"Stand by her, hell. I love her! She's carrying my child."

Clayton gaped at him. He hadn't expected that answer. "She's what?!"

"She hadn't told you?"

"No." He hesitated. So many things were beginning to become clear. "I suppose she thought I'd go through the roof. I might have, too. But not now. I can picture Nikki with a baby." He smiled in spite of himself. Then he looked up. "You said you loved her."

"I loved her the day I met her," came the grim reply. "I couldn't stop. I tried, though." Kane took a sip of the scotch. His head lifted and he glared at the other man. "You're a damned blackguard of a politician. You planted that waste at the dump site deliberately and led the media to it."

"No, I didn't," Clayton said honestly. "But I very much think Haralson might have."

"I'm getting that idea myself," Kane said slowly, remembering Jurkins' odd comments.

"I haven't had time to do much investigating, but I know why Haralson is after you, and it isn't for any political reason." As he recounted the long-ago episode to Kane, Clayton noticed his expression change from shocked disbelief to anger.

Kane whistled. "I must have been preoccupied because I never connected it. That was past history." He looked up and frowned. "But why are you here?"

Clayton didn't even blink as he replied. "Because I can't let him blackmail Nikki—or me, for that matter.

He's rattling one more skeleton in my closet and I can't fight him alone.''

''Who else is Haralson blackmailing?''

''My ex-brother-in-law.''

''Miles Townshend is gay, isn't he?'' Kane asked quietly, having long since worked that out for himself.

Clayton hesitated, but only for an instant. Lombard, like it or not, was going to be family. ''Yes,'' he replied.

Kane was silent for a long time. ''He has a broad base of support in Washington. Even his political enemies respect and like him. But it would be a pity to have him blackmailed for something he can't help.'' He glanced at Clayton. ''So Haralson knows.''

He nodded.

Kane looked down at the photo of himself and Nikki again. He grimaced. ''Nikki isn't going to like this, but I only know of one way to stop a blackmailer short of killing him.'' He picked up the photo with a regretful smile. ''I think you know what has to be done.''

''That's why I came.'' He got to his feet. ''You'd better marry her soon.''

Kane reached in a drawer and produced a document. ''That is a marriage license. You can come to the wedding, but after that, we will not expect you to be a regular visitor. Especially until after the election— which my candidate is going to win.''

Clayton found himself grinning. ''You bastard.''

Kane grinned back. ''It does take one to know one,'' he pointed out.

"You're going to allow that to be published?" he nodded toward the photograph.

"Can you think of another way?"

"Not off the top of my head."

"Then the sooner, the better. I'll fax it to my father right now. There should still be time to get it into this week's edition. Don't tell Nikki."

Clayton glanced at him. "You'd better make her happy."

"That's a foregone conclusion. She loves me," he added with quiet pleasure.

"Does she know how you feel?"

"Guess."

He looked back at Kane. "Like hell your candidate is going to win," he tossed over his shoulder.

Deep laughter followed him into the yard.

Secretary of the Interior Miles Townshend was fielding questions from reporters after a news conference. He'd supported the president verbally, and publicly, on a non-environmental issue, on the vote to assist United Nations troops in the Serbia-Bosnia hostilities. He cracked a few jokes and defused the grilling in no time. He had a gift for handling the press that amazed and delighted him.

A telephone call was waiting for him when he got back to his office. He motioned his secretary to put it through.

"Great timing, that!" Haralson laughed curtly when

he heard Miles's voice. "I caught you coming in the door, I guess?"

"Yes." Miles was curious, and sounded as if he were.

"Listen, I'm turning some photos of your ex-wife over to the press."

Miles went silent. "What sort of photos?"

"Pictures of her with Kane Lombard in a, shall we say, compromising position." He laughed. "I don't expect you to say a word," he added coldly. "I know what you are. Unless you want the media all over you, closet queen, you'd better do as I say."

Miles felt a shock like a gunshot. He stared at the window and saw a tiny spot where the painter had missed with his brush. He focused on it with a roughly beating heart and slowly his mind began to work again. What he feared most in the world had finally happened. And now that it had, all he felt was a sense of sudden relief. Did it really matter if people knew? It was a new age, a new world. Probably it was an open secret on the Hill anyway, and who cared? It was time he started believing in the basic goodness of people again. The people who cared about him would still care, no matter what secrets he harbored about his sexual preferences. And it wouldn't affect his life unless he let it. He was strong enough to take the occasional underhanded swipe.

He started laughing. He started and couldn't stop.

Haralson was shocked. He clenched the receiver in

his hand. "I'll tell the whole damned world about you!" Haralson threatened.

The laughter got worse. Vaguely, Miles was aware of cursing and the slam of the telephone receiver. There was no hope that Haralson had given up. But perhaps Miles had given him something to think about.

But when he got hold of himself, he remembered what Haralson had said about some compromising photos of Nikki. He really couldn't allow her to be hurt by his own blackmailer. He owed her a warning.

He had his secretary dial Nikki. But the number he had wasn't the right one. It had been changed. He'd have to call Clay. He hoped there was enough time to save Nikki from whatever diabolical fate Haralson had planned for her.

Slowly, he put down the receiver. No. This time a casual telephone call wouldn't do. He owed Nikki more than secondhand information. He thought for a minute, then he buzzed his secretary. "Get me on the next flight to Charleston," he said.

"But Mr. Secretary, you've got a committee meeting . . ."

"Call and explain that I have an emergency in my district. Tell them," he added, "that it's a family emergency."

"Yes, sir."

He hung up and reached for his attaché case. If he hurried, he might be in time to avert a disaster for Nikki—and, inadvertently, one for Clayton.

CHAPTER
SEVENTEEN

A tall, dark man wandered into the main offices of Lombard International. He was wearing jeans and boots with a long-sleeved red shirt and a denim jacket. His hair was in a ponytail and he wore dark glasses.

He turned his attention toward the executive offices. He flashed his credentials to the pretty, smiling receptionist and only a minute later was escorted into Kane Lombard's office.

Cortez introduced himself and shook hands.

"So you're with the FBI," Kane said heavily. "What am I being investigated for now, for God's sake? First the EPA, then the IRS, now you . . . ," he muttered to Cortez after motioning him into a chair.

"I don't have a bone to pick with you," Cortez

chuckled. "I just want to talk to a man who works for you—a man named Jurkins."

Kane scowled. "Will Jurkins?"

"That's him." He hesitated, his narrowed eyes assessing Kane. "There's something I'd better tell you up front. I work for the government, but I have no authority to make arrests in this particular case." He leaned forward. "However, if you'll give Jurkins to me for about three minutes, I think I can help you extricate yourself from this damned mess that I inadvertently helped John Haralson mire you in."

"You . . . ?" Kane's eyes flashed dangerously and he got to his feet.

"Sit down," Cortez said wearily, motioning an infuriated Kane back into his executive chair. "I'm a third degree black belt. Just take my word for it and don't ask for proof. I called the EPA when I found what I thought was evidence of deliberate pollution. I hate polluters. But I didn't count on Haralson taking an active part in your downfall. He's been under surveillance for another reason entirely. Apparently he decided to combine his normal business on the coast with the pleasure of framing you," he added enigmatically. "Why don't you send for Jurkins and I'll let you in on a few unclassified secrets about that toxic waste dump that was so conveniently uncovered?"

Kane only hesitated for a minute. "All right." He hit the intercom button. "Get Will Jurkins in here. Don't tell him I've got company."

"I wouldn't dream of it," came the dry reply from Gert.

* * *

The last person in the world that Nikki expected to find on her doorstep was her ex-husband. Miles Townshend looked tired, but he smiled as she stood aside to let him into the house. Out on the curb was a black limousine with a liveried driver and two men in dark suits wearing sunglasses. It reminded Nikki just how important her visitor was.

"Sorry to show up like this, Nikki, but I owed you a personal call," he explained, when they were seated in the living room.

"Haralson called me earlier," he told her. He leaned forward with his arms crossed over his knees. His eyes narrowed. "Nikki, he's got some photographs of you and Kane Lombard."

"So it was him," she said tightly. "But I've done what he asked me to. He won't print them."

"Yes, he will," he said firmly, watching her react. "Oh, not now, probably; but closer to the election. He's gone over the edge, Nikki. He doesn't care who he hurts now. He's after me, too."

"You?" she asked uncertainly.

"That's right."

"I'm sorry. He's angry at Clay because Clay fired him. He's angry at Kane, and at me, too. He'll cut us all down . . ."

"I'm not going to let him cut down anybody," he replied. "He thinks he's got me on a meathook. In fact, I know someone who can settle his hash for good."

She turned back toward him, her eyes wide as saucers.

"I've been silly, Nikki," he said, smiling sadly. "If I'd admitted everything in the beginning, who knows how things might have turned out. As it is, I'm going to let Haralson tell the world, if he wants to. I don't care anymore."

She looked suddenly worried, and he laughed.

"I'm not going to blow my brains out," he said gently. "If I do, who's going to protect that little spotted owl?"

She smiled despite her worry.

"It's just as well, you know. I can't go on like this for the rest of my life, risking blackmail and pretending to be something I'm not just to spare myself embarrassment. What happens, happens. My friends won't mind, and my enemies won't matter. I hope," he added wryly. He opened his attaché case while a puzzled Nikki stared at him. He tossed a packet of papers onto the coffee table. "Think of it as counterblackmail," he said. "Give those to Clay, with my blessing."

"What are they?" she asked, picking up the sealed envelope.

"Things you don't need to know. Tell Clay that I've already set these wheels in motion, and that the appropriate agency is about to close in on Haralson's real operation down here. It actually has nothing to do with politics or revenge; those were a fringe benefit for him when he discovered that Kane was living down here and supporting Clayton's political opponent. The material in there," he pointed to the envelope, "is just for Clay's information. He won't need to do a thing. Not one single thing. That is the thread that ties Haralson to an employee of Kane Lombard's on a totally unrelated federal investigation, and provides enough proof to have them both arrested. Haralson will be much too busy defending himself to do much more damage from now on. What he planned for Kane Lombard is now going to happen to him."

Miles smiled as he got up and moved closer to Nikki. His fingers lightly stroked down her cheek and his regrets were all in his eyes. "I'm sorry I ever caused you to suffer, Nikki."

Her eyes searched his. "It wasn't all your fault," she said softly. She smiled. "I loved you, you know. In my own way, I always will."

He chewed his lower lip and looked pained. He was faintly flushed. "I wish . . ."

"You needn't feel sorry for me, Miles," she said warmly. "But I'm concerned about what you'll do now."

He chuckled. "I may need to look for a new profession if Haralson turns his attention to me."

"Not a chance. People like you too much. Thank you for coming all this way," she said as she walked him to the door. She paused to look up at him. He was worried, even though he was hiding it well. "Everybody has skeletons, didn't you know?" she asked.

"Most people are lucky enough not to have them disinterred, though." He smiled. "Don't look so morose, Nikki. Dreams still come true. We'll deal with Haralson."

"I look forward to that," she said with venom in her voice.

"So do I. See you around." He smiled at her and left the house as quietly and unobtrusively as he'd entered it.

Nikki studied the envelope in her hand with a curious frown. What in the world could Miles have in there that would save Clay from Haralson?

Jurkins entered Kane Lombard's office for the second time in as many days. He was more nervous this time, though, especially when he saw the dark-haired man sitting across from Lombard.

He stopped just inside the closed door and stared from one man to the other.

"This is Cortez," Kane said. "Will Jurkins," he indicated the other man.

They shook hands. Cortez noticed that Jurkins' palms were sweaty and hot. The man was almost shaking with nerves.

He sat down heavily in the chair adjacent to Cortez's. "Yes, sir, what did you want?" he asked Kane.

Kane nodded to Cortez and sat back in his chair.

Cortez pinned Jurkins with his eyes. "I want to know how you managed to incur a 'medical bill' of several thousand dollars at a local clinic on the outskirts of Charleston, and how you managed to pay it in cash.''

Jurkins' gasp was eloquent. He shivered with reaction and his pupils dilated.

''You paid several thousand dollars in a lump sum,'' Cortez continued, and Kane Lombard scowled darkly as he heard.

Jurkins wondered at first if he could bluff it out, but these men weren't going to fall for any bluff. He was unprepared, caught red-handed. Well, there was one thing he could try; a dodge. He slumped and put his head in his hands. He deliberately let out a heavy, hard breath. ''I knew it would come out,'' he said huskily. ''I couldn't turn him down. The medicine costs so much, and I wanted my baby to have just a few pretty things.'' He lifted pleading eyes to Kane's. ''She's all I got in the world. It didn't sound so bad, when he explained it to me. All he wanted me to do was say that one company wasn't working out and hire another one to take its place. That's all. He never asked me to do anything illegal, Mr. Lombard. He just said I was to tell you the other company didn't do its job right. He said I was to do that, and to hire Burke's to replace it. That's all.'' Jurkins said miserably, ''I don't want my little girl to die.''

Kane felt the man's pain, but Cortez showed no such compassionate reaction. He leaned toward the man. His dark eyes were steady, intimidating. ''Your little girl has gone to St. Jude's for treatment,'' he said quietly.

"The only expenses you incurred were at the clinic and for medicine. Your daughter does have leukemia. She is also in remission, and has been for six months. However, Mr. Jurkins," he added very quietly, "it is not her bill that you paid at the clinic. It was your own. You are a cocaine addict. And your deal with Haralson was that he would pay off your drug bill if you would hire your brother-in-law, Burke, to replace CWC as the waste disposal company for the plant."

Kane had been prepared for the dumping charge. But this accusation came out of the blue, and his head jerked toward Cortez. He saw something in the man's dark eyes at that moment that chilled even him.

Jurkins' hands clenched the arm of the chair. His eyelids flickered and he swallowed, hard.

"No," he said hastily. "No, listen . . . !"

"You listen," Cortez said. He hadn't raised his voice or even changed his expression. "The clinic you frequent is the front for one of the most notorious drug lords in the Carolinas, and Haralson's main source of income. I'm sure that you care for your daughter's well-being, but the reason you took the money from Haralson to sell out your employer was to support a habit that you can no longer control."

Jurkins had jumped up to run, but Cortez had him in one lightning-fast motion. He whipped the man around and shoved him firmly back down into the chair. Cortez stood over him, powerful and immovable, and Jurkins decided to cut his losses while he could.

"All right. I did what Haralson told me to, and I took

money for it. Me and my brother-in-law just did what Haralson told us to. Burke's supporting five kids of his own. Haralson said he'd bail him out if he got caught planting the industrial waste in that marsh. I'm sorry. I couldn't help it," Jurkins groaned. "I couldn't, I couldn't . . . !"

"Would you telephone the local police, please," Cortez asked Kane. "I think we'd better have the assistant D.A. over here, too, and the Department of Health and Environmental Control field representative."

Kane sighed angrily as he studied the broken man before him. "Jurkins, didn't you have enough grief already?" he asked sadly.

"I had . . . too much," the man whispered, his head down. "Too much grief, too much pain, too much fear . . . and too little money and hope. It got to me so bad. At first I took just enough coke to make me forget how sick she was. But then, it took more and more . . ." He looked up at Kane. "It was just to hire another company to haul off your trash," he said, as if he couldn't understand what all the fuss was about. "And Burke dumped it in the swamp where he was told to. What's so bad about that? It wasn't as if he put it in somebody's yard. It's just a swamp! He just tossed it in the swamp where it wouldn't hurt anybody. I don't see what all the fuss is about. Nobody lives in it. It's just a swamp!"

Kane and Cortez exchanged glances. It was too much trouble to try to explain it to him. He wouldn't understand at all.

* * *

There was a brief conference with the police and the environmental authorities, and several loose ends were tied up. Jurkins was taken away. Kane had Gert send in a tray, and he drank coffee with Cortez, trying to find the right way to thank him.

"It goes with my job," Cortez said with a lazy smile. "Sometimes, though, I don't enjoy doing it. Jurkins' little girl is the one who'll suffer the most."

"No, she won't," Kane promised tersely. "I'll make sure of that. Jurkins will get treatment and maybe he won't get too stiff a sentence." He shook his head. "He's like a lot of these people who were raised way out in the country. They threw out their trash and tin cans and used oil in the back yard or buried it, and never gave a thought to the groundwater table. It's going to take a long time to make people understand the damage they can do. Even to 'just a swamp.' " He sighed. "He and Burke were pawns, though. Haralson is the real culprit."

"True enough. And he's put the rope around his own neck." Cortez finished his coffee and got to his feet. "I'm glad it worked out for you."

"It hasn't yet. But maybe it will, now." He shook hands with the other man and scowled curiously. "Listen, how did you get on to Jurkins?"

"Haralson steered me in his direction originally, hoping to use him to bring you down under an avalanche of polluting charges. You'll hear about it on the news soon enough, so I won't be breaking any confidences by telling you that we've been watching Haralson for several months," came the surprising reply. "He had a lot more going on than just getting back at you for past grievances, or even helping Seymour get reelected. He was supplying the clinic where Jurkins got his stuff. The clinic is only part of his money-making operation, and the place where he first met Jurkins. It would have been easy enough to pull strings and send the man over here to apply for work. Jurkins had a good background, and he was a good man for the position—once. Before he became an addict." He smiled knowingly. "I don't suppose the man Jurkins replaced left suddenly? Unexpectedly?"

"As a matter of fact, he left for personal reasons," Kane recalled. "And, yes, suddenly."

Cortez only nodded.

"I drove past Clayton Seymour's office one day on my way to a meeting," Kane remarked. "I saw Haralson getting into his car. I did wonder how a campaign manager could afford a new BMW. I drive a two-year-old Lincoln myself," he added with a grin. "The economy hasn't been that good lately."

"Tell me about it. Haralson afforded his life-style by selling drugs," Cortez replied. "I let him think I was here on an extended vacation. I didn't know what he was up to, but I was hoping for a link to that clinic. And I found it."

"Luckily for me," Kane said.

"What happens now?"

Cortez lifted an eyebrow. "I have Haralson arrested for drug trafficking and merge back into the woodwork in Washington." He lowered his voice. "I think I mentioned that I'm not really supposed to be working in this area."

Cortez held out his hand. "Good luck with the media. I hope they give you the same coverage now that they gave you when you were supposed to be a bad guy."

"Are you kidding?" Kane asked cynically. "They'll apologize on the classified page. But my family will attack them on the front page." He grinned wistfully. "There are times, mind you, when I don't mind having a father who publishes a tabloid."

Derrie was sitting in the outer office of Sam Hewett's headquarters when Nikki walked in the door.

"A spy, a spy!" Derrie exclaimed dramatically, pointing a finger at the newcomer.

"Oh, shut up," Nikki said pleasantly. "As one campaign worker to another, let bygones be bygones. The voters will pick the best man."

"Why, thank you!" Sam Hewett said with a bow as he joined Derrie and Nikki. Other campaign workers chuckled at the look on Nikki's face before they went eagerly back to work.

"You haven't won yet, Mr. Hewett," Nikki reminded him with a smile. She shook hands with him. "But you're a nice man to fight. You're a clean hitter. No low blows."

"I wish I could say the same for your brother," Sam replied quietly. "But I can't forget the way he's gone after Norman Lombard's brother Kane in the press. Norman is my campaign manager, you know, and he's a good man. So is Kane."

Nikki nodded. "I can tell you truthfully that you've seen the last of the sneak attacks."

"I do hope so."

"Can you spare Derrie for lunch?" Nikki asked. "I really need to talk to her."

"Certainly. Go ahead."

"Thanks."

Nikki waited until she and Derrie were out in the street. "Miles came through for us," she said excitedly. "He got something on Haralson and brought it down to me!"

Derrie stopped walking and smiled delightedly. "What is it?"

"I don't know. Some papers. I gave them to Clay about ten minutes ago. He looked at them and gave a whoop and took off out the door running."

"Good for him. I hope he nails Haralson to the wall."

"What's going on?" Nikki asked pointedly.

"I'm not quite sure," Derrie said, "except that Mr. Haralson has made a lot of people very angry. Norman Lombard got a phone call from someone—his brother, I think—and he also went racing out of here, grinning from ear to ear. Whatever is going on, I think most people know except us."

"Mushrooms. We're mushrooms."

"Why?" Derrie asked curiously.

"Because they keep us in the dark and feed us . . ."

". . . don't say it!"

Nikki chuckled. She linked her arm through Derrie's. "Let's have lunch. Then I want to ask you to supper at the weekend."

Clayton was trying to reach Nikki. But the telephone rang over and over, and there was no answer at the house. He hung up, and his face was troubled. Kane had just telephoned him to say that the photograph Clayton had given him was going to be in print and on the stands by early afternoon. He'd been fortunate enough to catch the presses the day before, just as they rolled off the weekly edition. Clayton didn't want Nikki to see it before he'd warned her about what was coming. The shock might harm her or the child.

The child. He smiled as he thought what a wonderful mother Nikki would make. If she loved Lombard, he supposed he could force himself to be civil to the man. He wouldn't admit for all the world that he saw something in Kane Lombard to admire.

CHAPTER
EIGHTEEN

The front page of the Lombard tabloid was shocking. It showed two people making feverish love on the beach; but only from the waist up. The headline above it was even more shocking. It read, "ROMEO AND JULIET FOR THE MODERN AGE; ADVERSARIES BECOME LOVERS."

The young woman staring at it on the shelf had gone a pasty shade of white. Her companion was tugging at her arm, even as one of the women in line belatedly recognized the face on the cover and matched it with the white face leaving the drugstore.

"He printed it!" Nikki gasped. "Haralson printed it, did you see? Oh, my God . . . !"

"Nikki, that was the Lombard tabloid," Derrie pointed out uneasily, helping her friend into the car.

"The *Weekly Voice*, the one that belongs to Kane's father."

"Oh, how could he! I hate him," Nikki whispered, sobbing with rage. "I hate him! How could he do that to me, to Clay?"

"Calm down, now," Derrie coaxed. "You'll make yourself sick. I'm going to drive you home, Nikki. It will be all right. You have to stop crying."

"I can't. I want you to drive me to Kane Lombard's plant! I will not go home in tears. I'm going to break his jaw for him!"

"No, you aren't." Derrie kept driving toward the Battery, ignoring Nikki's angry outburst that lasted all the way there.

"Thank God, Clay's home," Derrie said to herself as she pulled into the driveway.

Clayton came out onto the porch and she motioned furiously for him to come. He ran to help Nikki into the house.

"I'll make some coffee," Derrie said, leaving Clay to settle his sister in the living room.

"The animal. The swine. The filthy pig!" Nikki choked. "I'll break his neck. Have you seen it!? His family tabloid, and they printed that . . . that disgusting photograph! They're in league with Haralson, I knew they were . . . !"

"Calm down," Clay said, holding her wet face against his chest. "Calm down, now, and listen to me. I tried to fire Haralson and he showed me that photo, Nikki."

"What?"

"That's right. He tried to blackmail me." He grinned. "Nobody blackmails me. I took the photo to Kane Lombard."

She stared at him, heartbroken. Her own brother had sold out to his worst enemy.

"We compared notes about Haralson," he told her. "And then I made the comment that I'd like to skewer his liver for what he had done to you. That's when he explained things to me. It seems that you're marrying him very soon because you're pregnant."

There was a crash from just inside the doorway to the kitchen as Derrie dropped a tray of cups and saucers on the spotless lacquered wood floor.

"I hope you enjoy mopping," Clayton called out to Derrie. She stepped in from behind the doorway and stared at Nikki in disbelief. Then she turned to go back into the kitchen, a smile broadening on her face.

Clayton turned to her sister. "Two things, Nikki. Are you pregnant, and are you going to marry Kane Lombard?"

"I am not pregnant," she lied, coloring violently.

"He loves you, he says," he added.

Her face softened magically. "He does?" The softening went into eclipse. "That's a lie! He does not, or how could he have let his venomous relatives print that ghastly photograph of us and distribute it all over Charleston? Oh, Clayton, people stared at me as if I were some hussy!" she wept.

"We know you're not a hussy. But if you're pregnant, I don't really think Kane is going to let you remain single for long. He seems pretty intent on dynasty building.''

She studied a piece of lint on her sleeve. ''He lost his son.''

''I know. He told me. But that isn't why he wants to marry you, if the way he looks when he talks about you is anything to go on.''

''I don't want you to think I was meeting him behind your back deliberately,'' she began.

''I know that.''

''I know I should have told you, but I was so confused. I was sure that Kane was being set up. I knew he didn't deliberately pollute the marsh. But you wouldn't believe that.''

''I knew,'' Clayton said, grimacing. ''I wouldn't listen.''

''You're listening now,'' she said, smiling, and reached out to clasp his hand briefly. Whatever their differences, he was her brother, and she loved him.

He returned the soft pressure of her hand and let it go. ''Do you know, those documents Miles left for me had some fine investigative information in them. They contained more than enough to send Haralson to prison.''

''What sort of information?'' she asked.

''It's confidential, so I'm not at liberty to say. Even to you.'' He grinned at her. ''Kane knows. I'm sure he was waiting for the tabloid to hit the stands before he came looking for you.''

She touched her stomach with a wry grimace. "Poor little baby, with such an unfeeling, unspeakable animal for a father . . . ! To publish a photograph like that . . . in the paper!" She was getting red-faced all over again as the indignity and outrage claimed her. "Why?!"

"It was the only way to stop Haralson from giving it out in revenge to some less friendly tabloid," Clayton said, ignoring her protests. "You'd better announce your engagement pretty soon, nevertheless," he added, tongue-in-cheek.

"No need for that," Derrie said as she came in with a fresh tray of cups and saucers and a pot of coffee. "There's an announcement of Nikki's engagement to Kane Lombard right on the front page of the society section. I saw it just now in the paper Mrs. D. left on the kitchen table."

"He didn't! He wouldn't!" Nikki burst out.

Derrie chuckled. "He has," she said. "And Mrs. D. is going to have apoplexy because you didn't tell her before she read it in the paper. If you'd been home when she came, I expect you'd have caught both barrels of her tongue already."

Nikki glowered at both of them. "Well, I don't care what it says in the paper. I won't marry him."

They both looked at her stomach. She put her hands over it protectively. "I won't," she repeated.

"Have some coffee," Derrie invited, handing a cup of it to Clayton.

"Don't mind if I do."

"I'd like some, too," Nikki began.

Derrie handed her a glass of milk, smiling.

"I hate milk!"

"It makes babies big and strong," Derrie coaxed.

"So that was what the dropped tray was all about!"

"Yes. I was eavesdropping," Derrie confessed. "I learned from him." She pointed toward Clayton. "He's always standing outside conference room doors with his ear to them."

"I am not." He glowered at her.

"How do you think he knew how to vote while he was in the state legislature?"

"I studied the issues and made up my own mind," he reminded her.

"After I explained them to you." She polished her nails on her skirt and looked at them. "God knows how many mistakes you'd have made without me."

He started to speak, stopped, and shrugged carelessly. "Well, I'm not making any new ones. Why don't you come back and run my campaign for me?"

"I could run it," Nikki replied.

"You're pregnant."

"So?"

"Sam would never forgive me if I left him now," Derrie told him. "But we can be friends. Until after the election."

He lifted one eyebrow and smiled slowly. "Just friends?"

She laughed softly. "Well, anything's possible," she said demurely.

The phone rang and Nikki reached beside her to answer it. It was a well-wisher. She hung up. It rang again. Within ten minutes, it seemed that everyone in Charleston and North Charleston had recognized her in one paper or the other and wanted to comment on the Romeo and Juliet story. Nikki was fuming by the end of the day, and not at all in the sort of mood to answer the phone one last time and find a smug Kane Lombard on the other end of it.

"You!" she exclaimed. "Listen here, you snake in the grass . . . !"

"What time tomorrow do you want to be married?" he asked. "One o'clock would suit me very well, but if that isn't convenient, we can try another time."

"How about another century? I am not marrying you!"

There was a pause. "My father would love that."

"Excuse me?"

"He's got the next headline set in type already. Want to hear it?" He began to read, " 'MOTHER OF RO-MEO AND JULIET BABY REFUSES TO MARRY HEARTBROKEN FATHER OF CHILD.' "

"Oh, my God!"

"Yes, sad, isn't it? I expect people will call and write and accost you on the street, you heartless Jezebel."

"Kane, how could you?!"

"Well, you did help, after all," he reminded her. "In fact, you remarked that it felt very good." He paused. "I wonder how that would look in print?"

"You blackmailer!"

"I did the only thing I could, you know," he relented,

his voice soft and quiet. "Haralson would have published the photograph."

"I suppose he would have."

"As it is, I've cut the ground from under him. He now has photos that have no intrinsic value to shock or humiliate. Haralson, by the way, is about to become a resident of the county jail on several counts of controlled substance violation. I'm sure that he'll get a good lawyer who will work feverishly to have him released on bail at his arraignment hearing. I do not think much of his chances, just between us. And that reminds me. You and I have some unfinished business."

"This isn't the way it should happen," she pointed out.

"Probably not," he agreed quietly. "All right. We'll do it the right way. By the book, my dear."

"By the what? Kane? Kane!"

But the line was dead. She glared at the receiver. "You're a horrible man and I will not marry you!"

"Oh, I'll bet you will," Clayton said. He held out a glass. "Drink your milk."

John Haralson had finished his third glass of Scotch whiskey. He heard his motel room door open but it didn't really register until he saw Cortez and a uniformed man standing in front of him.

"Cortez!" he greeted. "Have a drink!"

"No, thanks. You'll need to come with us."

He blinked. "Why?" he asked with a pleasant smile.

"It's a pretty long list." Cortez read the warrant. "It starts with several local violations of the controlled substances act, possession with intent to distribute, attempted extortion, bribery . . . you can read the rest for yourself." He proferred the warrant.

Haralson took it and scanned it, frowning. He moved a little unsteadily to his feet. "You're arresting me?"

"No. He is. You're being arrested right now for violation of South Carolina state law. You'll be arraigned on federal charges for drug smuggling a bit later. There are a few formalities . . . extradition and so forth."

"You're on vacation."

Cortez smiled coldly. "I haven't been on vacation since I engineered the first meeting with you at FBI headquarters where you were trying to probe for some classified information," came the quiet reply. "And by the way, you'd better have this back." He handed the startled man the two dollar and fifty-cent gold piece.

"You bought it. You were obsessed with it!"

Cortez smiled faintly. "I don't have obsessions. Not even about coins."

"Of all the underhanded things!" Haralson roared.

"You wrote the book on that." Cortez slid his sunglasses back on. "He's all yours," he told the police officer. "Take good care of him for us. We'll be in touch."

Haralson yelled after him. "You don't have any jurisdiction down here or in this case! You work for the FBI!"

Cortez lifted an eyebrow. "Do I?" he asked with amusement, and kept walking.

The same evening, the front door at the Seymour home opened to admit a gift-laden Kane Lombard. He walked past Clayton into the living room, where he dumped his burdens on the sofa next to a startled Nikki.

"Roses," he said, pointing to three large bouquets, one of each color, "chocolates, CDs of romantic music, a personal CD player so that you can listen to them, two books of poetry, and a bottle of the best perfume. Chanel, of course," he added with a grin.

Nikki gaped at him. "But . . . what is all this?" she asked, aghast.

"The accouterments of courtship," he explained. He sat down beside her, ignoring Clayton. "The ring is in my pocket, somewhere. It's only an engagement ring, of course, and you can exchange it if you don't like it. You'll have to come with me to pick out the wedding band, anyway."

"But I haven't said I'll marry you . . ." she stammered.

"Of course you'll marry me," he said, extricating the ring in its velvet box from his jacket pocket.

"I hate diamonds," she began contrarily as he opened the box.

"So do I," he agreed. "That's why I bought you an emerald. It comes with a matching necklace, bracelet and earrings."

The emerald was square-cut and faceted like a diamond, with incredible clarity and beauty. Nikki stared at the ring, entranced. The stone had to be almost two carats.

She looked up, her eyes full of delighted surprise.

He smiled at her. "Never expect the obvious from me, Nikki," he said gently. "I'm not conventional."

She studied his broad, leonine face, reading the sorrows and joys of a lifetime there. Her hand lifted to touch it, to trace its hard contours. She did love him so.

"Marry me, Nikki," he said softly.

Her eyes searched his and read the adoration he no longer concealed from her. She smiled slowly. "Oh, yes. I'll marry you, Kane," she said huskily.

He smiled back, holding her hand to his cheek. His lips pursed. "It will break my father's heart, of course," he said. "He's gaining a daughter-in-law and losing a hell of a headline."

"He can always find another headline." She nuzzled her face into his chest. "Perhaps Haralson's arrest will make a good one."

John Haralson was later extradited on federal drug smuggling charges and sent to prison by a cold-eyed, very familiar federal prosecutor.

Miles Townshend didn't wait for Haralson to strike back at him. He went public with a startling announcement that he was gay. It made headlines in two newspapers and was repeated on several television broadcasts for two days. No fuss was made. No one suggested that he resign. In fact, the presidential candidate for the Democratic Party applauded his courage and honesty and offered to keep him on as interior secretary if he won the election. After that, Miles made speeches in favor of the candidate that gained him enormous support among the gay community.

Will Jurkins' daughter remained in remission. Her father, thanks to some financial assistance from Kane Lombard, got treatment. He was pardoned for turning state's evidence against Haralson. His brother-in-law was heavily fined and barely escaped a prison sentence. He moved to another state and started a new waste disposal business.

Kane Lombard was cleared of any criminal charges. He did, however, pay a hefty fine.

The presidential and general election was a week away. Nikki was knee-deep in invitations for her wedding to Kane, working feverishly on her carpools with the phone at her ear while she addressed envelopes. They'd spent the previous night at Kane's beach house. Now they were having second cups of coffee at the Seymour home in Charleston while she worked on her campaign duties. He was going over contracts at one end of the couch while she worked on invitations at the other.

"That's right," she was saying into the receiver. "And we'll be more than happy to make sure that your group gets plenty of media attention for your contribution to the carpool," she was saying. "Yes, it's most kind of you. No, we just want the people to vote. There will be no attempt whatsoever to coerce them to vote for my brother just because we take them to the polls. We want a world-shaking turnout this time. So do you? Good! Thank you again for your help, and I'll be in touch soon. Yes."

She hung up, her mind more on the addresses than her savoir-faire at manipulation. "So much for that," she said, pausing to check her calendar. "Now, there's a speech at the Arts Club in the morning, and a meeting with the League of Women Voters tomorrow afternoon. Then I have to appear at the opening of a new restaurant Thursday." She frowned. "I hope I can still get into my pink silk suit."

"Buy a new one," Kane said. He was watching her and smiling to himself. She radiated energy, even in her present condition. He adored her.

She felt his gaze and raised her eyes to meet Kane's. She beamed.

"I'm on the last one hundred invitations," she said. "I wish we could better coordinate the wedding with the election, though," she pondered. "It would give us such an advantage at the polls . . ."

"Forget that. He's your candidate, not mine," he teased, sweeping the contract aside as he got to his feet and stood in front of her.

"The carpools are for everybody's supporters, not just Clayton's. It's a unilateral political move that will benefit your candidate as well as mine," she added smugly. "Besides, my candidate is your future brother-in-law."

He bent down toward her, his dark eyes acquisitive and warm. "Did I mention that I loved you this morning?"

She laughed softly. "You mention it all the time lately," she replied. "But a few more times wouldn't hurt at all."

"Say it back."

"I do, every time I look at you. Kiss me, you mad fool!" She draped her arms around his neck and jerked him down onto the sofa with her in a tangle of arms and legs and laughter.

While he was trying to keep them from tumbling onto the coffee table and into her cup of cooling coffee, a throat was loudly cleared at the doorway.

They looked up. Clayton cocked his head at them. "Can't you stop that?" he asked pleasantly. "For God's sake, we've only just finished breakfast!"

They looked at each other. "Are you sure he's your brother?" Kane asked.

"He must be adopted," she murmured, smiling against his lips. "Otherwise he wouldn't be such a wet blanket after all I've done for his campaign. Something must have upset him."

Clayton took that as an invitation. He moved right to the huge coffee table, moved the coffee cup and invitations and contract aside, and linked his hands on his knees, ignoring their rather intimate entanglement as he began to speak.

"Something did upset me. Derrie's on that soapbox about the Endangered Species Act again and the election's next week. Now, listen, Nikki, we've got to get this owl off my back before people go to the polls. Are you listening? . . . Nikki, could you stop nibbling on your fiance long enough to pay attention to what I'm saying? This is serious!"

"So is this," Nikki chuckled. "But, if you insist," she sighed. She arranged Kane into a sitting position, curled herself into his lap, and gave her brother her undivided attention in a bit of physical diplomacy that left both men smiling.

"When this campaign is over, we've got to do something about Derrie," Clayton continued.

Nikki laid a hand on her belly and looked warmly at the two most important men in her life. "I'm afraid you'll have to solve that problem, brother dear." She curled closer to Kane and felt him envelop her with a contented sigh. "And I hope you've noticed that I've gone above and beyond the call of duty on your behalf," she added mischievously.

Clayton looked puzzled. "You mean with the campaign?"

"No, I mean that I'm in the middle of producing a new voter for you. The thing is," she added a little shyly, "I'm not going to be a lot of help to you after I finish this latest bit of organization. You see," she added with a wary glance at Kane, "I had to go to the doctor this morning for a checkup and he listened for the baby's heartbeat."

"Are you all right?" Kane said at once. "You didn't tell me you'd been to the doctor!"

"I was saving it for a surprise. I'm all right!" she said, exasperated by the terrified look in two pair of eyes. "It's just that things are a little more complicated than we expected."

"Complicated, how?" Kane asked tautly.

She curled up against him with a loving sigh. "He heard two heartbeats."

"Two . . ." Kane began.

". . . heartbeats," Clayton finished.

The men exchanged complicated looks and Kane's was positively arrogant.

"Twins!" Kane burst out, beaming down at her.

Nikki chuckled. "Yes. How's that for family loyalty, brother mine?" she added, smiling at her brother as she rested her cheek against Kane's broad chest. "I'm not just producing one brand new voter for you; I'm producing two!"